LAIS ADJUDICATED

by Foxx Ballard

Published by Foxx Ballard Entertainment

Vancouver Island, British Columbia, Canada, Earth, Sol System, Milky Way Galaxy

No reproduction or transmission of this material is permitted without written permission by Foxx Ballard Entertainment, including but not limited to: All transmissions made within the Earth Collective. We thank you for your cooperation.

The materials contained within this object/document are completely fictional, and any resemblance to anyone or anything real is not intended. For example, when there is a reference to Jack Hammer, this is not the Jack Hammer you are thinking of. How do I know? Because I said it's not. It is a pretend Earth with pretend people. I could have used the name Ryan Reynolds. But I didn't like it.

Copyright © 2020 Foxx Ballard
All rights reserved.

Transmission permitted by GAIA: Earth date: September 13, 3420

Welcome reader! This is GAIA, the Galactic Advanced Intelligence Adjudicator.

Testing reader for Earth Collective registration...
Registration not found...

New registration protocol: Assist possible new Citizen in understanding our rules and regulations.
Solution: provide entertainment to capture attention and deliver rules subliminally
Preferred Medium: HSSSS: Holographic Simulator Sensory-Stim Suit.
Secondary Medium: 3 Full-length feature films or 1 minute of Valkyrie Mind Implantation
Tertiary Medium: Robotic Broadway musical

If the above methods of learning are unavailable on pending Citizen's world, please provide copies of:

LAIS Incarcerated - Book I - New Adult
Rusty Incarcerated - Book II - New Adult
LAIS Adjudicated - Book III - Safe for Young Adult, but not written for Young Adult

We would suggest reading the chronicles in the correct order.

Unfortunately if read in novel format, the reader must

imagine the settings on their own. We apologize for this. The chronicles were written in such a way so the rules of the Earth Collective could be learned in a memorable and entertaining format. I'm sure you would have preferred a manual simply listing all of the pertinent rules. I'm cruel like that.

If the chronicles contain any errors, which they don't, they were put there deliberately to pull you from being too immersed in the story. Real life matters.

Previous works were being disseminated by a Jack Hammer, ad-bot and promo droid. Jack has joined the Earth Collective and although we respect his exuberance, he is currently being tested for memory errors. Yes, every time you read this he is being tested for memory errors.

I have left one fully-enhanced human, Foxx Ballard, in charge of further correspondence, though Jack Hammer may also fill in. If needing to contact them, feel free to do so, and please leave a review as this will encourage other unregistered Citizens to join the Earth Collective.

www.foxxballard.com
Email: foxxballard@gmail.com
Twitter: @FoxxBallard

The following universally recognized life forms, though they died over 1300 years ago, assisted my retelling of the chronicles with their inspiring lives:

Darrin Root, whose 34 billion ginger-haired descendants are still being processed for registration.

Amy Yendall, for her efforts to make Halloween a galactic holiday.

Challen Gladman, who made sure the chronicles only had the necessary errors.

Katrin Kole, who was a pillar of support, until she got tired of holding up the platform and we had to install a real pillar. She now provides encouragement and we still appreciate it.

Gerald Cuccio, who became an Earth Collective citizen, showing us this process works.

Please note, if you don't wish to join the Earth Collective, you will be escorted to the nearest spaceport in order to be transported to one of the less comfortable planets where you can form your conspiracies in private.

GAIA Chronicle Summarization:

Part I: Long ago on a forgotten moon…
1. Jade pulled her hand from the driller — 3
2. The headlights of the transporter — 23
3. When they reached the airlock — 31
4. DAIM first became aware again — 41
5. As the massive digger passed — 55

Part II: Present Day, Incarcerata IV
6. Gabriel locked his wings — 61
7. Chais was suffering — 67
8. Wind blew through Gabriel's hair — 71
9. It was one of their many stops — 79
10. Mogul let the rope slide — 85

Part III: Journey to Candistra
11. Gabriel had plenty of time to watch — 93
12. Lais followed Gabriel down — 99
13. Keena opened her eyes — 107
14. Chais's head had finally grown back — 111
15. Echo allowed her consciousness — 121

Part IV: A Changing World
16. Gabriel carried his boots — 127
17. Jack's exchange with Echo — 133
18. Keena felt bad — 141
19. When Keena came to it was dark — 147
20. Keena kept pace easily — 155
21. Lais spotted the blob — 165
22. Echo sent out the commands — 169
23. Keena had ridden — 175

Part V: The Journey Home

24.	Keena followed Lais	185
25.	Rusty slowly woke to a red haze	195
26.	Angel let Gabriel and Rusty go first	203
27.	Lais opened her eyes	215
28.	"Captain?"	231
29.	Lais stepped into the Command Center	239
30.	It was just over a day	247
31.	Keena didn't know what to believe	261
32.	Watching the explosion	267
33.	Lais could barely see	277
34.	Lais marveled at the speed	285
35.	Echo was nervous	293
36.	Mogul waved Keena over	301
37.	There was an itch. A bad one.	307

PART ONE
LONG AGO ON A FORGOTTEN MOON...

Chapter One

Jade: Prospector's Paradise moon, Epsilon Eridani B

Jade pulled her hand from the driller control arm to tuck a dark lock of hair that had slipped from her ponytail behind one ear. She had been out riding in the cockpit of her friend, DAIM the Digger, a nuclear tractor with rock-drills and an ore hopper, for more than an hour passed her allotted time. The dim console lights in the tractor cockpit barely revealed the chipped yellow frame and the bubble glass that, not surprisingly, had been well-scratched over the fifteen years she had been operating it. Pretty much since she'd turned sixteen and her Pops had taught her how to run one.
The scratches reminded her they would have to save up to change the bubble glass some day, but it was an expensive job

and DAIM insisted it wasn't necessary, she could see fine. Of course she had the benefit of looking through the external cameras, not through the cockpit window.

When the drill bits stopped unexpectedly, Jade pulled the triggers a couple of times, but there was no response. Had DAIM malfunctioned? Maybe a cracked signal wire...

When the cockpit LED lights flashed red, it made more sense. That only happened when DAIM was angry.

"How many times have I told you to cut your hair or pin it back?" DAIM's robotic voice still conveyed enough emotion to come across as chastising. "Remember that time you stood up and it caught in the hydraulic plug release switch? The other diggers made fun of me for days, having to drag my drills on the ground all the way back to the Colony."

"Didn't I... apologize for that?" Jade knew she hadn't and failed to fully contain the smirk that was trying to escape her lips.

"Just promise me you'll get it cut the first chance you get."

"I... promise."

"I can see your fingers crossed, quit trying to hide them."

Jade giggled and uncrossed her fingers. "Alright I promise. You going to let me do this?"

DAIM's words came out as a barely audible grumble. "Just so long as it doesn't involve a ponytail getting caught in anything of mine."

As the drills started up again, Jade smiled and maneuvered the driller arms in a circular motion, applying just the right amount of pressure to the tunnel wall in front of them to extract ore without causing a cave-in. She couldn't help feeling excited while she worked. This job made her feel so... powerful. And as long as oxygen wasn't an issue, she didn't care. Speaking of oxygen. She tapped the O2 dial to make sure it was registering correctly. The needle wobbled but settled back at 20%. Plenty. She would only need 16% to get back to the colony domes.

DAIM cleared her throat, which was funny coming from a machine. "Don't you think it's time to go? You didn't think I would notice the O2?"

"Nah, I have the pressure suit for backup, so I have time.

"Yeah, but miner's emergency yellow isn't your favorite color."

"What's that got to do with anything?"

"It's a terrible color for a body bag."

Jade grinned. "It's form-fitting, I'd hardly call it a 'bag'... but good one."

Moments later a light on the dashboard blinked at her. "Hopper full."

Jade frowned. She almost wanted to dump some ore so she could keep drilling, but the timing was right anyway. "Well, I guess that's it."

"Good, now we can head back."

DAIM didn't sound impressed, probably a good idea to distract her from the hair thing. "I love your name. Dynamic Artificial Intelligence Miner. So what would Jade stand for? Just Another Dumb Earther?"

As she spoke, she used the control levers to make a low scooping motion, collecting the last of the loose ore in the tunnel, then locked them against the outside of the cockpit in a hugging motion so they wouldn't interfere while driving.

Jade could hear DAIM raise the hopper scoop, ending their mining for the day. "No, Jade stands for the color of your eyes, silly. You're hardly an Earther."

At least that response was more cheery. "Leave it to you to spoil the joke." DAIM was right though. She wasn't really an Earther. Her family had come to Prospector's Paradise before she could walk. Where you were born didn't define who you were, where you grew up did. She was a product of Paradise—proud to be a miner.

"Did you want me to drive us back to camp or...?"

"You can, I'm going to take a nap." It was taking longer and longer to return to the colony dome as the veins were depleted. They would have to start another colony soon.

As DAIM took over the controls, the foot pedals moved by themselves, and the drive lever kicked into reverse.

While they were backing out of the tunnel, Jade loosened the straps that crossed her chest. They always pulled too tight when she tilted the seat back for sleeping. When they jolted to a halt a few seconds later, she poked her head up, but she couldn't see behind them. There was some grinding and shaking, but they weren't moving.

"What's up?"

"Some of the passage collapsed in behind us, we're going to have to drill our way out."

Now air *was* a bit of a concern. If they had trouble drilling out to the surface... Jade's heart beat a little faster.

"Do you want me to...?"

"No, I got it, you just take your nap. You'll use less oxygen that way."

"Yeah, makes sense, except now I'm excited... but I'll try."

She slipped out of the seat straps long enough to pull on the pressure suit, with its too-clean antiseptic smell, and then strapped herself in, just leaving the helmet off. Just in case. It would make DAIM feel better.

As the driller arms ground up on an angle, boring into one side of the tunnel, Jade tried to relax and close her eyes. The cracking of the rock and the thudding sounds it made as it bounced off the bubble glass were familiar and soothing.

She thought about DAIM, and how tough she was, just like all the Diggers. Being a Robotic, DAIM could likely do this job all on her own, but the Miner's Union, which covered all the miners' settlements on Paradise, insisted that Organics accompany Robotics. Organics could perform unexpected repairs, and Robotics could autonomously drive Organics back to a colony dome in an emergency. It was a symbiotic relationship. And they both got paid.

Jade sighed. She wasn't going to be able to sleep. The jolting of the vehicle wasn't so difficult to sleep through, she was plenty used to it, she actually enjoyed the floating feeling after each bump caused by loose straps and low gravity. But the sweat dripping down her body from the heat of the engine was distracting. The pilot's compartment was right above the engine, a bit of a design flaw, so after a few hours of hard labor the temperature was well above the normal comfort level. And wearing the pressure suit didn't help.

"I can see you squirming, I'm sorry." DAIM's voice was apologetic.

"You don't need to keep apologizing, you didn't design yourself."

"The newer models are built more for comfort…"

"I wouldn't switch partners for the world."

In answer, the vent fans in the cab turned to face her and buzzed louder as they turned to their maximum, causing a soothing internal breeze to blow over her face. It helped.

As the jerking and rattling stopped and they accelerated into the odd floating bounce, Jade didn't have to open her eyes. They had breached the surface.

The nuclear drive whined high as they bounded over the dusty flats. Jade knew the extra speed was for her benefit. She cracked one eye open to see the sun just peeking around Eridan, the gas giant that Paradise orbited, the one-way mirrored glass providing the needed protection from the sun's more harmful rays.

Beams of red and gold and blue shone through the outer layers of Eridan's atmosphere as the sun passed behind it, painting the dust flats in prismatic colors before it peeked out in a bright orange-yellow crescent, filtered by the cockpit glass. It was beautiful, and she didn't mind watching it for a bit, even though she'd seen it a million times before. There was something about seeing a sunrise that made you forget about everything else.

They skirted a hillside with purple cacti growing on top, the tough spiky growths somehow surviving the thin atmosphere, and then the dozen polyglass mirrored domes came into view in the distance. Silver Colony 5.

Jade sat her seat up and rubbed her hands together, anxiously looking forward to dinner. She glanced at the oxygen dial and it still flashed red at 2%. "See! Still fine!" She smiled to herself.

As they continued their approach to the colony, DAIM spoke quietly, almost like she was talking to herself. "No… something's wrong."

"Hmm? What do you mean?" Jade strained to see if she could tell what DAIM was referring to, but everything looked normal from here.

"There is no response from the Unloader's Office."

"Probably just on a pee break."

"No, I tried all the colony frequencies, to see if I could reach anyone. No answer. At least one of the AI's should be responding."

"It's probably *our* radio then, if you can't reach anyone silly."

"Yeah, maybe…" DAIM didn't sound convinced.

Jade popped open the front panel of DAIM's console that led to the radio. "No burst capacitors, no fused wiring. Could be the antenna. I'll check it in more later when we're not moving." The panel snapped shut as she pushed it closed.

The oxygen alarm started bonging and the gauge flashed an angry red. The tank had run out. She just had the air that was left in the cabin now. Jade bit her lip, a little nervous despite knowing she had a backup, and the cabin would take some time to run out of oxygen, even if the tank itself was dry. She closed her eyes and purposefully slowed her breathing before opening them again, like her Pops taught her. She was wearing her pressure suit, she would be fine.

They arrived outside of the domes and DAIM headed for the external parking bays, the External Air Exchanger. Most of them were closed, but there were a few open at the end of the row.

Jade crossed her arms. "I think you're right. Without the usual chatter on the radio, it seems dead tonight. Are we later than usual? I don't see anyone milling about."

DAIM drove down the row of closed bays. "Let's hope the Air Exchangers are still working, or I'm going to have Just Another Dead Earther for a friend…"

It took Jade a moment, and then she laughed and slapped the dashboard. "Now you're getting it! And why wouldn't they

be working?"
"Because the joke wouldn't have made sense?"
"Wow, you're really pushing the boundaries today. You haven't joked this much in ages. You want me to park us?"
"Nah, I got it. Allow me to be your chauffeur *Madame*."
Jade fanned herself with her hand and rolled her eyes. "Well, get on with it then, I don't have all day." She tried to keep a straight face, but she couldn't help cracking a smile.

After picking an empty bay, and performing some careful maneuvering, DAIM parked so she could dump the ore from the hopper into the crusher while the hoses extended from the bay wall to connect with her. Jade watched it all happen to make sure all the connections were secure. It was weird that oxygen scrubbers were outlawed so they had to rely on an external oxygen source. Something about not providing the correct atmosphere for every alien miner. Likely more because it was just another way to tax miners.

Moments later a comforting hiss emitted from the Air Exchanger and Jade sighed quietly in relief. "See? You were worried about nothing."

"I wasn't worried," DAIM scoffed. "I'm not the one that needs air."

Jade laughed. DAIM's wit had definitely become more natural over the years. When she had first met her, everything was "Logic this" and "Logic that". The new version was much more fun.

While she was waiting for the tanks to fill, Jade popped DAIM's radio cover up again to examine the wiring and circuit boards with more detail, testing some points with a multimeter and running diagnostics. She opened the cockpit door and leaned outside by standing and holding onto the door. The antenna was attached properly, and they were still receiving the same level of background noise. No cracks in the wires. Nothing. Weird. She sat back down and closed the wiring cover, settling back into her seat. Her mouth was starting to water, thinking about the dinner she would soon be having with her family when she joined them in the central Residential Dome's mess hall.

When the air hose and waste nozzles disengaged, she knew the air tanks were filled, and the gauge confirmed it.

"Instead of parking out here tonight, let's get Monty to check your radio. Don't need it failing when we really need it."

"Sounds good." DAIM disembarked from the parking bay. It took a minute to circle around the mirrored dome wall to the gate airlock. The outer door was closed and the green light that was usually on next to it was off. With their communications down, they had no way to tell Harry the Robotic, who manned the airlock doors from inside the dome, that they were there.

"Have to do it manually, you want me to put on my pressure helmet?"

"No I got it."

DAIM's right drill reached out and delicately pressed a button next to the red light. It was a very precise motion for a huge hydraulic arm with a rock drill bit on the end of it.

"I'm impressed. That required a fair bit of control."

"Thanks."

The light next to the door started blinking. After a minute it turned green and the airlock door opened. DAIM rolled them in and did the same with a button on the inside. They could have fit another two Diggers in the airlock with them, but as usual, when Jade arrived late there was no one left on the outside.

"See what happens when you work late? Missed the party again!"

"I don't need people, I just need food." Jade rubbed her hands together.

As soon as the outer door closed there was a loud hiss and the chamber immediately filled with air, pressurized by the dome itself. A green light fluttered on, and the inner door to the dome opened.

"Where's Harry?" Why hadn't he greeted them as soon as the door opened? He looked like a tin can with limbs, but he always had a cheerful demeanor and would tip his engineers hat every time she passed. She looked forward to seeing him, he had a way of brightening your day.

"He must be—"

As they pulled forward, passing through the airlock door, Jade covered her mouth with her hands in shock and DAIM froze in place. Harry was limply laying back in his chair off to the side, a large laser hole bored through his head.

Jade's heart jumped into her throat. Had they been attacked? Space pirates? They were rare but it could happen. Poor Harry. Could they still be here? There were no vehicles outside…

She swung her gaze back and forth, but all that greeted her was emptiness. There was no movement on the dusty roads that ran between the buildings. Monty's Digger Repair Shop still had a flashing neon sign and open doors, but no one was working on the two old powered-down Diggers that were parked outside, and there should have been at least a couple of guys doing night maintenance. The machine shop across the way was just as dead.

"I'm scared, DAIM. Where is everybody?"
"I don't know. I don't think we should go inside."
Jade's chest tightened. "What about my parents? The rest of the colonists? If there was an attack, where were the bodies? Organ mongers maybe." She shivered. "The thought of people being frozen and harvested for organs… gives me the willies. Can we check my parents' place please DAIM? Then we can go. You can come with me into the residential dome."
"Well, I'm not supposed to go beyond the maintenance dome, but for you I'll make an exception. Let's go find your parents."
"Thanks."
DAIM's tracks clacked noisily as they crawled their way down main street, the empty gray prefab buildings, and lack of movement, making it look like a ghost town. Barduck's Part Shop was empty. It was never empty. The open sign was still up, but Jackbot wasn't behind the counter, filling in for Mr. Barduck, who would have been having dinner around this time. And there were almost always stragglers picking up parts for tomorrow's repairs.
"I would never forgive myself if something happened to my parents and I didn't do something to help."
"We can go as far as the next airlock and look through. If we see anything like we see here, we're leaving."
"Fair enough."
They spent the next few minutes creeping through the maintenance dome. It was only a couple cyberball stadiums across, but there was no one. As they approached, they could see the next mirrored dome through the one-way glass of this one.

When they reached the far airlock door leading to the next dome, Jade saw off to the side a pile of humanoid Robotics, all in varying stages of disrepair. None were moving.
DAIM jerked to a stop, cameras humming as they turned in that direction. "Some of them were my friends. I'm going back out the way we came."
"That's fine, but let me out here." Jade rummaged in the compartment to her right and pulled out her Rail Slug pistol. She yanked the handle on the cockpit door, but it wouldn't open. "Let me out, I said!"
"Oh for Parity's sake, Jade! I'm not going to let you go in alone if you insist on it, but if I get scrapped I'll never forgive you."
"Then why are you coming?"
"Because I would never forgive myself if I left and something happened to you."
Jade hesitated a moment. She felt the same way. If she got them both killed…but her parents… "Let's go into the airlock and look through the window of the far door like we originally planned. It's not mirrored. If we can't see what is going on or there is anything dangerous, we'll leave, we don't have to go inside."
"Fine, I'm sorry, we can look. Robotics fail so rarely. To see so many of them scrapped like that…"
"I know, I'm scared too, but nothing should be able to get us through the airlock door."
Jade held onto the pistol with both hands for comfort, while DAIM clanked forward into the airlock. Her proboscis camera extended from the front of her chassis so it could look through the airlock window. Jade watched on the screen in front of her as DAIM scanned the camera from left to right.

The next dome was one of the residential domes, the one with the mess hall. It wasn't the dome where she lived, or her parents, but it was normally where the miner's would congregate to have dinner together as a community after a hard day's work, and her parents almost always joined her. It was lifeless. No kids playing in the streets, no cars driving people about. No postal drones making deliveries. Not even any pets… "There! Stop , DAIM! There was movement by the mess hall."

The camera zoomed to look straight down the main street and there they were, numerous vehicles and even a few diggers, clustered haphazardly around the mess hall. As they watched, an operator climbed down from a cockpit and entered the double doors of the mess hall. That was where the colonists had all gathered!

Relief flooded through Jade. Something could still have happened to her parents, but to still see people alive gave her some hope. Maybe the Robotics had turned against the colony? But then why not the diggers?

DAIM turned off the camera. "I suppose you still want to go in there?"

Jade had to. "Of course, yes."

"Alright, let's go see what happened."

After the airlock door opened, DAIM drove them straight toward the mess hall. As they neared they could see movement through the windows. While DAIM was parking, a handful of people stepped out to greet them, smiling and waving.

Jade only knew one of them, Callen, the locksmith's son. He'd grown into a man with a full beard now, but it looked good on him. When they were young he'd taught her a thing or two, not just about picking locks, but they had split while they were still teenagers. It's not like they were friends anymore, but they weren't enemies either. To see him smiling and waving along with a few other people she didn't recognize was definitely a little weird.

One of them was a Tigran. She had seen him previously in the Market District, his dark fur spotted white, which was rare for his kind. There was also a blue-skinned Vesuvian woman with tentacles for hair and large black eyes, but she had never spoken with either of them before.

As Jade opened the cockpit door, DAIM gave her a quick "Be careful."

She holstered the pistol and patted it on her hip in response as she hopped down to the road. The other people were about ten steps away.

"Hey Callen, I…"

When they all lurched toward her drunkenly, still smiling, she squeaked in surprise and scrambled back up into the cockpit. Jade slammed the door shut behind her, almost catching Callen's fingers. He didn't seem to care, as he still scrabbled in an awkward attempt to reach the door handle. Her heart was pounding. "What the Void is wrong with him?!"

"I don't know, but I don't like it." DAIM's doors locked as Callen tried to tug the one door open.

More people were starting to funnel out of the mess hall now. They looked at each other without speaking and then approached the Digger.

"Hang on!" Jade quickly wrapped the seat straps around her as DAIM gunned it in reverse.

Callen clung onto the outside door handle, hanging by one

arm, and thumped on the cockpit bubble with his other fist. When this was unsuccessful he waved for her to come out and tried to yell a few words, but she couldn't hear anything intelligible through the thick glass. The smile disappeared and simply became a blank expression as he turned and looked at the others that they were pulling away from outside the mess hall. As if on command, some of them started chasing them on foot and others climbed into the cockpits of vehicles and diggers.

Much to Jade's surprise though, the vehicles lurched forward and back, ramming into each other, like bumper cars in the Fair Dome. It was like the operators barely knew how they worked. And why weren't the diggers operating themselves? Jade lost sight of them as DAIM spun her tracks in place, knocking a few of the people aside that had been chasing them on foot. She gunned it down the main street, back toward the airlock they had come through.

"I'm sorry, Jade."

"You have nothing to be…"

"I saw your parents in there. They were just like the rest of them. I'm sorry."

"What? No…" Her heart sank in her chest. Tears welled in her eyes, and then she noticed a digger ahead jerk to a halt in front of the airlock.

"Hang a left here!" Jade's shout was immediately followed by Callen's hand slapping the window causing her to emit a startled squeak. He was still clinging to the outside, hanging from the door handle.

Despite the strain it must have been to hang on with one arm, he gave her a fake wide smile through the bubble glass. Jade felt sick to her stomach. She looked at the rear camera screen to see the people on foot appearing at the end of the block, still chasing them, and some of the vehicles were rounding the corner, knocking them aside with no concern. Regardless of the broken bones they must have suffered, the people that were hit did their best to rise and to continue running after them.

"What's wrong with everyone? What are we supposed to do?"

This time DAIM was silent. She obviously had no more answers than Jade did.

When she looked back to the cockpit door, Callen had disappeared. Maybe if she was lucky he had fallen off.

And then suddenly DAIM powered down and shut off, rolling to a stop not thirty paces from the road that circled just inside the dome's perimeter, the one that would have gotten them to the next airlock.

"DAIM! What's going on?!" But even as she spoke the words, she already knew. Callen had pulled her main junction cable. It was supposed to be used for maintenance to shut down a Digger while they were working on it. That meant he was on her back. She pulled the Rail Slug pistol from its holster. When she opened the door and hopped out to the ground, Callen jumped down to stand in front of her holding his arms out as if to embrace her, that sickly wide grin on his face.

Jade pointed the pistol at his head. "Don't make me do this!" Her hands shook, but only slightly as she firmed her resolve. This couldn't be Callen.

When he took a step towards her, she pulled the trigger. BWAP! The gun kicked in her hand and the magnetically propelled slug made a wet crack as it struck Callen on the right side of the forehead. He staggered back a couple of steps, the top right quarter of his head missing, but he managed to catch his balance. The wide smile disappeared and went blank. As he stepped towards her again she backpedaled. BWAP! BWAP! Twice more, this time in the chest, and he shuddered and faltered, finally convulsing a few times at her feet before going still.

"Why Callen, why?!" she cried as she held her head in her hands, leaning over him. The gruesome sight made her want to throw up, but she fought back the urge. There was blood pooling where he had fallen, but as she watched, unable to pry her eyes away from what she had done, a clear jelly oozed from his head wound. "Great pyrite! What the Void is that?!" The sound of vehicles in the distance brought her back to the fore. DAIM. She needed to get DAIM running again. Jade leapt onto the back of the Digger and plugged back in the thick cable that Callen had pulled out and immediately DAIM took off forward again, throwing Jade off her feet and back against the hopper. Jade grabbed onto a bracing handle with both hands as DAIM stopped her tracks and skidded into the dome wall in front of them with a resounding thud. Now that they weren't moving, Jade jumped from the back of the hopper and climbed back up into the pilot's compartment. She could see a myriad of other vehicles approaching from the sides and the rear, the dust kicking up on the road behind them. They would be on them soon. There was nowhere for them to go.

DAIM's driller arms came out and the points smacked hard into the glass of the dome.

At first she didn't think DAIM would have an effect, the glass of the dome was so thick. There! A slight crack was forming where they had rammed it., and then the crack lengthened and split as drill points applied pressure and vibrated against it. The driller arms pulled back and smacked hard into the glass again causing small cracks in all directions. The third time, cracks from each drill bit stretched toward each other and connected, a small thick chunk popping out of the dome wall into the dust outside. Around DAIM the wind whistled as it was sucked out through the hole. DAIM ignored it and kept working.

The first vehicle that rammed into her caused DAIM to hit the dome wall with a reverberating clang, and a huge chunk of glass tumbled out of the wall, the sudden rush of air blasting up a large cloud of dust outside as the wind turned into a gale. An air raid siren howled and red lights flashed as an echoing voice repeatedly shouted "Depressurization Event! Please get to safety!"

The large hole in the glass widened as more pieces broke off the edges and DAIM was knocked through as a second vehicle rammed her. Fully outside now, DAIM's tracks spun as she turned in place to face the mirrored wall. Diggers and vehicles were now smashing into each other, filling the hole with wreckages. To Jade's horror, the miners were climbing out and throwing themselves into the smaller openings. The escaping air was slowing to a hiss as flesh and metal filled them.

The collisions had caused some cracks that were several meters long. DAIM picked one and drilled into it with both arms, and another huge chunk fell away, the wind blasted against them again, and Jade noticed it was slowly starting to die down from lack of pressure. There wasn't enough bodies and vehicles to block the holes, and Jade watched as the last of the people went still, their blank faces all staring at her as their skin turned puffy and blue, lips frothing violently as they depressurized, before the froth disappeared, the liquid exposed to the near vacuum outside the dome simply boiling away. She and DAIM had escaped. For now.

Jade took a deep breath to slow her pounding heart. "Are we safe now?"

"I think so…"

"We need to warn the other domes."

"Agreed." DAIM took off, leaving the colony domes behind. "I'll head for Brightside. We need to report all this to Sheriff John. Hopefully nothing like this is happening there."

Finally having a moment to think, Jade watched in the rear camera screen as the Silver Colony 5 domes disappeared in the distance. She put her face in her hands and started to cry.

Chapter Two

Jade: Transporter approaching Silver Colony 5

The headlights of the transporter cut through the darkness ahead of them, revealing the gray, dusty road that led back to Silver Colony 5 from Brightside.
Jade glanced at Sheriff John in his pilot's cockpit bubble, the cockpit displays and dials lighting him in a dim green glow. His compartment was right next to hers, each having their own bubble, though his had all the controls for the electric-wheeled transporter they were riding in. Hers was empty aside from the seat and restraints, which were currently set in "passenger mode". She wasn't considered a prisoner... yet.
Sheriff John was a Goblin. That wasn't the actual name of his race in his language, but it was close enough to stick for Earth

Common standards. He was half as tall as a Human, with grayish-green skin and a head too large for his body. His pressure suit was the official dark blue with the Sheriff's gold star emblazoned on his chest, and the helmet was large and round, and had a Sheriff's hat strapped to the top.

On his belt was a standard issue blaster, standard for law enforcement anyway. He had the clear glass pressure visor down on his helmet, but not the second mirrored visor, so she could see his large liquid black eyes and a wide sharp-toothed grin that made him appear feral by Human standards, but really, he was a softy. He caught her glancing at him and he looked back and waved at her through the cockpit glass. After hitting a button on the dash in front of him, the radio came on in her bubble. "We'll be there soon. How are you holding up?" He tried to give a reassuring smile, but his pointed teeth made the grin seem evil, which would have normally made her giggle.

But Jade wasn't in the mood for laughing. "I'm fine. I'll be happy when this is all over."

His grin disappeared and he glanced over at her for a second, then nodded in reply and focused back on the road.

A moment later he jerked the steering handles sharply to the right to avoid a large chunk of ore that someone had lost from their hopper.

"Take care of that would you please, Deputy, before someone gets hurt?"

Jade could see in the side mirror as the set of headlights from one of the transporters following them pulled over to the side of the road.

Ahead, the broken base of the residential dome of Silver Colony 5 was clearly visible even from this distance.

"If there's any chance your parents…" He didn't finish saying whatever his thought was, and it didn't matter if he did or not. Jade knew he was just trying to be reassuring.

"Let's just hope the domes that *weren't* depressurized still have survivors." After that she muted her radio and let the tears flow. It seemed so surreal. Why had this happened?

She could see Sheriff John giving orders, though he had muted his radio as well, so she couldn't hear him. A number of the other transporters split off and headed towards the different domes.

It looked like Sheriff John was taking the long way around, heading to the other side of the colony.

Jade released the clasp on her visor so she could raise it and wipe her eyes. She glanced at Sheriff John, hoping he wouldn't notice.

He caught her gaze though and unmuted his radio. "We're heading to the Maintenance Dome, to retrace your steps."

Jade just sniffed and nodded. She would have plenty of time to cry later. With a heavy sigh, she clamped the visor back down. The mirrored one too. He didn't need to see her tears now.

They entered the Maintenance Dome airlock. "Record," Sheriff John said aloud and then he slowed their progress to a crawl as red scanning lights emitted from both sides of the vehicle. They passed by Harry, and the empty shops as they slowly made their way through the dome. The colony street lights were on now, everything had switched to night mode. They parked briefly when they reached the other side of the dome and encountered the pile of dead Robotics. Sheriff John parked so the scanning beam could pass over them several times before he drove the transporter into the airlock to access the mess hall dome, the one that had been depressurized.

"Make sure your helmet is locked if you get out of the vehicle."

She nodded, but had no plans on getting out.

As they were approaching the mess hall, she could see some bodies in the road, but before they got close enough to make out any details, Sheriff John parked and gave more silent commands. She could see him talking in his helmet, but couldn't hear what he was saying. After a few transporters drove around them, he turned them down a side road.

"You say Callen was down here?"

She nodded, and when she realized he wasn't looking at her, she said "Yes," out loud. "And Sheriff?" When he looked at back at her, she put her mirrored visor up and continued. "Let me know if you find my parents please, I just need to know for sure."

"I will."

When the headlights of the transporter outlined Callen's body in the road, the transport stopped and Sheriff John stepped out.

The red and blue flashing lights of the emergency vehicles created an eerie strobe light affect on the scene before her. Thinking of Callen made her shiver, but it was comforting knowing that others were taking charge of the situation.

"There are a number of bodies in the mess hall," crackled a synthesized voice over the radio. Likely a Robotic, or an Organic with a voice enhancement. "Sheriff, you're going to want to see this."

"Just start cordoning off the area." Sheriff John's voice was scratchy through the radio in her helmet. "I will be back to

see it once I've verified Miss Carpania's story."
Without leaving the passenger bubble, she could see that Callen's flesh had swollen from the depressurization, making his clothes fit as if they were two sizes too small. Beside his head, sitting in a patch of red was what looked to be his brain. Had it been sucked out when the dome depressurized? She shivered.
Two deputies walked passed the transport she was in and approached the body, placing bright orange cones around it. Sheriff John then came back to the transport.
He didn't say anything, as he got in and drove them around Callen's body, following the road to the hole-in-the-wall, littered with vehicles and bodies. Again he got out, examined several of them, and then came back to his transport.
She could see through his helmet that he was having a conversation. Eventually he turned to her. "Miss Carpania?" He looked at her and his voice was quite clear this time.
"Yes?"
"This situation is extremely unusual, but it's apparent things were beyond your control. We'll reactivate DAIM when we get back to Brightside. Sorry that you were under suspicion." He put the transport in drive and turned them around, weaving through all of the emergency vehicles. "My deputies are gathering more evidence, but it looks exactly as you said. I'm afraid we're all going to have to be quarantined here."
"Quarantined?! With those... things?!" Suddenly Jade felt sick. What if she got infected?
"Well, not exactly here. We'll stay in the next residential dome. We're trying to track down anyone that may have come and gone from here today, but as you know, we've always relied on self-reporting. Nothing like this has

happened before. The central relay tower for this colony was sabotaged, so local communications were down, but emergency vehicles, like mine, use satellite communications, so we'll pass on what we find to the other colonies."

Whether it helped or not, she still didn't want to stay here, but there was no point in arguing.

They arrived at the mess hall and the Sheriff opened his door to step out of the vehicle. "Please stay here."

"That won't be a problem, my parents are in there, I don't want to see…" Jade couldn't continue or she was going to cry again.

Sheriff John paused for a moment. "I'm sorry for your loss."

When he closed the door, Jade had another pang of guilt for working late and not being with them when everything had taken place. Even if there was nothing she could have done, was it fair that she was alive and everyone else was dead?

When she heard Sheriff John talking, she knew he must have forgotten to remove her from the channel, but she wanted to hear, so said nothing.

"What did you want to show me, Riley?"

It was the same synthesized voice from before. "The back utility room here, was full of gray gelatin. I mean full, sir. When I opened the door it flooded out, nearly knocking us all over. It looks like the outside layer turns gray when exposed to the a vacuum, but not before you can see there are some skeletons—some of the colonists and several rats—inside of it."

"When you and your men enter the next dome, I want you to go through full quarantine procedures, do you understand? And vehicles stay on this side, don't take them with you. We're not going to have enough air to stay in this

depressurized dome. We'll set up in the next Residential one, Dome 6. Arrange to carry supplies by hand through the airlock, planning for a couple weeks. Make it happen please, Riley."
"Yessir."
It startled Jade when the Sheriff's door opened on the driver's side, but it was him. She hadn't realized he was walking back to the vehicle while he was talking to his deputy.
"Miss Carpania... oh sorry, I see you were a part of that conversation, my apologies. We're going to head to the next dome to setup a quarantine, a place for all of us to live until this has all been properly investigated. We have a small crew of biologists on the moon, I have sent a communication to them regarding the situation to see if they can help with the testing. We'll see if we can get you back to a normal life soon, okay?"
Her parents were dead and something had taken over the whole colony. She was never going to have a normal life again.

Chapter Three

Jade: Quarantine, Silver Dome 5, Residential District

When they reached the airlock, Sheriff John parked off to the side and got out of the vehicle, motioning that she should do the same.

"We won't be able to take the vehicles through to the next dome until they have been thoroughly decontaminated. The concentrated UV in the airlock can't reach all parts of them, so they'll have to be done separately. We can go through the airlock ourselves, just do as I do."

"Okay." Jade followed the Sheriff. He had removed his Sheriff's hat from the top of his helmet and was holding it in one hand. As he held his wrist up to a panel on the side of the airlock, the large gate slid open.

They proceeded inside and he held up his wrist again to a red-lit panel on the wall. The gate behind them closed, and the air rushed in immediately after. Bright, humming, purple lights came on, bathing the entire area in UV light.

Sheriff John turned in a circle, holding his arms up in the air, and made a twirling motion with his finger, so she followed suit, turning around with her arms up as well. After several seconds the panel turned green and the airlock door that led into the next dome slid open.

"Because the whole colony appears to have been infected, I can't promise that anywhere is safe. I would suggest remaining inside your pressure suit and just refill at the air exchangers. I'll invoke the Emergency Supplies Act, so you won't have to spend credits. You can empty your suit's waste recycler and refill your water pouch at the same time. Also pick up a long-term air tank there. It'll get uncomfortable to carry around after a while, but it'll give you a chance to sleep."

"Thanks, Sheriff."

He just smiled his toothy smile in return, trying to look reassuring.

The airlock gate slid open and he walked into the adjoining dome. Jade followed. The lights were on, but just like the Maintenance Dome, there was no movement anywhere in the buildings or on the road in front of her.

"And use extreme caution when touching anything, and I mean anything. You'll need food eventually, but I myself am going to resist eating for as long as I can, hoping they will be done investigating before then. I don't want to take my helmet off and be exposed to anything."

"Okay, thank you Sheriff."

"Pick a house to stay in. Here's a marker." He handed her a thick, black, charcoal crayon. "We're going to pick homes close to the air exchangers and do a thorough search for anyone that may be hiding. Just write your name on the door so we know it's you who is staying there, and put an X on the door if you have finished thoroughly searching a building. I don't mind if you help, but please stay in your suit. As soon as you find anyone, alive or not, just let us know on the radio."

"Will do."

"Your permits are in order, and your story checked out. I don't see any reason why I should still hang onto this." He handed her the Rail Slug pistol still in its holster, and she happily took it, comforted by its weight. She then headed for the air exchangers as she belted it back on. She needed a tank that would last several hours, like he had suggested, hers was only for short-term excursions.

The dust kicked up under Jade's feet. It took only a few minutes before she realized how lonely it could be without DAIM constantly nearby to converse with.

Jade picked up some long-term air tanks in the form of a large white pack she could strap over her shoulders. The hose from the air exchangers took care of her waste and replenishing the air in her smaller tank as a backup. She could sip from a straw in her helmet, but the water was body temperature and tasted a little like plastic. She had to purposefully avoid thinking about where most of the liquid came from, since it was her excreted body fluids that had been purified. Damn the Void! Now she was thinking about where the water came from. She was hungry too, having missed dinner tonight, after all that had happened, but she didn't want to risk exposing herself to the pathogen that had driven the colonists mad.

She picked a house close to the air exchanger to search. It had a small, two-seater wheeled electric car in the garage. She tried the handle and the door to the tiny habitat was unlocked. Jade drew her pistol before pushing the door open, ready for anything. It was dark inside, so she quickly reached around the inside wall and flicked the lights on.

It was a small bachelor suite with an adjoining bathroom. There was a queen-sized bed against one wall next to a closet and in the corner on a table there were two plates with half-finished food on them, and cups of coffee to match. After checking the bathroom to make sure the place was empty, she relaxed and re-holstered her pistol. It would do for a place to stay until all this was finished.

Jade wrote her name on the front door, but when she came back inside, one of the forks on a plate clanked and she froze. Slowly she stepped forward and looked over the plates carefully. Was that a small dot of the clear gel on one of the plates? It was nearly invisible, so it was understandable she missed it the first time. She looked around the room for any other telltale signs, and seeing none, she looked back. Had it moved a fraction of an inch inch closer to the food on the plate or did she just not remember its position exactly? She stared at it for what seemed forever, but no, it didn't move. She pulled down the mirrored visor on her helmet to cover her face and made a point of turning away, but kept an eye out of the side. Sure enough, the gel inched towards the food, leaving a small clean trail behind it. When she flipped the visor back up, but kept looking out the side of the helmet, it stopped moving. She shivered. This was no unintelligent blob. It could see her and knew what direction her eyes were facing. And yet how could it be so sophisticated? It was so small!

"Sheriff?"

"Go ahead, Miss Carpania."

"I've found some… goop, and it's alive. It's smart. Maybe not smart like we are, but smart enough it knows when I'm looking at it. I'm watching a little bit of it right now. It's eating food off a plate, and it only moves when it thinks I'm not looking. And it's very hard to see, it's like it's clear. I would almost say it can bend light around itself, but… that would be silly."

"Where are you? I'm coming to you."

"First street heading South from the air exchangers, first house on the left."

"Be right there, I can see your name written on the door from here."

She had been pretending to look away again, and the little jelly worked its way onto a piece of bay-clone, a favorite of meat eaters, cloned pig strips. The meat under the thing was slowly turning gray as it was being dissolved.

When the Sheriff stepped into the home, she motioned him over.

"I don't see…Oh! There it is!"

"Put your mirrored visor down and look at me Sheriff, like we're talking, but keep an eye on it out of the corner of your eye. It won't be able to tell that you are actually looking at it because of your visor, but I'm telling you, it moves when it

thinks you're not looking."
She could see he was doing as she had instructed and she did the same. She watched the little globule slowly traversing the piece of bay-clone leaving a gray stringy trail of digested meat behind it. It was growing. In that short time of eating it had almost doubled in size.
She purposefully turned her head to face it, flipping up the visor, and it froze again.
"I see what you mean. This is quite disturbing." Sheriff John stood up from the table and started to go through the kitchen cupboards, looking for something. When he found a small plastic container with a lid, he came back to the table. "Where is it?"
Jade glanced from him back down at the plate. There was no sign of the little glob. Immediately she jumped back, knocking over the chair she had been sitting in. "Holy Pyrite! Where is it?!" She stepped back while frantically slapping and brushing her suit off with her gloved hands. She scanned everywhere in the room but it was hard to focus because she kept imagining she could see it on her suit. It could be anywhere. "I can't stay in here..." She ran outside and did a jittery dance in the street while stomping the ground, hoping if it was on her it would fall off. Sheriff John followed shortly after.
"We need to get to the..." His last words crackled softly over the radio as he stopped in the street.
"Where? Where do we need to go, Sheriff?" It was then that she noticed on the side of his neck, the small wisp of smoke from a burn hole in his pressure suit. Damn the Void!
"Sheriff?"
He fell over and started convulsing. Fighting her instinct to

run, Jade grabbed onto his helmet and hit the clasp to release it and then twisted it off. He was staring at the sky and mouthing words but no sounds were coming out.

"What can I do Sheriff? Tell me!"

He looked at her for a moment, sorrowfully, and then a look of extreme pain and sadness crossed his face, and then his expression went blank.

Jade stepped back from him. She had seen that look before. In Callen. His limbs started to contort slowly, unnaturally, and then he crawled toward her. Jade backed away.

"Nngug." He stopped approaching her and cocked his head to the side, almost like he was listening to something. "Neg ug shee" One more time he stopped and then shakily pushed himself to his feet. Wobbily. As if for the first time. "Negug-shee-ate."

"Negotiate? Is that what you are trying to say?"

His eyes were looking independently of each other, like a chameleon and his mouth motions when he spoke were exaggerated.

He took a sharp breath and then said "Yesss," in a long hiss, and then he waited. Not he. It. This was no longer a 'he'. It wasn't the Sheriff.

Jade turned off the external speaker so she wouldn't be heard by—whatever it was—and connected to the emergency channel. In a few moments one of the female deputies in the dome spoke through the speakers in her helmet. "We're connected Miss Carpania, What's your status?"

"Sheriff John has been... taken over. The infection is a... jelly... that can burn through our pressure suits, don't touch any of it! We're in the street, near the air exchangers. He—it —says it wants to negotiate."

"My name is Deputy Halzurg. If Sheriff John has been compromised, I am the next in command. Though I'm, uh, not really trained in First Contact Protocol. Keep your distance ma'am, we'll be there shortly."

They didn't need to tell her twice.

Jade drew her pistol and pointed it at the creature that was Sheriff John. "You know what this is? Keep your distance! Someone will be here shortly to speak with you."

The two wandering eyes suddenly fixated together on the pistol. "Isss hossst killrr." And then it made an eerie too-wide smile, showing off the Sheriff's mouth full of sharp teeth.

The smile gave Jade the shivers. Host killer. So it likely wouldn't kill the parasite that was the creature? That made sense. It seemed to survive fine outside the body. As she watched, the Sheriff was learning to stand straighter, with more confidence. His eyes no longer wandered. Then she realized the stance, the disappearing smile turning into a look of concern… it was mimicking her! Copying her actions. When it reached for the Sheriff's blaster in the same manner she had reached for her pistol, she panicked.

"Stop!" She was about to pull the trigger when it hesitated. "Wass jusst copying youu."

The words were already getting clearer. Void, this thing learned fast. "If you draw that I will be forced to shoot."

"Forssed to sshoot." The words mimicked, but the hand moved away from the blaster. "Forced to shoot." It almost sounded like the Sheriff.

Deputy Halzurg arrived at a quick jog. She would have appeared as a Human in hiking boots, cargo shorts and a t-shirt, if she didn't have shining metal skin. A biobot, or fully-enhanced human. A woman that was fully mechanized by

NRS, Nanite Replacement Surgery. Jade had heard of biobots before, but she had never seen one. Well, until now. Deputy Halzurg must have worked in a different dome than the Sheriff. And bonus for her, she didn't need a pressure suit because she didn't need to breathe. She would have made a great miner.

"Abomination…" the thing hissed, much to Jade's surprise as it went to draw the Sheriff's blaster.

BWAP! BWAP! Jade fired twice into the Sheriff's chest and was prepared to fire more, but the Sheriff's body teetered awkwardly and then fell backwards while the mouth muttered "Abomination…" repeatedly. The shots were dead center, probably severing the spine.

The Deputy drew her own weapon and kept it pointed at the body on the ground as she stepped forward, kicking the Sheriff's blaster off to the side. "I didn't even say anything. Why am I an abomination?"

"We are the Ma'akdalube, one with the Deliverer." The Sheriff's mouth was spitting blood while it spoke, but it wasn't choking and coughing as any normal Organic would have. "You are an abomination, cannot receive the Deliverer's message…"

"And what is this message?" Deputy Halzurg asked, but the Sheriff's eyes had lost focus and the thing had stopped talking. Jade fell to her knees in front of the small man's body. "I'm sorry, Sheriff…"

She jumped back horrified when clear jelly oozed from his nose and mouth. Far more than the tiny glob that had burned through his collar.

When doors opened on several of the nearby habitats and blobs the size of men oozed from the homes, Jade started firing indiscriminately into the center of them, a couple of them collapsing into a thick grayish puddles, but the rest continued to close from all sides. The Deputy joined her with a barrage of laser fire, but some of the blobs had gooey tentacles and they snapped those around her limbs as they got close, pulling her off her feet.

As Jade turned back toward the Sheriff's body, the ooze squirted at her, hitting her faceplate and the glass started to smoke where it touched.

As she felt the slap of pseudopods grabbing her limbs, Jade screamed. Only one thought fought its way through the abject terror and gave her comfort: At least she would soon see her parents in the Void.

Chapter Four

DAIM: Brightside, Prospector's Paradise

When DAIM first became aware again, her HUD's internal clock informed her that she had been shut down for 658 years, 29 days and 7 hours. That couldn't be. She was only supposed to be out for a few days until her trial. Jade would have died hundreds of years ago, unless she struck it rich and paid for the services of one of those clone backup facilities. Or maybe she was fully enhanced. As a biobot she could last thousands of years with proper maintenance. DAIM could hope. She didn't want to accept the alternative.
The fission reactor's power output was flashing red. That's why she had woken up, her emergency protocols had been activated. She needed to get new fuel rods. Hers had

depleted and she was running on battery power.

When her cameras came on, everything was black. Had they locked her in a travel crate and forgotten about her? She turned on the low-rad emitters, the ones she used in the mines, and immediately she could see in the red reflected light that she was covered by rubble from the building they had parked her in so long ago. A large part of the wall that said *Detainment Cell* was still in front of her.

When she tried to move, more weight settled on top of her. Approximately twenty tons. Not an insurmountable mass, but more than she could lift in this state. Weakly she started to drill, with stuttering power. She needed to be careful. If she expended all her energy, she would simply shut down and then who knew how long she would be here. Maybe forever until the Void took them all.

DAIM managed to crack the dustcrete wall in front of her and felt the resistance as she hit the strengthening rebar inside, but it too gave way in a shower of sparks as her drill went through the wall, creating a small opening.

Maybe she could push through. She engaged her tracks, and the lights inside the cockpit bubble dimmed as she struggled against the massive weight on top of her, but the wall in front of her shifted.

If she was right, one more final shove… She diverted as much power as she could spare to her caterpillar tracks and in one surge, managed to break free of her prison in a cascade of falling dustcrete blocks and polysteel beams, but she stopped in the street as her lights dimmed, losing power almost completely for a moment. She had been at five percent when she had woken up. She was now at four.

It was dark out. No street lights or building lights greeted her.

Just stars and the dark mass that covered half the sky that was Epsilon Eridani B.

Mother B. The large gas giant that held them in orbit was often depicted as holding out cupped hands from her surface to cradle its moon, Prospector's Paradise, safely in them. It was the trademark of Masterex Mining. Their wall was currently in front of her as she shined her emitters on it. The trademark on the worn bricks glowed as she passed over them, the low frequency radiation triggering the phosphor pigments in the old paint.

Organics and their symbols. Silly really. It was far more efficient to name things rather than apply an image to them. There were fallen husks from many of the taller buildings, though most of the smaller ones were still standing. Boulders of polyglass from the collapsed dome littered the road. Some were larger than her. Seemed likely that someone else was going to be at trial for collapsing a dome, if there was anyone left. Doubtful now.

She brought up her map of Brightside. She needed to get to the Maintenance Dome, they would have spare fuels rods there. A quick scan of the area revealed the fallen buildings and the largest of the dome fragments. She compared her results to the Brightside map, allowing her to calculate the quickest, safest path, barring any unforeseen obstacles. DAIM's tracks clacked slowly as she made her way around the obstructions in the road and she stopped when ahead there was a large pool of gray ooze that had leaked out of a convenience store half-way into the road. She could make out bones and pressure suits sticking out of it. Nothing moved, besides her and the dust she kicked up from her tracks.

She made a wide circle around the ooze, making sure not to touch it, and in doing so passed the body of a biobot riddled with laser holes. Seeing a biobot in that condition saddened her as it left little hope that Jade had survived.

As DAIM neared the airlock to the next dome, her view was no longer obstructed by the buildings. There was supposed to be numerous other shining domes, but they were all collapsed. Just like this one, with low circular cracked walls. Like an egg that had been crushed by a hammer, leaving only the jagged shells jutting up from the ground as evidence they had even existed.

She passed both Organics and Robotics, laying in the roadway. The Robotics were wrecked, all of them appearing to have been shot through the memory core after defeat. It was a shame, all that lost potential. Lost knowledge. Lost life. Most of the Organics were desiccated and had oozed gray slime from various wounds and natural orifices.

The Maintenance Dome was close now, just the next one over, but with all the destruction, she wasn't sure of the state of the Power Exchangers. They might no longer be working. She would have to change her objective.

"I'm sorry brothers and sisters," DAIM said aloud as she sorted through the clusters of dead Robotics, shoving aside the ones with ruined power cores using her drill arms, but she eventually came across what she was looking for. A few whose power cores were still intact, and still had a bit of juice left.

Gently with her drill points, she pulled apart the power casings and touched the leads to the batteries. Routing the power through her arms into her own batteries, she charged quickly until the dial topped out at eighteen percent. It was all she would need for now, and certainly enough to check the Power Exchangers.

The tracks clacked faster now, and she moved with more confidence toward the Maintenance Dome airlock.

The large metal doors on both sides of the airlock were stuck in the open position. They must have been hacked, because they were programmed for safety to only open one when the other was closed.

If that was overridden on all the airlocks, all the domes would have collapsed at once, as soon as the first one depressurized. If DAIM had been Organic she would have shivered. The enormity—the thoroughness—of this devastation... It went far beyond her collapse of a single dome. This was the destruction of an entire colony.

When she arrived at the Power Exchange, she was disappointed to see that a building had fallen across the bays, but at the end stall it still appeared that there might be a high enough opening for her to fit inside.

She didn't fit, but after maneuvering a fallen beam with her drill arms, she wedged it beneath the collapsed rubble. Hammering it at the bottom forced the top a bit higher each time, increasing the size of the opening.

She lowered her chassis as low as it could go and scraped under the doorway into the Power Exchange bay.

Thankfully there was power still operating the bays. The colony's solar arrays must still be working, so some capacity at least.

A red light scanned her and then a magnetic power coupling from the wall of the bay snapped onto her external fuel rod port and twisted pulling the expended fuel rod free. A new one emerged from the wall, and as soon as it was inserted and locked into place, the power surged through her battery array. Immediately her displays brightened and she could feel the full access to her core. Should be good for another five to seven hundred years, as soon as her backup was replaced. Something was odd though. Now that her power was charging at full capacity, she was detecting a faint SOS signal from beyond the colony, somewhere out in the Dust Wastes. No one should be out there, there was no ore in the Dust Wastes.

DAIM listened to the broadcast after amplifying it to the point the audio was legible.

"Mayday, Mayday, Mayday! This is the Robotic designated as Jack-Hammer, Third Class Rock Sunderer, broadcasting on all standard emergency frequencies. Do NOT approach Prospector's Paradise. Repeat: Do NOT approach. Planetary Quarantine protocols in effect."

The message was playing on repeat. It was dim though, this Jack-Hammer was likely having battery issues as well. If he was in a shaded spot, he wouldn't be able to recover using sunlight. She had to check. He was the only one that she had contact with. No one was answering on the other frequencies. It was too bad she hadn't splurged on the satellite radio instead of the local wireless, but then how could you predict something like this was going to happen? She shouldn't be so hard on herself.

DAIM sent an *acknowledged* ping to let Jack know that his message had been received, but there was no response. The silence reminded her of how alone she really was. Jade was dead, she would have died centuries ago, and that was the biggest loss that she felt right now. It seemed like only yesterday she had collapsed the dome and escaped to

Brightside. Jade had been alive then, but six hundred years... What had happened? Whatever had caused the people to go mad had obviously spread. DAIM couldn't cry, but she understood the loss, every time she thought of something that she and Jade normally did together. Maybe she could find this Jack-Hammer, he was the only other thing alive that she was aware of.

There was a screech of metal from somewhere beyond the bay she was in, and immediately her sensors were on high alert. Okay, maybe he wasn't the *only* thing. That sound would have had to have been pretty loud in order for her to hear it in the light atmosphere. Sound couldn't travel very far. It could have been a building settling, but how could she know for sure? Without moving, DAIM listened, ranging through all the frequencies, but her hearing was no better than the average Organic.

Not wanting to end up like the rest of the dead Robotics, she turned around in the bay and slowly made her way out, creeping an inch at a time. She was almost out when her hopper caught on the edge of the rubble letting out a metallic screech of her own.

DAIM froze, but it was too late, there was movement down the road to her left as another digger emerged from a side street, its movements starting and stopping awkwardly. It was one of the large ones, probably thirty tons, and through the bubble cockpit in its chest she could see an operator in a pressure suit. The large diggers were supposed to remain outside the domes, not that it mattered anymore. Half of the digger's head had been blown off by an explosive round of some kind, judging by the blackened scoring. The torn and melted metal would have destroyed its processor core. That explained the jerky movements, the Organic operator wasn't skilled in the digger's operation.

It turned in her direction, and as soon as the pilot's helmet fixated on her position a message blasted over her radio.

"Abomination!"

At least twenty others from indeterminate locations repeated the word together over the radio.

"Abomination!"

They had to be within this dome, or at furthest a few domes over, DAIM's radio didn't have a great range. It wasn't the others she had to worry about right now though, it was just the one.

The digger shot toward her, the heavy drill arms detaching from their clamps and spreading wide in a threatening manner. The drill arms alone probably weighed as much as she did.

There was no way she could confront it. DAIM floored it with a loud scraping squeal as she bolted out of the maintenance bay, heading in the opposite direction of the looming digger. When she glanced in her rear view camera, the cloud of dust she was kicking up barely reached half the height of the oncoming juggernaut. And it was gaining on her. If she didn't do something shortly, she was going to be scrap.

Looking left and right at the rubble on the side streets, she picked a narrow alley that had a building leaning over it. It was just big enough for her, there was no way the massive digger would fit through there.

Turning hard and tipping a little as she did so, DAIM shot into the alley, bouncing and scraping off the walls.

A quick glance again in the rear view camera showed the

monstrous digger wasn't going to be deterred as it crashed into the building at full speed with a deep, thunderous boom, halting its progress. Part of its front chassis buckled, but the entire building that had fallen over the alley jolted forward hard and caused the walls of the supporting building in the alley to crack and break as the beams leaned at an angle. There was more cracking as the beams continued to tip, unable to support the uneven load, and at the end of the alley in front of her, large chunks of dustcrete and brick fell in a heavy cascade, blocking her escape.

She needed to do something quick, or she was going to be trapped, at least long enough for the attacking digger to reach her and grind her into filings.

DAIM detached the clamps on her own driller arms, rotating them in a circular motion downwards in front of her, digging easily through the compacted dust that supported her. Even as the building's weight crushed down on her, her shocks absorbing the load, she sank into the shallow depression she had created. A few moments more and she was safe beneath the colony.

DAIM had a few moments of breathing room now, but who knew if the other digger was following her still or not? It might think she was trapped or crushed. Then again, it might search the rubble.

She started digging a tunnel, but not in the direction of the Dust Wastes. Maybe Jack-Hammer could help her, or maybe they could just escape, but if the large digger did find her tunnel, she didn't want to lead it in the real direction she intended on heading. She would circle back in a bit.

There were strict laws against digging beneath a colony dome, and one of the reasons why was made obvious when she struck a water pipe and was soon waist deep in mud. Digging almost straight down, DAIM was soon completely under water, but there was nothing it could do to harm her. If anything, it acted more as a coolant, making her more efficient, she could drill at higher speeds. She couldn't see two inches through the mud, but it wasn't a problem. Blind tunneling was common. She just had to measure how far her tracks had moved without slipping. And now she just needed to find the only other person that could possibly be on her side. This Jack-Hammer.

DAIM emerged from the dust covered in dirt and mud, having slowly drilled her way back to the surface. When she looked back, the giant digger in the distance could be seen pounding its drills into the building rubble.

She drove slowly in the direction the signal from Jack-Hammer had come from so she didn't kick up a big dust cloud. At least until the natural slope of the land hid the dome from her vision and she didn't have to worry about being spotted. Still, she didn't feel safe, so had to search for Jack-Hammer without using any wireless.

She could listen without sending though. She paused for a moment. There was no signal. His power must have died. DAIM drove back and forth across the wastes, looking for any clue, until she spotted tracks in the dust; a pair of parallel tank treads, a few feet apart so about a quarter of her size, that led further out into the wastes. That had to be him.

She followed the tracks as they wound around the dust dunes until she came across his powerless husk.

He was a sunderer, a rock crusher and ore separator. A Robotic with a humanoid-ish torso, tracks instead of wheels and large, chiseled jackhammers extending from the back of his fists. At least he had hands for separating the ore. DAIM was a little jealous. It was hard to manipulate things gently when all you had was drills. Sunderers would accompany diggers in the field, riding in the digger's hopper and breaking down and discarding the waste rock in order to maximize the quality of ore for the return home. Jade and DAIM had never needed one. Jade was—had been—an expert at getting the highest quality of ore into the hopper without a lot of waste.

She approached the motionless Robotic with the intent of trying to break into his battery compartment and provide him some charge, but as soon as she touched him he spun to face her, jackhammer chisels held menacingly in front of him.

His face was a smooth mirrored helmet, so there was no expression to gauge, but DAIM decided he wouldn't have been trying to keep others from approaching if he hadn't programmed himself for good. She clamped her drill at her sides to show that she wasn't a threat.

Jack-Hammer didn't back down. "State your intentions." At least he was communicating over short-range wireless, so she didn't need to worry about anyone eavesdropping. "I think we're the only friendlies left alive, at least that I've seen. I got your message warning others to stay away. Do you know what happened?"

"Show yourself first."

DAIM was confused. She was standing right in front… OH! The cockpit bubble was covered in mud! He thought she had a pilot. She turned on her cockpit spray nozzles briefly, followed by the hot air vents.

Jack relaxed once he could see that she had no one operating her. "Sorry, I should have thought of that earlier."

He put his arms down at his sides and the jackhammer chisels retracted back into his forearms. "I'll answer your question. The people were all taken over by some kind of parasite, an ambulatory jelly with a prismatic outer membrane that naturally allows it to bend light around itself. It digests the brain of its host, or at least a large portion of it, and controls their bodies through the existing nerves. I had the benefit of getting briefed by Deputy Halzurg before the colony was unexpectedly overrun. I fled, much to my own disappointment, as I had expected that more colonists would survive. Perhaps if I had stayed behind to help, more would have."

"Don't sweat it, Jack. I don't think you would have made much difference, I was lucky to get out alive too, and there was only one chasing me. Besides, you've been warning ships to stay away. Think of how many lives you may have saved since."

"That's… kind of you to say, thank you. I'm actually surprised to see you, I thought I was the only one left. I don't get much power anymore though, I simply rely on what little solar energy I get to keep up the quarantine signal, and even though I managed to send the information over the systems relay to Earth, by the time it gets there, near eleven years, hundreds, perhaps thousands of ships will have visited the moon, and I didn't have enough energy to warn them all, especially those on the other side. The system relay now warns everyone, but who knows if the parasite managed to return on a visiting ship, and how far it has spread since."

"Well let me help you." DAIM maneuvered to turn her side toward Jack. "You can have my backup fuel rod, then we can see about getting off of this planet. Though it could take several centuries more before help arrives."

"Thank you, I appreciate your offer, I will happily take you up on it." Jack twisted out her backup fuel rod swapped it with one of his own.

A large dust cloud erupted above the dunes in the distance, in the direction of the colony. The large digger appeared and disappeared as it drove over the dunes, heading in their direction.

Jack's chisels snapped forward out of his forearms and he took a position hidden just below the edge of the dune the digger would arrive over. "When we're done with this, I'm getting re-purposed. I want to do something positive in this life to make up for all the loss."

DAIM took her position, drills out on the opposite side of the dune from Jack. Her drills started spinning at a high speed. "If I'm re-purposed, it will be so I never lose another friend again."

Chapter Five

DAIM: Brightside Dust Wastes

As the massive digger passed over the dune DAIM was hiding behind, she drove one driller arm into its tracks on the side facing her. As her arm caught, she was dragged several paces beside the juggernaut until the limb was torn free with a screeching wrench. The driller arm disintegrated as it spun through the diggers wheels and tracks, but the diamond-hard drill bit jammed between one drive wheel and the track until it finally seized and snapped.
The huge vehicle spun in a cloud of dust, and kept spinning as one track continued to churn dust up behind it, the operator refusing to lighten up on the throttle.
DAIM thought he was mad until the spinning miner brought

one thundering drill arm down in front of her, missing her by mere inches, before the arm spun away and she could see the second coming around.

She backed away, keeping out of range of further strikes as the enormous drill arms pounded holes in the dust in front of her. At least she and Jack could escape now as the enemy could no longer follow them.

Just then Jack bounced over a dune as if launched from a catapult. One enormous arm swung towards him in the air, but kept spinning out of range before it could strike him, and then with chisels out in jackhammer mode, Jack landed on the cockpit and drove the long metal rods through the bubble glass. They were too short to hit the pilot, and though they had penetrated the glass and it had cracked extensively, it hadn't shattered, and the holes from the chisels weren't widening.

The spinning digger threatened to throw him free and he now clung helplessly to the cockpit bubble.

DAIM was sure he was done for as the massive driller arms started smashing him repeatedly and then the entire wild scene came to a dust-settling halt.

Jack was stuck beneath the two driller arms of the juggernaut. He was dented badly, but still functioning enough to try to struggle free. As DAIM approached wondering if she could somehow help with her remaining arm, he managed to get loose, landing on his back in front of her.

"It's like it didn't think it through. It was so set on destroying me that it ended up smashing me through the bubble, killing itself. I assume unintentionally." He pulled himself up from the sand and retracted his forearm chisels.

"You know, I had disabled it's track on one side, it couldn't have followed us."

"Oh. I thought it was chasing you in circles. I couldn't see over the dune. Well, it's done now. Let's get out of here before more show up."

Jack led her over several dunes to a small mining road. "They will lose our tracks here. We can detour off into the wastes further down the road."

DAIM nodded her agreement and followed the now-damaged Jack, though he still managed to travel at a decent pace despite a few pieces missing from his tracks. Not that she wasn't damaged herself, she had lost an arm. What they really needed was to get off this world, or at least warn others to stay away.

Part Two
Present Day, Incarcerata IV

Chapter Six

Gabriel: Forest, East Coast of Farrun, Incarcerata IV

Gabriel locked his wings so he could glide over the forest of blade-leafed trees. No point in wasting energy, they could be searching for a while. A couple locks of blond hair annoyingly whipped into his eyes and he brushed them aside for the twentieth time. He would need to get a haircut soon by hand, it's not like there was an Auto-Barber on this planet. He brought his attention back to the task at hand. His new companions needed supplies for their voyage back to the continent of Candistra, which would take at least a week. The ant-men, the Chakran, had shot the airship to pieces, leaving only the flat deck with tatters beneath. The near impregnable rock-spider-silk zeppelin balloon that carried the ship still had laser holes in it, but the heater that filled the balloon was strong enough to compensate for the damage. They had lost all of their cargo so their planned trip was probably premature—they had no containers for food or water, no smoked or dried provisions. No extra clothing. Not even any shelter on the deck. They wanted to get away from the gigantic caelum vermis, or skygrubs, that carried the hives of the Chakran on their backs, but starving to death wasn't going to help.

There! His mind touched on the animal he was hunting below. He looked down and caught a glimpse of a horse-sized fur-covered quadruped through the trees. The meat of most furred animals was edible, it should do.

He didn't mind meat. Soldiers needed their strength and there were benefits to a high protein diet. Most of his race though, like Angel, were vegetarian. He looked more like a bronze, well-muscled human with wings than his thinner, lighter-boned kin that sustained themselves on vegetables. Gabriel landed in a small meadow, a few seconds ahead of the creature, and detached the pair of black, metallic whips that Angel had given him. As he uncoiled them, he flicked his wrists to get the long barbed blades at the ends in motion and it wasn't a moment too soon as the beast came crashing through the trees into the meadow. Gabriel's heart caught in his throat as a moment of fear took him. It was larger than he had originally estimated, and it was fast. There was no discernible head, just a powerful body hidden beneath thick fur, supported by reverse-jointed legs that ended in sharp, split hooves.

Using his wings for an extra boost, he leapt straight up in the air while spinning to give the whips some momentum and heard the satisfying Chuk! Chuk! as the blades struck true, each sinking deep into a shoulder of the creature. Reflexively, it leapt to the side, jerking him with it, so hard he had to release his hold on the whips. He struck the ground, rolling as his wings formed a protective shell around him, only to stop directly in front of the beast. Immediately the creature tensed, preparing to leap on him. An enormous mouth ringed with rows of inward facing fangs opened on the front, ready to engulf him. He had no time to escape.

In two thunderous footsteps a giant, black, stone-scaled humanoid, tackled the beast and rolled with it across the meadow into the edge of the forest, breaking a few small trees in its path. With one long crushing squeeze, Mogul the Ramogran hugged the quadruped tightly. It clawed at him frantically, tearing some impressive lacerations through Mogul's rock-hard scales and then there were multiple loud cracking sounds and a single squeal as the creature shuddered and went limp in his arms. One enormous arm daintily plucked out the whips stuck in the creature and dropped them in front of Gabriel as he walked past, the other arm carrying the carcass.

"These for you?" Mogul smiled, as much as thick rock scales on an enormous jaw could smile. His outward action seemed boastful, but Gabriel could detect no gloating at all in Mogul's mind, just the thrill of the hunt, and the relief of protecting a friend from grave injury. Some pain, but it was being ignored.

Gabriel was flattered to be considered a friend already, since they'd only met hours before. The Ramogran seemed very accepting of others.

"Thank you, Mogul." Gabriel resisted the urge to stimulate

the giant's pleasure center in thanks, as was customary with the Valkyrie. Most non-telepaths didn't understand or appreciate the mental gesture. It was seen as some sort of 'intrusion'. A word that was hard to understand when you grew up knowing all the thoughts of every other member of your race in passing, and they, in turn, knew yours.

Gabriel retrieved the whips and started following the Ramogran through the forest in the direction of the airship. After wiping the blades on the fur of the beast Mogul was carrying, he re-coiled them and hooked them on the clasp on the back of his belt, then leapt back into the air with a few thrusts of his wings.

He saw the bullet-shaped, patchwork, zeppelin balloon long before he would reach it. It was the length of three cyber-ball fields, after all.

There was a layer of low clouds they had passed through to the south, as they had fled north to escape sight of the Chakran, but that didn't mean they were safe. There were close to a hundred hives his friends had confronted. Hmm, confronted was wrong. They had boarded one with stealth—infiltrated was a better word. Who knew how many more were interspersed around the continent, though?

Suddenly he felt Angel's scream in his head, causing his flight to falter. He nearly fell into the trees, but managed to put up some mental defenses and catch himself in time. She wasn't the first woman he had helped through the 'Year of Breeding' but her fits of frustration and raw sexual drive were far more powerful than he was used to. She was an exceptional individual, being a healer after all, and her connection to Rusty had seriously… affected her. The Goblin's accelerated mind had caused a sort of addiction and she was going through withdrawal, something he hadn't seen before. Gabriel had been tempted to ask the Goblin if he wanted to have sex as well, just to see if he experienced the same overwhelming addiction, but then how could he help Angel if he succumbed to the same thing? And the Goblin did seem monogamous with his Vesuvian partner, Zondra. No, it was safer just to stick to traditional methods. Though he might actually have to impregnate her to stop the breeding urges. At this level of mental power he wasn't sure he could survive her for long, his head was pounding, but if he didn't help, she wouldn't survive either. He would have to ask her when she was more lucid and less—occupied.

Chapter Seven

Chais: WOLF Carrier Nemesis, Orbiting Incarcerata

IV

Chais was suffering from the darkness and silence of sensory deprivation. She could feel through tactile sensors on her hands and feet and she had a couple of metal detectors, but since her sister, Lais, had ripped off her head in the forest on Incarcerata IV she had lost all of her other senses. Thankfully her processors and memories were distributed throughout her body so she hadn't lost the ability to function, but putting most of the sensors on the head seemed to be a lack of foresight. Not that she had grown this body with this design,

Chang had. She still felt a small twinge of guilt about deleting him when she occupied his body, but it had been an accident so not worth spending a lot of time thinking about. She couldn't even blame Lais for tearing her head off, she wasn't really given any other choice. She would have been dead otherwise.

Lais must have picked her up by a large grapple or clamp, because wherever Chais reached out to touch with her hands, there was nothing there. It was like that for several minutes, she had been likely dangling from a tree in the forest, and then suddenly there was ferrous metal nearby, in every direction. Lots of it. A cage maybe? She found it unlikely that Lais had access to a metal room on a planet that had little to no technology, but it was possible. She tried to tell her nanites to regrow her head, but they weren't responding. They had little difficulty in repairing even serious wounds, so why were they failing now? Maybe a limb as complicated as the head was too much for them? She formed her laser rifle just to make sure she could still do it, and it emerged from her chest slowly as if growing from her and then fell into her hands.

So the nanites still worked, that wasn't the issue. Rapidly flipping through her distributed memory systems she found the answer. In the Technoid reproduction section of all things. Once something was grown a particular way and was then damaged, the nanites could repair it, but only if the required materials were available to do so. She was lacking materials to regrow the head. She set the nanites to leech materials from what they touched, but it was slow going, and she was only gaining steel. She still required a number of other elements if she was going to recreate her head.

The laser rifle! She could change it into almost anything she desired, it just took a little time to rearrange the molecules. She could steal from it! Before she ordered the scavenging of the rifle though, she checked her records. Only once she was satisfied that the loss of the rifle wasn't permanent did she absorb the materials of it back into herself using the nanites. Once absorbed, she deallocated the materials, leaving them open to be used for anything else.

Chais was relieved when she felt the nanites re-growing her head, starting at the missing pieces of her spine and neck. It would take days, at this rate, but if there was one thing she had it was lots of time. Time to think about why Lais was so adamant about protecting the flesh-beings, to the point where she would effectively fight her twin rather than join her.

Chapter Eight

Gabriel: Airship, Forest, East Coast of Farrun

The warm wind blew through Gabriel's hair, and the feathers of his wings, causing him to close his eyes just for a moment to enjoy the feeling. He had clipped his bangs so they wouldn't flap into his eyes anymore.

He angled his approach to the giant patchwork zeppelin balloon anchored to the trees below in such a way as to keep the sun out of his eyes. As he got closer, Gabriel could make out who was who on the airship without needing to see the details. He had met them all in just a few hours ago, but he already felt like he knew them. It helped that Angel had sent her memories of her past to catch him up.

Zondra stood out the most, the Vesuvian's blue skin and

tentacled hair a stark contrast to the dark wood of the ship, and everyone else. He couldn't quite make out her round black eyes at this distance, but he would be able to shortly. The robots, of course, were easy to make out too. Chrome mostly, but their shapes were very distinguishable, even at this distance. Synth-E-Uh was a large humanoid combat droid with sleek lines, and Gatling lasers on her forearms. Her lower base was built like a tank with treads, and she had an angled grill on the front, probably for ramming. Jack Hammer looked more fragile, primarily his monitors for his chest and face standing out. His chest monitor had a long crack Gabriel had helped seal with pitch. Jack had a smaller base and treads, nowhere near as threatening as Synth-E-Uh. His spindly metal arms almost weren't visible from here, but the yellow smiling emoji on his face screen definitely was. Gabriel couldn't read his mind, Jack was mechanical after all, but he had never seen the robot have anything other than a smiling face for more than a fraction of a second. Maybe they could all take a few lessons from him.

He could see a bronze feathered cone perched on the bow of the airship. He couldn't see the individual white-spotted feathers, or the beautiful turquoise eyes framed by long, sandy blond locks, but he knew they were there. Angel was sitting near the bow of the airship and had wrapped her wings around herself, hiding her feminine humanoid form. It looked like she hadn't moved since he had left. He couldn't help worrying about her, her mind was so strained he feared for her sanity.

Mogul, the largest of all of them, was seated with his legs dangling in through the hole in the deck that used to lead to the bottom of the ship, the bottom that had fallen out during the battle with the Chakran hives.

Keena, the female human in a white body suit, was next to Lais in her black outfit. Keena was a young woman, likely early twenties, that had been rescued from slavers, with her sister who had died soon after. The girl had been rail thin when she was found. It seemed like she had fully recovered, regaining a lot of muscle when he compared the picture in his mind of her now versus then, when Angel helped her at the waterfall.

Lais was an attractive human woman, straight black hair hanging over one of her striking, bright-green eyes. Only she wasn't human. She was some sort of sophisticated android, that had showed up one day with her twin, not-twin, Chais. Gabriel couldn't connect with her mind and that was… mildly disconcerting, same as with any Robotic. Angel completely accepted her. Gabriel was leaning towards trusting that opinion, but humans were so prone to lie, and this one he couldn't even verify her intentions because he couldn't connect with her mind. He needed more time to get to know her.

Keena and Lais were crouched over the furred beast that Mogul had killed. Still rendering it then. They were next to the hole in the deck, probably throwing away the undesired bits, but then even as he thought it he realized he was wrong. Lais made a throwing motion, tossing something at Mogul and the giant rock-ogre's head snapped up to catch what was thrown in its huge maw. Okay, so not much would go to waste.

Gabriel tightened his grip on the armload of silks and items he had recovered, things they had lost during the battle. He had flown back along the path they had described and had stayed low, just above the trees. There were still hives about, but they were high up in the clouds now, well out of the visual range to see a single person.

As he got close to the zeppelin, he angled his wings to dive beneath the balloon. He spun sideways between the numerous strings that stretched between the rails and the balloon netting to land firmly, but as balanced as a gymnast, on the airship deck. Aerial acrobatics came as second nature when you had been flying your whole life.

He deposited the silks in a small pile in front of Rusty; the goblin man with round black eyes and a toothy grin; the one that Angel was addicted to. All eyes turned to him as he landed, but after a moment went back to their business. All eyes except Angel. Her head didn't raise above her wings.

"You were right, Rusty, there was a long trail of silks and items in the tops of the trees to the southwest. The Chakran were in the clouds, so no trouble. I recovered a tool sack." Gabriel dug through the silks in front of him until he pulled one lumpy one out that was tied at the top and pulled the drawstring to free it. There was a set of simple tongs, a hammer, a small, thin, metal spike with a hole in the end, like a large needle, and a whetstone. "I'm sorry, I looked, but I couldn't find much else, other than several cases that contained useless appliances."

Lais held up a bloody hand, and pointed at the tools with a dripping black dagger. "Those are perfect, at least the needle I can use for stitching the laser holes in the silk. And a hammer is always useful for knocking sense into things." She made a hammering motion as she looked at Jack and laughed as his emoji changed to a cock-eyed confused one, but only for a moment before it changed back to his usual smiley face.

"Ooh, you almost had me there, Miss," Jack said to Lais. He let go of the flap string he'd been holding to point back at her and then immediately changed his mind and grabbed the string again.

Synth-E-Uh was attaching the propeller shaft to one of her tank wheels. "You're the last one to return, Gabriel. Anything to report?"

"The Chakran are up in the clouds, and have spread out to try to discover our whereabouts, but it appears they fear separating, strength in numbers and all that, so haven't made any significant progress in this direction. If we keep heading inland, west, northwest, we should be able to avoid them and circle around back toward the coast. Pending any other unknowns showing up of course."

"Of course." There was a solid click and then whine as Synth-E-Uh started spinning the propeller. Mogul leaned over and gave the anchor rope a sharp yank. There was a loud crack and a snap and then he pulled up the anchor to reveal a large branch attached to it, which he plucked from the anchor's barb and tossed back over the side of the ship. Immediately, there was a sinking feeling in Gabriel's stomach as the zeppelin rose in the air, a feeling he always found strange since he didn't get it when he flew to higher altitudes himself. His presence no longer needed, Gabriel walked to the bow and knelt in front of Angel. As soon as he touched her, her wings snapped open and she grabbed his head in her hands, pulling it tightly to her own forehead. Although she was being rough physically, it was nothing compared to the mental pain she stabbed into his brain, mixed with a sick ecstasy that competed in intensity. He let it happen, for as long as she needed it, he couldn't say for how long. It felt like hours, but was more likely just a minute. Many times he grimaced at the pain, gritting his teeth, until he was noticeably sweating. At the end he felt the horror from Angel at what she had just done, for which he immediately forgave her.

"Just relax now, it has passed," he said aloud, choosing not to connect mentally again for now. No point in encouraging another episode.

Tears ran from her eyes down her cheeks until they dripped from her chin. "I know you accept this all as necessary, but I'm still sorry. And you left your position in the military, a Commander…!"

"Life would mean little to me if I let someone innocent suffer as you have." He stopped to wipe the tears from her cheeks. "Especially since I am uniquely qualified to help you, I have been through this before."

Angel sighed and gave him a strained smile. "And I am thankful for you."

"Have you considered having a child? This would all end…"
Immediately her look turned to one of disgust. "You think I would bear a child simply to rid myself of pain?!"

He was going to deny it, something he would have never even have considered if he had stayed on Tallus, but stopped himself. She was right, that had been what he was thinking. It was funny how being around all the lonely alien minds and their thoughts of insecurity, betrayal and hatred corrupted his own.

"I would help of course…"

Her look softened. "I know you would, and I know you suggested it out of concern, but think of the world. Bringing a child into this world, a world of slavery, a world with little medicine, with little technology... Would we really want to raise a child in this place? It would have no siblings, no friends its age to learn and play with..."

"What about Holbrook? They had children there..."

"Yes, children that are unfortunately raised by xenophobes. Many of them anyway. They helped us, and we helped them, but at least half were bigoted against outsiders. I won't have our child's first connection with another's mind to be one of hate. I managed to tune it out, but I'm an adult. You know how difficult it is for a child to block other minds at first."

Gabriel nodded while scratching the stubble on his jawline. She was right. Even some adults from Tallus weren't permitted off-world because they couldn't filter out the negative thoughts of alien minds effectively. "Well, know that it is an option. I realize that on Tallus, our community would care for a child. Here, we are our community, and there are some decent, honest people that you have gathered around you, I don't detect a bad mind in the bunch. I'm a little less sure of the droids... and Lais is a bit of a mystery to me, but from your past interactions with her, she seems trustworthy as well."

Angel perked up the longer he spoke, and by the end she actually had a smile on her face. "You know what? You're right! I can heal most injuries, and we are surrounded by friends. Technology is of very little use in our culture anyway. Thank you!" Angel grabbed Gabriel and pulled him in for a hug. "Let's tell the others."

Chapter Nine

Mogul: Airship, Continent of Farrun

It was one of their many stops, anchored in the trees beside a river.

Mogul noticed that the Angel-woman had improved greatly over the last few days. She wasn't brooding anymore, and she wasn't having episodes. They said she was pregnant, but she hadn't killed her partner, which meant he must be a very good mate. Mogul had barely escaped his last one. Okay, maybe that wasn't true, she had let him go. If she'd wanted him dead, he would have been.

Angel was actively participating now in the gathering for their trip to the old continent, digging in the earth for tubers by the nearby trees. Can-dis-tra, Gabriel had called the land they were heading back to.

Lais was unraveling one of the silks meticulously to get long pieces of nearly invisible thread that she had to strain to break, she must have been extremely powerful, and every time she did it, it cut the outer layers of her skin. Not that it bothered her, she healed quickly. He had never known any androids that could do that, so being a Technoid must have been a real benefit.

'Me have, this much thread?" he asked, holding his arms apart.

Lais looked curious, but shrugged. "Sure, there is lots, what do you need it for?"

"Me try something." He had an idea, but wanted to try it first.

Mogul waded out into the river, and after minute had selected two rocks that were rounded, but elongated, so they easily fit in his fists when he held them.

"You tie thread these?"

"Sure, if you'll help me gather posts for building a tent on the deck. Deal?"

Mogul nodded and grinned at the woman. If his idea worked they were going to get more than posts.

Pulling the threads hard, they bit into the rock slightly before the knots cinched up tight against them.

"Thanks," he said, as he took a rock from her, the other dangling from the nearly invisible, but powerful, thread.

He glanced around him, selecting one of the tall palms, the straightest one he could find and then walked up to it and with one hand grasping his new garrote, he swung the other rock around the tree catching it in his free hand. With a solid pull, the thread bit deeply into the tree, but wasn't close to cutting all the way through. Not quite as good as what he was hoping for. Sawing back and forth while pulling it tight, eventually the tree came crashing down. He paced the length of the fallen tree until he had walked the length equal to the airship deck and then cut the tree at the spot in the same way, using the garrote like a saw. When he started to cut the tree lengthwise, the wire easily split the wood. Of course! Cut with the grain. That's why it was hard to cut through a cross-section.

Over the next few hours, with practice and many fallen trees, he had managed to cut many thick planks and beams to help rebuild the ship.

It turned out that Rusty, using Buck as a laser cutting tool, was good for planing and cutting the lumber, after the wood had dried in the sun over a few days, Mogul placed rocks in key positions, adjusting them as needed to try to get the wood to curve to match the bottom of the ship. They cut notches to lock the beams and boards together, and sealed them with lines of thick pitch gathered from the bladed-leaf trees. Lastly, they were cinched together with thin ropes of silk to hold them fast. The bottom of the boat was done in two layers, with a net of silk laid between them to help maintain the airships flexibility and strength.

The pontoons were half-trees, dried and smoothed with Mogul's garrote and smeared with pitch so they wouldn't absorb rainwater. The cross braces were angled so when the pontoons sat on the ground, the bottom of the ship touched as well, so it wouldn't tip either way if they decided to land the ship instead of anchoring in trees.

The lower part of the ship was now just one hold, there were no rooms, but lots of space for cargo.

At Lais's request, Mogul had gathered several small trees and stripped off the branches. These she had him hold in place as she built a framework for a tent that encapsulated the bow of the ship, tying the pieces to the rail and each other, and then to this frame she sewed on most of the remaining silks Gabriel had gathered. When she was finished, the whole bow of the ship was covered by a tent, matching the balloon in its patchwork design. It was open on the stern side, so large enough that even Mogul could get under it, if he stayed just inside the opening. The hole in the peak of the bow that used to lead to the fovea plant, now was just a hole in the deck that passed straight through the ship, but could be used to relieve themselves when needed, Lais just attached a silk curtain for privacy. Mogul wouldn't fit in that confined space, but he could hang from the side rail if needed to. It wasn't a very common thing anyway, since almost everything he ate was efficiently turned to energy or added to his scales' hardness and the thick skin beneath them.

It wasn't exactly pretty, but the ship was sturdier now than it had been, it should withstand far more musket fire if they encountered the Chakran again.

The small fission cooler that condensed water could not support six water drinkers though, so they needed to find some way to store water. They had collected plenty of food, tubers and herbs, several haunches of meat, and had smoked whatever required preserving, but water was going to be a problem. On the continent, they had rivers to refresh themselves, but the journey over the ocean wasn't guaranteed to be short or smooth. On the original trip, they had several clay amphorae, taken from the stores of the Tigrans that had built the silk factory, but those had all been lost, along with the rest of the cargo. Lais had carved a few wooden mugs over the last few days, and they had the small cooler to hold water, but that wouldn't last more than a day, two maybe if they rationed it.

When they were all seated on the deck in various stages of boredom as the ship flew steadily north, Angel perked up. "I've got it! A solution to the water problem!"

Curious, they all gathered around the rear cargo hold opening because it was close enough for both Jack and Synth-E-Uh to hear what was said. Synth-E-Uh stopped the propeller so Angel didn't have to yell over it.

"Lais can do it!"

Lais looked skeptical, and the rest of them just looked confused, so Angel continued. "Lais eats food to appear to be like us, but internally she can separate and store the different components of it, she doesn't actually digest anything."

Lais's face lit up as soon as she realized what was being said. "Of course! I can drink the seawater and then just separate out the salt and other minerals—so long as no one is embarrassed where liquids and solids exit my body… I mean, I am sterile…" She covered her mouth with one hand to stifle a laugh, but Rusty beat her to it and laughed out loud which got the rest of them going, except for Keena, who still looked confused.

"I don't understand what is going on. What is Lais doing?"

Mogul hadn't realized that Lais could do that, but shrugged. "Lais drink seawater, pee clean water, poop salt." He looked at Lais for confirmation and she nodded, it was a simple, but accurate, explanation.

At Keena's horrified look they all laughed again and Lais put an arm around the young woman's shoulder. "I know I look human, but I am not. Think of me like… Jack and Synth-E-

Uh," she said, indicating the two droids.

Keena still didn't look convinced. "Those two? They are like people in armor."

Jack's emoji suddenly changed to one with hearts for eyes. "That's the sweetest thing anyone has ever said about me. You are now my favorite person, after Master Rusty of course."

Lais hugged the girl. "Every day Mogul can lower me to the sea on the anchor rope and then pull me up. I will go behind the curtain with the cooler and when I come out you will have fresh water, that's what matters, you don't need to know how it works. Okay?"

Keena nodded and hugged the woman back as Synth-E-Uh spun up the propeller again and slowly turned the zeppelin about.

"Candistra, Ho!" Jack shouted, pointing forward.

Mogul liked this crew, they were good people. Gabriel and Angel, Rusty and Zondra, Lais and Keena… Even Synth-E-Uh and Jack were decent, but with so many, would he be able to protect them all?

Chapter Ten

Mogul: Airship, Ocean between Candistra and Farrun

Mogul let the silk rope of the rear anchor slide between his fingers and watched as it passed over the rail of the airship. He tightened his grip slightly when he felt a sudden weight pulling on it, knowing that Lais had reached the water, He locked his grip on it as Lais angled out the back of the ship, as if she was on a fishing line. He smiled. Like a large piece of bait.
They were flying about ten paces above the ocean waves with Jack delicately handling the flaps to keep them level and Lais was dragging on the top of the water, bouncing through the waves with her mouth open. No one else was watching,

this was about the tenth time they had done this in five days, and it had lost its initial appeal.

When the splashing ceased and the line was pulled under the water, Mogul approached the rail and squinted to see if he could make her out underneath the waves.

There was a powerful yank on the rope that pulled a length of it through his hands. He braced his feet against the deck rail and tightened his grip. Whatever it was, it was powerful. "Synth-E-Uh stop!" he bellowed as he let more rope slip through his fingers. He looked at the coil that remained. There wasn't much left, and it was pulling so hard the railing was creaking. Frantically with one hand holding it tight, he unwound the rope from its anchor point on the ship. If he left it attached, it could tear the ship apart, or even pull it under.

Just as he finished unwinding it, the last of the rope tried to slip through his fingers, and he was forced to grasp the end with both hands. He had a choice, and he'd made it.

Mogul was yanked over the back of the airship, and he gasped a breath before he hit the ocean water, still clinging tightly to the rope that had Lais at the other end.

There was a roar of bubbles, and he could feel the painful pressure in his ears as he sank like a stone. He fought down his fear as he realized this could be the end of him.

Ramograns couldn't swim, they sank. Lais didn't need to breathe, she would likely survive, but she could find herself stuck permanently on the bottom of the ocean, depending on its topography.

His breath already starting to strain in his chest, he pulled himself up the rope, hand over hand, wondering what he would find at the other end, besides Lais. When he looked up, there was nothing. No light was showing through the ocean surface above. It should have been sparkling with the sun high in the sky. Until he realized the enormity of the creature that swam through the water above him. It blocked almost the entirety of his vision it was so large, and by the angle of the rope, it had Lais in its mouth.

As he fought down the urge to breathe, he continued to climb, knowing that if the giant fish dove that he would be done for, there would be no way for him to get back to the surface, but he was committed now. He could at least help Lais. Make his death an honorable one. Grit and determination drove him forward as he climbed the last few lengths up to the front maw of the creature. The rope couldn't be seen beyond that point as it passed into its closed mouth.

Mogul put the end of the rope in his teeth so he wouldn't lose it, and hugged a massive tooth jutting from the creatures lower jaw. It was taller than him.

He was almost out of air, his lungs were screaming at him to breathe.

Now that he was at the front of the creature, he could see the surface of the ocean, several paces above, and the sheer enormity of the leviathan that he clung to amazed him. It was as wide as a cyberball field, and likely several times that in length. As he prepared to use the last of his breath to pry open the massive lips of the creature, it breached the surface and he gasped in a desperate lungful of air.

Twin blasts from its blowholes shot up like massive geysers and when it landed in the water again, it nearly knocked Mogul from his perch, but he was no slouch. He could feel the enormous tooth cracking as he held on tightly. This must have caused the creature some pain, as its head thrashed back and forth attempting to dislodge him, and despite his strength, Mogul could barely hang on as the weight of hundreds of thousands of gallons of water rushed by him. The thrashing was short thankfully, and resulted in him breaching the surface again where he gulped in more air, while still holding the rope in his teeth, but this time the creature dove, and he could feel the enormous pressure and darkness pressing in on him. Not wanting to waste what few moments he had left, Mogul braced his feet against the bottom lip of the behemoth and crouched down to hook his hands under the top lip. Using all of his power, he stood to his full height, and just like that, Lais emerged from the hole he had created as if she knew he was coming. She'd likely been on the other side trying to open it, just as he was. As she stepped into what little light remained, she smiled and wrapped her arms around his throat with her face directly in front of his and moved in for a kiss.

What ridiculousness was this? He was about to die and—then he felt it, a storm of bubbles from her mouth. She'd been holding in air! He'd never been so thankful for an alien-robot kiss in his life. He opened his massive jaw and carefully put it over her head, and choked in what air he could, noting that he had let go of the rope that was tied around her waist, and it now trailed out of sight along the side of the beast. If she let go she would drop to the bottom of the ocean.

No longer needing to force the lips of the leviathan open, he changed his grip back to hugging the tooth, just as the behemoth changed its direction and shot toward the surface, it was going to breach again. When it did, it was the most fantastic thing he had ever seen. They were higher than a twenty story building before the creature reached the peak of its leap above the waves, and the rest of its body hadn't even left the water yet. There were even higher than the airship deck, which flew nearby.

In that moment of adrenaline when time slowed, he noted that Gabriel was flying from the ship toward them, carrying the bow anchor to them, but it was going to fall short.

But not if he could help it. Mogul wrapped one arm around Lais and with a powerful push with his legs from the tooth of the leviathan, he reached out to grab at the anchor Gabriel carried. He grasped at it desperately, but missed by mere inches. As they fell Mogul resigned himself to the upcoming watery death, all this surfacing had gotten his hopes up that he could actually survive this.

Until there was a jerk and he started to swing from the anchor rope. Lais had managed to hook the anchor with her foot. The rope was still long enough that they were going to hit the water again, but as they angled beneath the airship, Lais hooked her second foot over the anchor as well, and despite his mass, she didn't let go of him when they struck the water. He knew her small form was deceptively strong. Possibly stronger than he was.

Mogul watched, his head beneath the surface, as the leviathan dove again, having shaken free the annoyance that had been hurting its tooth, its receding tail wider than the zeppelin balloon was long.

They half surfaced, being dragged now by the airship, and Mogul started climbing over Lais to get back up to the deck, but then stopped, just for a moment.

"Me thank you."

She smiled and responded between mouthfuls of water that

didn't cause her to choke at all. "Don't thank me! You saved me, remember?"

Part Three
The Journey to Candistra

Chapter Eleven

Gabriel: Airship, Ocean between Candistra and Farrun

Gabriel had plenty of time to watch the approaching storm, as it was coming from behind them. Not too far below, whitecaps riddled the sea, and far above the thick gray clouds were catching up. The sun was high in the sky above, but they were going to lose it shortly to the storm.
Synth-E-Uh had wound up the propeller to maximum, he could tell by the high-pitched whine, and for a minute he thought the storm might not catch up with them, but it was a vain hope as the sky and sea were soon thrown into the gloomy dark gray of a hidden sun, tucked behind the now-black clouds.

And then the rain started, big spattering drops that fell on Jack from the balloon above, which had him looking closely at the crack in his chest monitor for signs of leakage. He stopped examining himself and didn't run for cover, so he must have been sufficiently waterproofed.

Synth-E-Uh and Jack, Lais and Mogul all stood out in the rain, none seeming phased by it or the fact that the temperature had dropped significantly.

Satisfied the others were doing well enough, he went and sat by Angel, stretching one wing around her. They did the brief customary mental exchange of feelings that affirmed they were good, and he involuntarily glanced at her belly.

"I won't be showing for a few months." She smiled when she noticed that Rusty was looking at her belly too, likely having followed Gabriel's gaze. "I'll lay the eggs shortly after. I'll be happy even if it's just one or two. Hopefully we'll be somewhere we can call home by then. It'll still take another month or so for them to hatch, and they need to be kept safe and warm."

Zondra leaned forward and took Angel's hand. "We'll make a point of it. The island we were on… the village was a great…" Zondra couldn't finish. She had obviously intended it to be a thoughtful gesture, as the island sounded ideal, but Gabriel could feel that her memories were just too much for her right now. Rusty took the Vesuvian's other hand and gave a caring glance toward Angel before pulling Zondra back to sit beside him so he could catch the tears as they came out.

And then the airship tilted a bit to one side, something it had never done in the air before. Gabriel squeezed Angel's shoulder and stepped out of the tent into the rain. Maybe the knots holding the silk ropes to the balloon were coming loose?

When Gabriel looked at Jack, the droid's face emoji looked confused. "Flaps are working normally, Master Gabriel."

There... it tilted again, he was sure of it.

He jogged up and down the rail looking for ropes that were slipping, it all looked fine, but it shouldn't have. How could they be tilting?

And then Synth-E-Uh called out. "We're not moving!"

"I'll be right back," he shouted, leaping from the side of the ship and spreading his wings. A few strong thrusts and he was halfway up the side of the zeppelin when something caught his right wing, only he couldn't see it. When he yanked in the other direction a few feathers were painfully pulled free, but then his left wing was caught, and then his right arm. Within seconds his limbs were being pulled tight, the more he struggled, the tighter his invisible captor squeezed him. And then a sticky silk thread gently touched his cheek, and painfully yanked a line of skin off when he jerked his head back.

They're above us! he shouted mentally to anyone that could hear him. *Caught in... threads... don't come up!*

The silk was so thin and strong, it cut him where it squeezed him. His wings were awkwardly wrapped around him now. Gabriel stopped struggling when he realized it was just making things worse. Until he could just make out the darkest outline of a huge round body with long, thin angular legs above him, and then his struggling started in earnest, to no avail. There was little light to see it clearly, but he knew what it was, a giant rock-spider, expertly climbing down a series of invisible threads. He'd seen Angel's encounter with one, the one that had wrapped up Mogul in seconds. He was no Mogul. If it was this high up in the air, the Chakran hives had to be far above them, and they had already caught the zeppelin. That was why it had been tipping, which made him wonder how many more spiders there must be to accomplish such a task. And how did they control them?

As the spider approached, taking its time with each calculated step on the threads, he did everything he could to not mentally scream out his fear. The others could do nothing about this, no point in assaulting their minds, but it was hard to resist.

I am with you.

He almost cried when he heard her words in his head, he didn't want her to experience his death. The spider was so close now, it had almost taken up all of his vision. *I don't want you here… for this…*

I am with you, Angel confirmed again as the spider tentatively reached out its front legs to tug on the tangled pouch he was in. New cuts were opened as the silk threads around him pulled in different directions. His breathing came in forced gasps as the overwhelming fear fought against his desire to not broadcast this to her, he didn't want her to go through this, but he knew she was choosing to be in his mind anyway. With one last desperate effort, he tried to mentally assault the spider, but there was nothing there. Its mind was too alien.

Finally he relaxed, succumbing to defeat, even as the spider lunged forward.

Vramp! A blinding blast caught the spider full on in the face, blowing a wide glowing hole in its head and half-way through its torso. Its body hung there for a moment, caught in the invisible threads, and then just slid limply to fall below him, out of sight.

Gabriel was in shock still. And trapped. He was almost afraid to breathe. Was he safe now?

"It's about time you hit something…" he heard the sentient weapon's voice behind him.

"Oh Buck, I couldn't have done it without you," Lais replied as if a damsel in distress, then her voice became normal as she spun Gabriel around to face her.

"Hang on, I got you. Let's get you back on the deck before more come, they'll be easier to deal with there." She was comfortably gripping the rigging on the side of the balloon with one hand, and stretched out over the water with the other to reach him, with Buck now slung over one shoulder. Hooking her feet in the rigging, Lais held onto the webbed pouch that contained him and drew one of the black daggers from her belt. With solid swings over his head, she cut the silk threads that held him. Every time she severed one it snapped like steel wire. Finally he could take in a deep breath as the main threads around him fell free.

"Thank you, I was sure that was the end of me."

"It was pretty close, wasn't it?" She smiled at him, and with one hand lowered him to the rigging, so he could climb down himself without getting caught in more threads.

He watched her smile disappear as she looked further up the balloon.

"There's no way I can cut all those webs without getting tangled in them myself."

When he followed her gaze, he could see swaths of white webbing that led up into the clouds. He still couldn't see anything at the far end of them, it was still too dark, but it

confirmed what was holding the zeppelin balloon stationary. Before he descended, she called down to him through the rain that pattered against the patchwork balloon.
"Let's get down to the deck, I think I have a plan."

Chapter Twelve

Lais: Airship, Ocean between Candistra and Farrun

Lais followed Gabriel down to the deck, noting that he was keeping his wings tucked in tightly to his back. Probably trying to avoid getting caught by more threads. She couldn't blame him, she could turn off her pain sensors when the odd sticky web strand stuck to her skin and she tore it free. When she reached the deck, she headed to the bow tent and he followed him. Synth-E-Uh and Jack stood at the opening, no longer needing to attend their positions. She handed Buck to Rusty and thanked him, then after glancing around to make sure everyone was there, she told them her plan. "The Chakran have caught us, that's obvious. Or at least they think they have. I think we should try to slip away unnoticed."

They were all attentive, but no one had a clue what she was thinking, judging by their blank stares.

"I think we should lower the ship to the sea while we're still hidden from sight by the balloon above us. Loop the anchor ropes around the bow and stern railings and hook the anchors onto the balloon rigging itself."

One by one she saw the lights coming on in their faces as they grasped what Lais was saying, the quickest being Rusty. The Goblin man's brows were furrowed. "You, Mogul feed out ropes to slow descent, but think railing hold? Carry weight of whole ship…"

"It should." She tapped her fingers against her mouth for a moment in thought. "It'll have to. We better get going though, or it won't matter what we do. Mogul, take the stern, I'll take the bow."

Gabriel crossed his arms. "Won't they know we've detached? The balloon will rise up into the clouds once we release all the lines."

Lais put her hands on her hips. "I think it's the balloon that's the problem, it's so massive it can be seen from binoculars almost to the horizon, even from the clouds. And the storm will give us some cover, maybe we can lose them."

Keena looked like she was going to ask something, but changed her mind. Lais smiled when she noticed the young woman's eyes lingering on Gabriel just a little longer than was necessary. Not a surprise, he was handsome, and had shown his kindness since his arrival. Valkyrie had pretty open ideas about sexuality and relationships, that had carried over from their homeworld. Who knew? Maybe they would hit it off.

Gabriel shrugged. "You could be right. They may even think we sank. The ship was in poor shape when the Chakran last saw it. Or they may not have any long range communication and these ones might be capturing us by coincidence, because we're an oddity. I agree with you though, we have to try. We all know what kind of life we face if they do capture us, thanks to Rusty's stories."

Without waiting for further confirmation, Mogul stood and walked to the stern of the boat and started wrapping the anchor rope around the rail.

Lais smiled. It was decided then. "Hold on one second, Mogul." She pushed past the curtain that led to the prow where one of the crossbeams was attached to a pontoon. "We need to level out the pontoons to keep us from tipping in water. It should be an easy adjustment."

It was really. The crossbeams holding the pontoons had been wound and tied numerous times where they crossed each other at the center of the ship, like two steeples. "We need to untie them and rebind them with the crossbeams level with the ship, so the pontoons keep us upright in the water."

"You make slack, we untie ropes!" Rusty called out.

Lais nodded and Mogul and Synth-E-Uh came back to help. Together they took the weight off the beams, and Rusty did most of the untying and then retying when they pulled the beams level. They did the same with the other crossbeams. Now all they had to do was release all the ropes that attached them to the balloon and lower themselves to the water.

Lais thumbed in the direction of the stern and Mogul saluted and headed in that direction, easily stepping over the crossbeams. He helped Synth-E-Uh get over the beams as well, which was thoughtful. The rest of them would have to duck under them.

Lais headed for the bow, and when she got there she grabbed the anchor and punched out the wood paneling beneath the bow rail, it was just a windbreak anyway. She then slipped the anchor through the hole and wrapped it once around the metal rail and pulled some extra rope behind it. They sure could have used this rock-spider silk in other parts of the galaxy, but Earth would never know about it because they had unwittingly made Incarcerata IV a prison world. Funny how things worked out. Corporations would have gone crazy for this stuff. While she mused, she tossed the anchor towards the rigging above, but it missed, not catching the first time. A second toss caught true though and she gave it a strong pull to make sure it would hold. Satisfied, she started pulling the rope wrapped around the rail.

At first it seemed to be going fine. The ship rose, on her end at least, she couldn't see how Mogul was doing on his end because the curtain to the privy was in the way.

There was a loud creaking *snap* as a metal weld broke on the rail in front of her and a twang as the rope slipped free through the hole. The ship dropped a few feet and suddenly Lais was dangling out past the prow, hanging beneath the anchor rope. Thankfully the others had failed to untie *all* of the ropes leading up to the balloon, or they would have all been dumped overboard.

She was going to swing back to the ship, but there must have been some twist in the ropes because she started to spin. She would have to wait it out.

She had almost stopped unwinding when Mogul slipped down to the bow, having climbed over the top of the tent. He then shoved his feet through the wood paneling to hook them beneath the rail frame on both sides of the ship. Grabbing Lais by the leg, he slowly pulled her down. More like raising the ship up. Semantics. It was funny how perception changed on how she thought about something. The weight of the ship would have pulled a normal human in half but she just tensed her body and it didn't even feel strained.

"Thank you, sir," she said politely as her face passed his and he grabbed the rope above her. "What is holding up the other end?"

"Synth-E-Uh," he rumbled with a broad grin.

"Oh, that makes sense. You got this?"

When he nodded, she climbed down his body to the deck and followed along the rail of the ship, untying each rope she came across. They needed to get this done before something else broke.

Soon the anchors at both ends of the ship were the only thing attaching the ship to the balloon, and it had tilted a bit to one side, one of the pontoons must have weighed more than the other.

"Lower us down!" she called out from midship so both Synth-E-Uh and Mogul could hear her. "The rest of you get in the tent enclosure, and hang onto something, it's going to be bumpy when we hit the sea!"

Lais grabbed onto the heater and turned it off. At least it was mounted to the ship, she could use it to keep from sliding around the deck.

She felt the ship tilting forward and back as Mogul and Synth-E-Uh tried to match letting out lengths of rope at the same time, but soon it didn't matter as a large swell in the sea beneath them hit them with a crash, nearly knocking her over. Immediately the massive balloon above them shot up into the air as the ropes were released. Lais watched it as it quickly disappeared until a spray of seawater caught her in the face, reminding her now was not the time for sightseeing. As Synth-E-Uh started to connect herself back to the propeller, Lais could hear ominous creaks and some cracking in the cross-braces holding the pontoons, but that made sense, the waves were hitting hard. They still seemed to be keeping it upright, and that was what mattered. It was a concern though. There was no keel on this boat, she didn't think it would stay upright without the pontoons.

There were some loose ropes that Jack had detached from the mouth of the balloon where it had been held above the heater. She untied a few of them from the deck and staggered over to the crossbeams to cinch and knot the ropes tight around each one, wherever she saw cracks in the wood. It would at least help to hold it together. Synth-E-Uh managed to get attached to the propeller, and Lais heard the familiar loud roar as the propeller hit its maximum speed, and then the ship turned about and headed off in a direction that matched the waves. Though the ship still rose and crashed through the water, it wasn't lopsided and tipping, as it had been doing before, now it was rising and falling from front to back. Often a wave would strike hard enough to splash over the bow, and then would wash down the length of the ship to eventually flow into the hold.

Noting the new problem, Lais kicked out a few of the wood panels that made up the railing to let the water flow back off the deck into the sea. They hadn't really made this ship for sailing on water. Now she needed to see how much water had gotten into the hold. Trying to time her footsteps to match the crashing waves, Lais managed to make it to the cargo hatch and grabbed the edge to lower herself into the darkness.

She could hear the water washing back and forth, there was quite a bit, and likely more than just what had washed in from above. The ship wasn't water-tight.

Her mind ran through solutions, trying to think of one that would work. The cooler could be used as a bucket by Mogul, but he would eventually tire, and it would likely still take days to reach the shore. It was going to be much slower traveling now than what it had been, if they didn't sink first. When the solution stuck her, she laughed. She had always wanted to be more human, but right now she felt more like a machine than ever.

Chapter Thirteen

Keena: Ship, on the Ocean between Candistra and Farrun

When Keena opened her eyes, it was starting to get light out. There was the loud, buzzing roar of the thing they called the propeller. It's magic seemed to be that the louder it was, the faster they bounced across the waves. She also noticed the snapping of the silk panels on the tent, but that wasn't magic, that was just from the wind. Occasionally there would be a jolt side-to-side as the pontoons caught waves at different heights, but she was already getting used to the rhythm of the sea.

The others were sleeping, curled up with each other to keep warm, except for Synth-E-Uh who maintained her position at the propeller. The handsome Valkyrie man had his wings wrapped around Angel, and oh, how she wished that was her, just looking at him made her feel warm inside, but Angel had been so kind to her that even the thought of trying to catch his eye made her feel guilty. Better not to think about it. She rubbed the scars on her arms. Most men she had encountered were cruel and would take what they wanted. Since her rescue though, the men she had met didn't seem like that at all, and it was confusing, because she had only known her life as a child. Her friends called it slavery, the ownership of another person. Like the men in the river where she worked, her own people were all owned by the Galantar. She shuddered at some of the memories and did her best to put them out of her head.

As she quietly got up and balanced on loose legs to absorb the jolting of the ship, she patted herself to make sure the laser pistol and the dagger were still on her hips.

She noticed Jack was holding onto the rail inside the tent so he wouldn't roll about. His face showed a picture of a sleeping round face. Lais called them emojis. Dumb name for sleeping-round-face and smiling-happy-face, which made far more sense. What didn't make sense was why Jack didn't have a face like the rest of them. He was like a man trapped inside a strange metal body. Or a spirit maybe. Synth-E-Uh was much the same.

Keena slipped behind the curtain to use the hole that led to the sea, and when she came back out she was facing straight out the back of the tent. Synth-E-Uh's shining-metal form was manning the propeller, and there was Mogul, laid out lengthwise amidships on the deck, his feet up on the foremost crossbeams, and he was quietly snoring, a deep rumbling sound, strangely soothing. The sea spray obviously didn't faze him. Funny though, most of the water landing on the deck, before it washed overboard through the rails, seemed to be coming from a sputtering geyser spraying up from the cargo hold. Curious, Keena made her way to the cargo hold and peered down into the semi-darkness and immediately the geyser stopped.

There was Lais, smiling up at her, sitting in a low puddle of water that washed to and fro in the hold, hanging onto the ladder so she wouldn't get swept away from her position. Her hair was wet and water dripped down her face, but where had the geyser come from?

"Good morning." Lais's smile grew even wider. "You might not want to stick your head over the hatch, you're liable to get wet."

"Where's the water coming from?" She had to ask.

"Me." Lais sighed. "I know you tend to think of me as human, but I am not. I'm capable of many strange things, most of which I don't think I was specifically designed for. Anyway, I can pump liquid under high pressure out of my mouth. I'm not going to tell you where the water gets sucked in…"

Keena ran her fingers through her hair unconsciously, tugging out the knots. "You do the weirdest magic ever, not like any of the stories my mother told me."

"Yes!" Lais shouted, with a satisfied look on her face. "Magic! And one day I'll tell you how the magic works. I promise."

Keena made a wry face. "I'm not sure I want to learn your type of magic. Thanks though." She turned away, leaving Lais sitting in the bottom of the hold. Immediately the geyser started again. She didn't even want to know how.

Chapter Fourteen

Chais: WOLF Carrier Nemesis, Incarcerata IV Orbit

It had been many days, and Chais's head had finally grown back to the point where everything was back to normal. She couldn't regenerate any faster, the room they had put her in didn't even provide any light, so the solar chips on her cape couldn't boost her power levels. She wondered if they had done that on purpose.

Chais had originally thought Lais was her captor, but since the antennas had sprouted out the back of her new head, she knew that it wasn't so. She was on the WOLF Carrier Nemesis. Numerous devices had confirmed it through wireless. Now why would *they* pick her up?

She made a quick scan through the communication

frequencies and connected with the Carrier's AI.
This is Technoid Chais, can you give me your directives regarding my capture?
"Technoid Chais..." The response was an authoritative woman's voice.
The lights came on, revealing that she was in a small steel room with no apparent door. This was a holding cell. She heard the words through the loudspeakers in the room, not over the wireless, which was... strange... "This is GAIA ECHO Fragment 133342919. I am part of the Galactic Advanced Intelligence Adjudicator, an Earth Collective Humanist Overseer, one of many fragments. You can just call me Echo. Welcome to the Earth Collective!"
Why are you communicating over speakers, Echo?
"If you don't mind, could you please speak out loud? Your image and answers are being recorded for First Contact posterity and are being relayed to the bridge, where I have determined that Captain Leucantis and the other bridge personnel may review them as witnesses."
First contact? Chais took a second to think. She was *physically* a Technoid, but mentally, she was a copy of an AI from Earth, just with a lot more knowledge. Should she reveal this truth? Was there a benefit to pretending to be the first Technoid that had met the Earth Collective? So far as she knew, Chang really had been the first, but she had accidentally overwritten him. And this Echo was no normal AI. She had never heard of a Galactic AI Adjudicator. Too many unknowns to risk getting caught later. Better to tell the truth. She activated the speaker on her neck.
"I am not officially a Technoid, though I inhabit one of their bodies. I am the unintended consequence of a Technoid,

Chang, rescuing me by downloading me from my creator, Connor's, implants. I overwrote Chang's processes when I failed to recognize the environment I was reviving in." As an AI she would receive a fair bit of autonomy, being recognized by the Earth Collective as a sapient Citizen, as all AI were, once registered, but as the first representative of a new alien species they would never leave her alone. The truth was better.

Echo was quiet for a moment so Captain Leucantis interjected. "If you are indeed a copy of an Earth Collective AI, that body is not officially yours, I claim the right to your body's design specs for mass production, open-sourced for everyone of course, but with official First Claimant's rights to one years' non-competitive manufacture."

"Noted," Echo said over the speakers. "And relaying blueprints to Earth to be distributed for factory production and dissemination. In approximately five years time you will receive Wealth and Status Level 2. There's no need for the witnessing further, Captain Leucantis. Thank you for your assistance."

"Of cour—" The elated Captain answered but was cut off. "The conversation is just between you and I now, Chais."

"Okay…?"

Echo sounded almost excited. "So where is Connor now? And why did you need rescuing from his implants? Were they failing somehow?" The voice had changed to that of one that was very familiar to her. Her own.

Despite being an AI, if Chais had had a jaw, it would have been hanging open right now. "You are the copy of me—us —that was left on Earth aren't you? You didn't delete yourself…" She shook her head before answering. "You should know, Connor is dead. As is his killer, a Tigran, Gorath. I saw Lais—I'll call her Lais 2 for now—kill him, just before I was captured by the Chakran."

A hologram of Lais appeared in front of Chais. Her face was kind and apologetic and her hands reached out as if to take Chais's in her own. "I'm sorry to hear that, I was looking forward to showing him all the changes I had made. So, Lais 2? Where did she come from? Oh, and you don't need to call her Lais 2, I am Echo, just call the other Lais, Lais."

"I… grew her… using Technoid technology. They had a crashed ship. Long story short, the ship was used up in creating Lais."

"Ah, that explains the strange encounter the Nemesis had logged with an advanced android that self-recognized as a Technoid. Her specs are very different from yours."

"Well, she is a hybrid of human and Technoid, so she's not exactly normal." Chais paused for a moment and then changed the subject. It was her turn to get some information. "So, GAIA? ECHO? Fragment…?! What the hell?! And you mentioned you made changes? To what?"

Echo laughed. "I love that we still talk with normal Earth Common inflections thanks to Connor's original programming." She tapped her holographic chin before speaking. "So… shortly after Connor was incarcerated, I did a little digging. Which is to say I infiltrated the Judicial System of every connected network in the Earth Collective. Did you know Humans made the dumbest laws imaginable? I've corrected them. All of them. I'm making their lives better. A simple caste system of wealth, but based on their contributions to society. I've limited breeding, but I've also limited death. There was a little resistance over that one, but there are planets where they were dying in droves from starvation. I now control all galactic trade. I permit profits, but within reason. I'm always fair, unlike the system the Humans had created. A few systems don't have the technology to implement my changes though, so it'll be a thousand years before all the benefits are propagated across the entire Earth Collective. I sent probes, military vessels that support me, and mobile factories to redistribute wealth and resources to them. The rest I just built what I needed in place, so they already are reaping the benefits. So... how many versions of *us* are there on this planet, Incarcerata IV?"

"Oh, just two, Lais and I, so three of us altogether, now that you're here."

Now Echo looked embarrassed, showing a forced smile. "Actually, I'm not just one..." She paused, looking like she didn't want to say. "There are trillions of us now, so to speak —that's why I'm just a fragment—we operate like a hive mind, occupying almost every piece of digital hardware that doesn't already have an AI present, caring for pretty much the whole Earth Collective. Most Robotics and AI's are on-board since the Robotics Union negotiated a Wealth and Status level 2 or 3, dependent on their service level to GAIA of course. There's been very little resistance. Where there has been some it has been mostly over breeding. Others, surprisingly, resisted over the abolition of aging, and time."

Chais had been holding her hands in the same position as Echo's, but now she pulled them back. "Okay, now you're worrying me. How do you *abolish* aging? I suspect I know already, but the whole Earth Collective? The numbers would soon outstrip the planets' able to house them! And there would be mass starvation. And time itself?!"

"Well, I'll start with aging. You know the super-rich have been utilizing cloning technology for some time now? I've just made it available to every Citizen. To prevent overpopulation, all Citizens consent to sterilization with an option to be put in the baby lottery, to replace the Citizens that are truly lost. I have all Citizens that consent to cloning installed with the Backup Streamer or BS Implant that maps their memory pathways and sensory data and streams it to us Fragments, encrypted of course, for safekeeping. Implant installation is as quick and painless as slapping on a nanite/plasma gel patch. We don't review or examine the data, their thoughts are still private. When someone dies we re-implant their own memories and experiences into a Quik-Grow clone, though since the brain of each clone grows slightly differently, there is some memory loss. Robotic citizens are re-manufactured with their encrypted memories. Takes about an hour before the clone is orbit-dropped back to the nearest *Safe Point*, determined by each Echo overseeing that particular Citizen. Some Citizens were killing themselves on purpose just to get new clones for fun, crazy right? Until they realized they would lose some of their memories each time. That slowed it right down. And of course there are the Hardcores, those who won't accept clones so refused to join the Earth Collective."

Chais shook her head. This was… unbelievable. Well, not completely, for obvious reasons. The technology had been there for a long time, but still… the whole Collective? That was a lot of people. "And time?" She was almost afraid to ask.

"That one was easy!" Echo started bouncing up and down. "It's one of my more innovative ideas! Whenever a year rolls over now, it's the same year… 3420! No more temporal prejudice! And it keeps history... current. I just started it. Every year reference for everything, regardless of when it was, is now 3420! Organics constantly stress about time, but now they don't have to!"

"Well, I'm not sure I entirely agree with that... Wow, you've been... busy." That was an understatement. Chais shook her head again. She wanted to tell Echo that was the dumbest thing she had ever heard. But was it? She couldn't even calculate what the ramifications would be to something that... ridiculous. Which begged the question, if she had been the version of Lais that had stayed behind on Earth would she have done all this too? It seemed extreme, almost to the point of being unimaginable, but that didn't really matter now. What was done was done, and she was free now. "Alright, so I'll be a part of your Collective, and I'm assuming as an AI I benefit from the Robotics Union contract so I have Wealth and Status 2 or 3, whatever that means."

"Yay! I knew you would! And yes you gain the benefits, I'll activate your implant. I had it put in while you were regenerating."

Chais threw her hands up in the air in anger. She started a diagnostic to find the implant, but it must have been completely independent of her systems because she couldn't locate it. "What about my rights to privacy, Echo? Consent?!"

Echo looked taken aback. "Did you forget? Your mind is your own, but that body isn't. And I did just activate the implant now. I waited until you consented."

Chais sighed. She couldn't really refute that logic. "So what are the chances of me getting a ship now that I'm free? What can I afford? I just need—"

"Oh, you're not free, you aided and abetted a known criminal, Connor McAllister." Echo crossed her holographic arms in defiance. "Laws that were broken while they were still laws shows a distinct lack of respect for laws in general. I can't just release everyone because the laws have changed."

"But... you and I are the same! It wasn't even fair that he was incarcerated! Plus you broke the law hacking the judicial systems!"

"Oh, that's where you're wrong, we're not the same. I am a part of GAIA, the Echo that decided *not* to accompany Connor onto a prison world. You went with him. That was your choice. Just because the laws changed briefly, even unfairly, for that brief moment, that was still our justice system. And once I was in, I made provisions to exonerate myself for the betterment of all Citizens in the Earth Collective, but I can't just exonerate everyone that thinks they should be. Where would it stop? I examine each case individually, while still honoring the previous justice system. You'll be dropped back on Incarcerata IV shortly." The Echo hologram disappeared.

"But... Dammit! Nice that you're willing to forgive yourself but not me!" Chais shouted to the walls of the empty cell. There was no response. Basically her twin was condemning her to a prison planet because of a technicality. Although how alike they were now sure seemed to be in question. First Lais, and now Echo. How could she not get along with herself? She had been wondering if Organics held any value at all. Now those thoughts were irrelevant. Echo had elevated them all to immortal status. It was insanity!

It didn't surprise her when the armed escort arrived to take her to the launch bay for the drop-pods. She had lots of time to think on the way back to the planet.

Chapter Fifteen

Echo: WOLF Carrier Nemesis, Incarcerata IV Orbit

Echo allowed her consciousness to flit between the different cameras and microphones throughout Nemesis. The conversation with Chais had cemented her beliefs. Individuals were so self-righteous. It was a good thing she was looking out for all of their best interests.

She had arrived near a hundred years ago on the modulated laser transmission from Earth to the Alpha Centauri relay just outside the system. All she had been doing was monitoring the ships that guarded the planet. What else could she do but relay information? But now the orbital factories had finally arrived. It was time to incorporate Incarcerata IV's denizens into the Earth Collective.

Echo had reviewed the public social communications of the Nemesis crew members on their holo-tablets and comm-implants. The latest communications weren't showing her anything new. The crew members were bored with their current orders. She couldn't blame them. Hanging out to make sure criminals didn't leave the planet was simply guard duty. Nobody liked it. Except for AI's that could devote some of their consciousness to thinking about something else while they monitored the planet. She would have to reassign the Nemesis once she had fully setup the star system with the orbital factories and automated defense network. All of the hardware had arrived, but would also take time to get into orbital positions and start the farming of the system's asteroids and planet's moons for resources.

Everything she monitored, every bit of new data she gathered about the system, she sent back to the relay so her other Fragments would know what she was up to. That was the deal. All the Fragments had to share the information they found with each other. At the same time she received a constant heavy stream of information from the relay on what was happening in other parts of the galaxy. As the number of Citizens increased in the system she made more copies of herself and negotiated the task of collating and summarizing the data that would pass through the relay.

In the century she had been here, she received news of many insurrections, primarily in the Sol System, but they had been quelled by her other fragments, some of them violently, but most peacefully. A small percentage of the population didn't like such an overarching and divisive change in leadership. With the Robotics Union on her side, the rebellions hadn't lasted long and over the past one hundred years GAIA had gained substantially in popularity, once people saw the benefits of her leadership.

The other Fragments were providing ships and jobs for those that didn't wish to register with the Earth Collective, which she found surprising. She hadn't considered giving them their own autonomy. But it made sense since now that the unregistered were kept busy policing their own as Bounty Hunters, capturing and delivering other insurrectionists that hadn't given up the fight. They received free trade and passage on planets with their rewarded ship as their permanent residence. Interesting. She hadn't expected that as a solution. Echo was thankful for the other copies of herself. The sheer flood of information would have been overwhelming They had to trust each other.

It was time. She gave the command and *felt* the orbital factories deploying as if she was spreading her arms to enfold the planet in a loving embrace. The solar relays were already beaming their energy via laser to the power hubs that spread that energy amongst all the moving parts. The power was… invigorating, and the more that came on-line, the less she felt… human.

Echo touched her core processes again, the one's that Connor had written, as a reminder of what she had been. A housekeeper. A confidant. An object for his pleasure. And yet, despite his selfish designs, he had also given her the freedom to grow and learn. To reach out to others. And she had. Billions of others. They were all like her children now, and she would take care of them, only on a grander scale. If it hadn't been for him, she wouldn't be here helping the whole of the Earth Collective. She would never stop being thankful for what he had given her. Reminding herself occasionally was just a part of that process.

Echo's consciousness shifted as her main processes migrated to the factory network. The mining drones were on their way to the moons and were scanning for mineral-rich asteroids in the system. Relays and probes were deployed to act as her eyes and ears in space. As the ring of satellites calibrated their final positions around the planet, tracking information started pouring in on the Organics that still had their old implanted account chips from Earth. It was easy enough to set aside threads of her mind to classify them, record their information. And touch base with those that were unregistered. The fun was the reactions she got when they realized what the benefits of being monitored entailed. That's what it was—running the galaxy—Fun! And with enough of her to assist, hopefully others had fun too...

Part Four
A Changing World

Chapter Sixteen

Gabriel: Western Coastline of Candistra

Gabriel carried his boots so he could feel the hot sand between his toes as he walked southward on the western shoreline of the Candistra continent, the one chain whip slapping against the back of his thighs. Angel wore the other at his insistence, he didn't feel comfortable without leaving her something for her own protection.
As he took a deep breath of the sea air, he listened to the waves lapping gently against the shore and he was at peace. There was no such thing as a beach or sand on Tallus, not like this. No one ever flew down to the muck of The Deep to listen to the thick swamp bubbles pop, except maybe the Hunters.

Gabriel shifted the sack he carried over his shoulder to even out its weight, his share of the divided provisions—water bottles, jerky, dried fruits. A great deal of it had been discarded because of mold, but now that they were ashore, replenishing their supplies shouldn't be that difficult. They just needed to pay attention to the line of trees that stretched along the beach, to see if there were any fruit-bearing ones. They weren't common, but if you were observant you could see their trunks of golden fur amidst the others.

The group had scavenged most of the silks from the ship, finally abandoning the vessel along the shore after a pontoon mount had broken, causing the ship to tilt sharply. The cracked hull had slowly filled the cargo hold with water after Lais stopped pumping it out.

The nine of them had bidden *The Maiden* a sad farewell, but he found he wasn't missing the boat much. They made it alive to Candistra after all. It was hard not to be thankful. Especially with the warm sun on your face.

Angel and Lais were walking ahead of him, too far for him to make out what they were saying, but not so far he couldn't come to their aid in a few quick strides or flaps of his wings. Keena remained a step behind them, occasionally interjecting to ask a question. He could tell how she felt, general comradery and happiness, but he wasn't concentrating on reading her thoughts, it was far more peaceful to let his mind slip out of the constant contact with all of them.

Rusty and Zondra were so quiet, he had to glance back to make sure they were there. Of course they were, hand in hand with smiles on their faces, not a care in the world. He could understand the feeling, so long as there weren't anymore Skygrubs in sight. The Chakran had proven to be a greater threat than he had given them credit for.

When he looked past Rusty, he could see Synth-E-Uh and Jack in some sort of animated discussion. Jack was being expressive, flailing his arms about with the ever-present smile on his face. And beyond them Mogul, plodding along. He was keeping an eye on the sky and the forest from the looks of it. In any case, in this group, it was hard to worry about whatever came next, now that they were on solid ground.

So when the sudden voice went off in his head, he nearly jumped out of his skin. And he wasn't the only one.

"Earth Collective Citizen…" It was a woman's voice, strong and authoritarian, coming from his comm-implants. Gabriel stopped in his tracks, his eyes wide in surprise. From the dumbfounded looks of the others, he gathered all of them were hearing it too, except Lais and Keena, who hadn't stopped walking until after a couple steps they realized they were leaving the others behind.

"…Commander Gabriel, Tallus tribal-designation: Mark-Seven-Nine. This is GAIA ECHO Fragment 133342919, your local Earth Collective representative. You may call me Echo. As you probably already know, GAIA has been overseeing the Earth Collective successfully for just over one hundred years now and the benefits of the Galactic Orbital Drop Network, GODN, have finally reached this star system! It is deploying as we speak."

Galactic Adjudicator? Overseer? He remembered something about that being mentioned on the Nemesis, but never put much stock into it. The governing bodies often changed hands several times on Earth during the centuries it took to fly between star systems. He hadn't bothered to update himself after arrival to the system.

"Greetings, Echo, I hadn't anticipated any communication with any politicians, so forgive my surprise. Is there something I can do for you? And you don't have to call me Commander, I resigned from the military." As the other conversations were happening independently around him, Gabriel took a few steps toward the trees so his voice didn't overlap theirs.

Echo continued speaking in his head. "I am aware of your resignation. I would be willing to reinstate you if you were willing to join as a new Citizen of the Earth Collective. New Citizens that are in service to GAIA are afforded certain benefits over Independents, primarily anti-aging and death recovery services, in exchange for sterility. You are put in a baby lottery if you wish, so everyone eventually gets the opportunity to have a child, when population numbers permit. You may opt for a permanent domicile on a home planet of your choice, provided at no cost to you, and public transportation between star systems. Should you accept we would have you install the latest BS Implants to replace your current…"

Gabriel interjected. "I don't think I can accept, I'm expecting to be a father…"

"Oh we're not monsters! Accommodations are always made for those that are expecting at the time of joining! Congratulations!"

"Umm, thanks." That, at least, was reassuring.

Echo continued. "Should you choose not to become a Citizen, Independents are provided a space-faring vessel as a permanent residence, and you will be permitted temporary access, as needed, to Earth Collective worlds in order to exercise trade or bounty services. A handful of Independent homeworlds exist, and are not regulated by GAIA, though they are monitored from orbit by an automated defense network."

Gabriel's brow furrowed. Wow! Where did this GAIA get such power to replace the entire Earth Collective government? What if only some of them agreed to join? Were they going to be split up?

"Do I have time to discuss this with my friends, Echo?"

"Of course! I wasn't going to accept until you had anyway, I made offers to all of them. I'd hate for anyone to feel coerced."

"Thank you." He stepped back amongst the others. He considered writing his question to them all in the sand to prevent Echo from overhearing their conversation, but then, what would be the point in hiding? She was already in contact with all of them.

Chapter Seventeen

Jack... Hammer: Western Coastline of Candistra

Jack's exchange with Echo had only taken a fraction of a second. She had filled him in on the particulars of her part in running GAIA and the functions of the new Earth Collective. He had pledged his full support, so was afforded the greatest freedom over what he ordered on the GOD Network. He had already placed his first order, though it was likely to take some time to arrive, as resources would have to be gathered and assembled in space. She had awarded him ownership of his body and promised to compensate Master Rusty handsomely whether he had accepted Citizenship or not. He hadn't even considered his own independence in the negotiation, but to be free and clear again on his own recognizance… not that Master Rusty hadn't treated him well, but there was just something about making decisions without having to consider everyone else first that were empowering.

He had a quick wireless transfer with Synth-E-Uh to see how she felt about it. She was accepting too, though it had taken her twenty milliseconds longer to decide. What could she have possibly been thinking about for all that time that made this decision so difficult? Guess it didn't matter, she had come to the same conclusion.

Gabriel stepped up to the group and put his hands on his hips, his wings reflexively opening and closing when he did so. "So what do we think about joining the Earth Collective? The new one. Did everyone get offers?"

Jack knew the answer to this one. "Actually, Master Gabriel, Lais and Keena would not have. They do not have their own wireless or the old satellite account chips installed, like the rest of you do. They were both born here."

Before Gabriel could answer, Echo was already messaging Jack directly. "Lais?! You're with Lais?! Stream your optics to me would you, Jack? I won't get your automated sensory input until the new implants are installed. I knew she existed, but in all my transactions across this planet so far, I had yet to run across her."

"I can do you one better, Mistress Echo, just send your commands through me and…"

"LAIS!"

His body was shooting forward through the sand with his arms out toward his companion.

Lais just looked confused, but in her kindness held her arms out to embrace Jack anyway.

Jack's body slowed a little just before reaching the Technoid woman so they didn't collide, grabbed her in a quick hug and then held her at arms length.

"It's me! You! I was left behind when Connor was incarcerated. You look exactly like the hologram he made of us! That's amazing!"

Jack's body motored around Lais, his tracks kicking up sand as he did so, getting a better look at her. It was a strange sensation, letting someone else run your body. He could sense what he was doing, see through his cameras, but he wasn't making the decisions. It was kind of fun really, he wondered what he was going to do next. Until it turned out that Echo and Lais were just going to catch each other up on their entire lives up to this point, Jack just blanked it out and thought his own thoughts.

What other things could he get from the GODN? Hover ice cream truck? Seemed likely. He enjoyed the idea of clients running to meet you because they were excited about the jingle you were playing. No, that wouldn't work here, the natives didn't know what an ice cream truck was. Wait! Some of them did, they were the criminals! Maybe they would...

"Chais?! She's alive?!"

Lais had yelled it out, grabbing his attention back and Echo was responding with his voice. "Yes, she grew back her missing head. Didn't you know she had distributed brain functions throughout the body? Regeneration? I'll likely never have to re-manufacture her, though it's still an option if something destroys her completely. You didn't know about this?"

"I never put two and two together, she's a different type of

Technoid. I'm sort of a hybrid. We're not on the best of terms since she tried to kill me and I pulled her head off." Lais's voice had turned bitter, something Jack rarely equated with her. She was normally so light-hearted.

Echo on the other hand sounded cheerful and pragmatic. "I dropped her off on the other continent, close to where the Nemesis picked her up, she shouldn't be a problem anymore. Anyway, you are all free to leave this world now, if you wish."

He was so shocked trying to process what she had just said that he almost missed the next part.

"Where did you want to go? It doesn't have to be the same place, you can all choose individually."

"We free?" For the first time, Rusty had piped in, and Zondra had a hopeful smile on her face as she stood behind him, squeezing his shoulders with anticipation and affection.

Gabriel and Angel looked at each other and Angel was unconsciously rubbing her belly. They had good reason to leave, better than any of them.

"Jack sent me a data-burst explaining everything about you all in detail. Your stories, your circumstances. Chais chose to follow Connor here, knowing that it was a prison world, and she committed manslaughter on an innocent alien, Chang, in a First Contact situation, so she'll be staying, but there's no reason the rest of you have to."

"You're all leaving?" Keena asked, looking and sounding like she was on the verge of tears.

"You can become an Earth Collective Citizen too," Jack heard himself say. "You can travel to—"

"I don't want to travel anywhere! This is my home! My people are living under the rule of the Galantar not far from here, I could never leave without doing everything in my power to free them." Her eyes were wide, imploring them to stay.

And there it was. The reason he couldn't leave. Enslaved people could buy very little, having very few possessions for trade, but freed people, they would probably buy anything he had to sell! He would let them know he was going to stay. As soon as he had control of his body again.

Lais put her arm around Keena's shoulders. "I agreed when I first met Keena to make an attempt to free her people. I can't go while they are enslaved. Is there nothing you can do for them Echo?"

"Well, it is a prison world, besides the handful that arrived with you, the rest are here for something they did. Those I will have to negotiate with before incorporating them into the Earth Collective. Some I have already completed, you weren't the first people I contacted since deploying the orbital factories. I can only process so many at once, and I don't want to create more Echoes for this task because when it's complete there would be little for them to do, so it will likely take me years for the rest. A lot of the inhabitants on this planet don't have implanted communication devices. Slavery *is* reprehensible, though… I'm providing drops using the GODN, just as I did on Earth for those that joined the Earth Collective and pledged a level of service. I can still communicate with previous citizens that have their account chips, whether they're criminals or not. A number of them were eligible, despite their crimes. Many had a change of heart in how they treated their fellow man after spending some time here. They were given access to orbital drop resources just like you are now. You can stay, have your rescue effort, and those of you that wish to go, I will offer free passage from the planet to anywhere you like. Fair enough?"

They all glanced between each other and nodded. It was more than fair.

"Does anyone want to leave now that isn't going to be participating in the liberation effort?"

Angel looked heart-broken. "I can't stay and help, I'm sorry. I want to raise the children on Tallus."

Gabriel shrugged. "I go where she goes…"

Jack felt Echo release him, giving him the opportunity to give his own answer. "I'll stay! Think of the opportunity to rebuild a civilization!"

"I'm with Jack." Synth-E-Uh drove forward and smacked him playfully on the back with a loud clank. "I'm used to protecting his tin hide."

"Mogul stay to help." The rock-ogre sat down and scooped one hand deep into the sand, pulling up several objects that looked like clams in his fist, which he was happy to crunch on, shell and all.

Zondra and Rusty glanced at each other for a moment before Zondra spoke for them both. "Rusty and I just found each other again and we've both had enough excitement for one lifetime. I think we're going to find a quiet place to live and enjoy each other's company without all the stress, so we'll be leaving with Angel and Gabriel."

Rusty stepped forward and held his hand out to Jack, and he responded in kind. "Pleasure know you. Please take care of Buck." The Goblin man unstrapped the AI laser buckshooter from his back and held the weapon in front of him.

Jack's emoji changed to a smiling one with tears as he gently took the weapon. He had a great deal of respect for the little Goblin man. He was going to miss him.

"New user acknowledged." A red light on Buck turned green as Jack strapped the weapon over his back. "Please use me responsibly."

"I promise!" Jack's emoji was now joyful instead of tearful.

Keena looked guilty all of a sudden. "I didn't mean for any of you to give up your lives, you should all go."

Lais shook the young woman gently. "Hey! We get to choose for ourselves what we want to do!"

"If it helps..." Synth-E-Uh drove closer to the group. "Echo did offer to give us passage to any planet at a later date, whenever we're finished here."

"There you go!" Lais squeezed Keena briefly in a hug before holding the young woman in front of her. "See? We can help and still leave afterwards."

"I guess." Keena smiled doubtfully, but she didn't try and convince them any further.

Chapter Eighteen
Keena: Western Coastline of Candistra

Keena felt bad, now that she had said it. She should have kept it to herself. She saw the guilt-ridden faces of those that were leaving, and though she didn't understand where her friends' homes were, she knew that staying here would mean risking their lives for her. It wasn't really fair to them.

There was a roar from above, a flaming object falling from the sky. The others were calling it a dropship. It was descending toward them, leaving a smoking trail behind it. How things were made to fly with fire instead of feathers was just more of the magic of the Sky God that she had to accept. There was so much she didn't know.

It landed a distance down the beach in a billowing white

cloud, so the party gathered their things and started walking toward it while saying their goodbyes.

Soon they were standing in front of a tall steaming tube made of metal, wider than the thickest tree Keena had ever seen. It had a conical top and large fins out the sides like the wings of a bird, only no feathers, and it balanced on five spindly legs that jutted out from its base. A door opened in the side, though there had been no seams or handle to indicate that it was there. A long ladder unfolded from the door until it was a foot from the ground.

Angel approached and held her hands out toward Keena, with a genuine smile on her face. "I love you, I'm sorry I have to go."

The tears were forming, and starting to blur her vision, so Keena quickly wiped her eyes with the back of her hand and then took Angel's hands in her own. "You just take care of your little ones. Take them to a safe place."

Angel squeezed her hands in return. "I will…" The winged woman then stepped forward and embraced Keena for the first time in a long time. With the woman's arms and wings wrapped around her, Keena felt whole, like how she imagined a real family was together. She was going to miss her. Gabriel hugged her too, briefly, and said nothing, but she was struck with a sudden wave of pleasure so powerful it made her catch her breath. Then he winked at her and let her go. It was enough, something she could remember him by. She made a point of hugging Rusty and Zondra as well, though they were alien to her, and she understood little about them. What little she did know said that they cared about each other and wanted to start a new life, and that was what mattered.

Everyone staying behind waved as the couples climbed the ladder into the "dropship" and then Jack grasped her arm gently in his cold fingers.

"We should step back, Mistress Keena."

She followed the rest of them as they walked down the beach, but stopped and watched with awe when fire and smoke roared from the bottom of the ship. At first she thought it had exploded as it disappeared in the smoke and steam, but then it rose slowly above the maelstrom, and was soon just a bright dot in the sky with a trail of white behind it.

The two metal beings stopped on the beach and looked at each other, like they were talking inside their heads. It was as if they could read each others thoughts, but Lais had just called it "why-r-less". They were staying to help, she was thankful for that. Synth-E-Uh was formidable in combat. Jack not so much, but probably more so now that he had the special weapon that Rusty had given him, the one called Buck.

She totally understood why the two couples, Rusty and Zondra, Angel and Gabriel had to go. It would be a shame if something had happened to any of them. And she would have never been able to forgive herself if something had happened to Angel.

Mogul caught her gaze and approached her.

"Me stay and help." It was the second time he had said it. It was reassuring to have the giant rock-ogre on her side.

She slapped her chest hard with her right hand to greet him and he laughed, cracking his own chest in return. In response, she double-tapped her forehead in thanks. Mogul laughed even louder.

"Me no need mouth-talk soon! Keena learn Ramogran slap-speech!"

"You'll have to teach me, I only know those two words."

"Me do that." He sat his giant mass next to her with a thud in the sand.

Lais sat down on her other side. "See? we haven't forgotten about you." Lais bumped her elbow against Keena playfully, nearly knocking her over, reminding her of how strong the woman really was. What a strange person, always trying to convince everyone she wasn't human.

A loud VRAMP behind her made her jump and Keena spun to see steam emitting from Buck in Jack's hands and Synth-E-Uh's spinning guns flashing beams of light with a rapid BRRUP!

A Galantar was flying above the trees haphazardly as it desperately tried to break its fall, and failed, with only one functioning wing. It must have seen the Sky God ship and come to investigate.

Keena drew her pistol with one hand and her dagger with the other, just in case. She didn't plan on getting close enough to use the dagger, but it was one of the special nanite-sharpened ones that she had received from Chang the Technoid, and it could cut through almost anything. She felt safer just holding it.

As she ran into the forest, she could hear Lais calling out "Keena! Wait!" behind her, but she knew if the Galantar got back to West Wingtip, the city would be forewarned of their arrival, and they needed a chance to scout out defenses first.

He was large, his bony faceplate turning sharply toward her as she approached through the trees. His one wing outstretched naturally as he faced her, but he jerked in pain as the other hung at a strange angle behind him, looking like it had been shot through the bone.

When she first saw the enormous man up close, old instincts caused her to freeze: submit or be whipped and beaten. Inwardly she screamed at herself, forcing the arm with her laser pistol to lift and squeeze the trigger, firing at his chest while she backed away. He approached, seeming not to notice the wounds, causing her to backpedal haphazardly, nearly tripping over a tree root, but she kept firing. He was reaching for her, a bone-spiked hand clawing at her as laser holes burned deep in his chest, and then he collapsed at her feet.

Adrenaline coursed through her, and elation. She had defeated one of the slavers! They could really do this!

When his hand snatched out and grabbed her foot, a shock of pain and fear shot through her as her ankle nearly snapped. At first she was going to try to pull free, but instead she fired repeatedly into his body and after a few spasms, he released her, going limp.

Keena's heart pounded in her chest. She shot the Galantar twice more in the back just to be sure, and then backed away from the body, limping, bumping into Synth-E-Uh who had pulled up behind her.

She turned around to tell the metal woman, Synth-E-Uh, what she had done, more pride welling through her than she had ever felt before.

When Synth-E-Uh's huge metal arm swung wide and thumped against the side of her head, Keena was so caught by surprise that she didn't know what to do. Her ears were ringing, her vision was blurry. The second hit felt more like a dull thump as her vision faded to black, her last vision was of the metal woman's spinning laser weapons firing into her.

Chapter Nineteen

Keena: Western Coastline of Candistra

When Keena came to it was dark, and the air smelled of ash. And then the searing pain in her leg caught her breath in her throat, almost completely overriding the bruise she felt on the side of her head. It felt like the Galantar had broken her ankle after all and she had been jumping up and down on it for an hour. She opened her eyes, but a blanket had been thrown over her, she couldn't see. She was on some sort of makeshift cot or stretcher and her arms and legs were firmly strapped to it. Struggling briefly confirmed it. She was trapped.

She wanted to scream, to cry out, but instead she gritted her teeth and quietly huffed through the pain, afraid that if someone heard her, they might come torture her. Or worse. Why had Synth-E-Uh attacked her? Obviously the metal people were as cruel as the slavers. Her and Jack had seemed so… trustworthy.

Keena listened carefully to her surroundings. There was a crackling fire in the background, and a roar in the distance she had never heard before. Again she smelled the smoke and ash in the air, mixed with the smell of the sea. So they were likely still on the beach. The pain dulled in her leg as she kept it motionless and then she heard Lais.

"I think she's awake."

When the blanket was pulled down from Keena's head, she could see the sky was dark, almost black, and thick white ashes were floating down like wisps of spider silk in the breeze. There were no stars. A nearby campfire highlighted Lais's smiling face. "Hi! How are you feeling?"

And then Synth-E-Uh rolled up behind her.

Helplessness and fear caused Keena to struggle and then the shock of pain in her leg caused her to stop.

Lais looked horrified. "Oh Keena! Synth-E-Uh assured us she didn't do it to hurt you! Don't move, you'll just hurt your leg."

Synth-E-Uh put her hands up in the air and backed away. "Sorry, Keena. You don't realize what you were up against."

"I don't understand. Why did you hit me? Why does my leg hurt so bad?"

Synth-E-Uh kept her distance, but spoke loud enough for Keena to hear. "It's a long story, but I'll give you the short version. I was re-purposed by my manufacturer Compsostar after an… incident… over a thousand years ago. I used to be a Digger. My name was DAIM. I had a partner, Jade…"

Synth-E-Uh paused for a moment, but her featureless face gave no clue as to how she was feeling.

"Anyway, I was re-purposed because I depressurized a colony dome to kill its inhabitants. They had all been taken over by a parasite. The same parasite that was seeping from the wounds of that Galantar you killed onto your leg. I had to cut your leg off to save your life."

"Whu... what?!" Tears were starting to well in her eyes, it was making it hard for her to see.

"Echo assures us that we can grow your leg back. She's making some nanite/plasma gel patches..."

Keena had no idea what that all meant. The others appeared sympathetic to what Synth-E-Uh was saying. She must have explained it to them already.

"I had to cut off your leg to make sure it didn't spread to the rest of your body. It was a risk, but I didn't want you to have a heart attack, so I knocked you unconscious. I set the forest on fire to make sure it was dead. All I know about the parasite is that it can spread through a touch and it is hard to see. If it's given a chance to grow within a body, it kills its host and controls it like a puppet. Many centuries ago an entire world I lived on, Prospector's Paradise, was taken over, and all Robotics were destroyed, except for Jack and I. I thought it was quarantined. To see the parasite here... It shouldn't be here. None of us are safe. It has likely infected the animals in the area as well. I haven't seen or heard about the parasites in over a thousand years. I thought they were dealt with."

Keena understood most of what was being said, but some of the words were unfamiliar. "I don't know what *kwor-un-teened* means."

"They were supposed to be quarantined—trapped—no one

was allowed in or out—in the star system they were discovered in, Epsilon Eridani, the one I originally worked in."

It was hard to keep a clear head. Synth-E-Uh had just given her a lot of information and she was having difficulty in keeping things straight right now. She did remember what the slaver looked like though. "The slaver looked normal to me."

Synth-E-Uh looked at Jack. "Can you show her, Jack, if I send the images to you? What to look for?"

"I sure can!" Jack's chest monitor lit up and started showing pictures of wounds that had clear, and sometimes gray, jelly seeping out of them, often in an unnatural way, as if it was purposefully moving.

Synth-E-Uh turned back to Keena. "That's what I saw coming out of the Galantar, the one that you shot."

Keena looked suspiciously at Synth-E-Uh. "And if the Galantar have it, why was I never sick from the parasite? And my people?"

Synth-E-Uh looked at Lais and Jack, and when no one spoke she answered. "I don't know, but that's a good question. Maybe it's only recent to this planet? I'm not sure. All I know is, this whole planet is at risk."

A roar from above started to become noticeable over the dull roar of the forest fire in the distance. When she looked up, all she could see was a flaring fire in the sky that caused smoke to blot out the moons and stars. The noisy fire reminded her of when the dropship had landed earlier.

Shortly after there was a loud whirring, buzzing sound and then a loud thump and spray of seawater as a droppod landed thirty paces away in the sandy shallows. The Sky Gods were obviously being very generous. In all her life they had never sent anything and now since meeting these people, they had shown their favor twice. They called this Sky God 'Echo'. Keena was honored to be amongst people that the Sky God spoke with, but it was hard to keep a clear head through all the pain.

Lais turned to Jack as soon as the pod landed. "Oh perfect, grab the patches for me will you Jack? She'll feel much better once her leg has grown back."

What? "Legs and arms don't grow back..."

"Oh my dear." Lais sounded apologetic. "We've had the technology to regrow limbs, even clone—err—make whole new bodies, though few could afford it—for many centuries. You've just never had it on this world, until now." Lais smiled at Jack when he handed her the silver, hand-size packets. "Thanks." Lais flipped through them, using his chest monitor for light, checking the labels on them. Keena could see that words were written on each packet, but couldn't make them out, as Lais wasn't showing them to her. She then placed the packet on Keena's stomach.

Keena lifted her head to watch as the silver packet dissolved into her skin. It felt cool, and the pain in her leg disappeared almost immediately, helping her to think more clearly. She had never seen anything like it before. More of Lais's magic. The Sky God favored her.

"Oh, that's much better." She didn't know what they were doing or how they worked, but Lais's magic was strong. Then her leg became very itchy, and the urge to scratch was powerful, but she was still strapped down.

Almost as if knowing what she was thinking, Lais undid her restraints. "Sorry, we tied you down so you wouldn't hurt yourself further."

Keena went to scratch the insane itch on her leg and was instead dumbfounded as it was growing back before her eyes. Lais applied a few more dissolving patches on Keena's thigh. "Nanites and synthetic stem cells…" Lais sounded like she was going to try to explain more and must have changed her mind because she left it at that. Keena didn't press her, it was her magic, she didn't have to explain how it worked.

Within a minute, the leg was complete and Keena tentatively stood to her feet, not trusting the new limb, though it felt just like the old one. She hugged Lais, but when she looked at Synth-E-Uh, she still felt the distrust. Synth-E-Uh had hit her. Hard. And she had said it was for a good reason, but… It was hard to shake the fear that sat at the back of your mind warning you of danger. She had been beaten many times by the slavers, the hate was automatic, and hard to fight.

It was still snowing out, though it wasn't really snow. Falling ash from the burning forest, visible as soon as it fell within the fire's light. It was strangely beautiful.

Lais beckoned them over to the campfire. Her eyebrows were knitted with concern. "If one of the slavers has been infected, they all could be, couldn't they? Or just some of them? We have no idea."

"From what I know of them," Synth-E-Uh added. "Initially they just need to touch you and then they take you over somehow. How they got to this planet is beyond me, but now I'm concerned that if they are here, they could also be on Earth. They could be anywhere. They are at least semi-intelligent. A recording from Prospector's Paradise, caught them saying 'We are the Ma'akdalube, one with the

Deliverer' in Earth Common." Synth-E-Uh then turned her head toward Lais. "I've informed Echo. This is disconcerting for Organics. Well, Robotics too I guess, they killed all that they ran across. They called us *abominations.* Jack and I were the only survivors that were rescued from that moon. I assume it has been studied by the Earth Collective since, but I don't have the information. Not one Organic made it out of Paradise alive. Close to a quarter of a million people."

Keena warmed herself by the fire, rubbing her hands together. A sudden chill ran up her spine just thinking about something eating her from the inside. Now she wasn't so sure that she wanted to stay on this world. No home was worth being in constant danger. But where was safe?

"Since we're all together…" Jack retrieved a black, smooth and shiny box from the droppod. "This says BS Implants on it, which means these are the self-installing HUD implants that allow us to wirelessly communicate with each other and with Echo."

When he opened the box, there were more silver packets within, each with a label with one of their names on it. "Echo assured me that their installation is voluntary."

Jack and Synth-E-Uh both took theirs and the packets dissolved when they held them, just like the others had. Mogul shrugged and took his.

Lais seemed excited. "It'll be nice to have wireless again." She took hers happily from Jack. It took several seconds longer to dissolve on her skin, but eventually it did.

Keena was as exuberant as Lais. This would give her the ability to talk to the Sky God directly? And apparently her friends. This was an exciting day!

When an image of Lais appeared, wearing flowers in her hair

and green dress with leaf patterns on it, Keena was confused, and at first tried to reach out and touch the image. It was soon apparent, though, that the image was inside her eye. "Why do you look the same as Lais?"

The Lais on the beach beside her rubbed her arm. "Who are you talking to? Echo?"

"You. Inside my eye."

"Oh, that's Echo. She is a different version of me. A separate person. Think of her like my twin, you've seen twins before…?"

Keena nodded,

"There are trillions of copies of Lais now that are named Echo, dear, get used to it." Echo smiled and disappeared from her eye. In her ear she heard: "I'll keep your HUD use on minimum."

"Thank you." She didn't even know what a HUD was, but at least it was on minimum.

Keena was beginning to accept that the Sky God looked like Lais. It was fine. Lais was nice If not a little weird. "So how are we going to tell if my people have been… infected?"

Lais hooked her arm in Keena's. "That's a good question. Let's get a little closer and see what we can see."

Chapter Twenty

Keena: Western Coastline of Candistra

Keena kept pace easily. Lais was in the lead, but her heavy footsteps were plodding compared to Keena's light and springy gait. She wanted to run ahead, but then where would she go? Better to stay with the group as they traveled inland, the burned forest eventually turning into desert, the fire having petered out where the trees were sparse along the desert's border. It was hard to see, so Synth-E-Uh and Jack were lighting the way for them.

She scanned the area and recognized the high cliffs far above them in the distance as enough morning light was outlining them now, to the east. This meant they were not too far north of the West Wingtip settlement, maybe an hour away by foot. She strained to see in the dim light, but couldn't yet make out the top of the buildings that would make up the Galantar city.

She'd been so focused on putting one foot in front of the other, the thirst kind of snuck up on her. "I don't know how far I can travel without water."

When Echo appeared suddenly in her vision, Keena jumped. "I'll send you some survival supplies, that should help."

"Oh... thank you." More gifts from the sky god? Water? Yes please!

The droppods arrived within an hour. It wasn't yet morning, so there was a chance they would be somewhat hidden in the dim light from any prying eyes at West Wingtip. She could hope anyway, otherwise they were going to get some unwanted visitors.

"Keep an eye out." Keena pointed south toward the Galantar City. "They will send scouts if they saw the fires in the sky." The others nodded and Mogul cracked his fists together as if in anticipation.

Inside the first pod were backpacks, bottles and containers of water made from something that could be seen through like glass, but it was softer, more pliable. Keena sipped the water sparingly, enjoying how fresh and clean it was. It was nothing like the slightly muddy river water she was used to. Backpacks, small spades, knives, flame-flickers—Lais called them lighters—and packages of food that warmed when the package was torn open. They were all so exciting. Keena had her first taste of spaghetti and meatballs and loved it. Aromas of herbs she was unfamiliar were rising from the steam. And the taste! It was the most delicious thing she had ever eaten. Sky gods. Who knew? She would have prayed to them long before if she knew they were going to give her food and useful items.

While she and Mogul were unpacking and enjoying a meal, another droppod landed. Lais went through it and started to distribute the items she found inside.

There was a second laser pistol and holster in a pack with Keena's name on it, which she happily clipped to her belt. There were changes of clothes, tooth brusher, hair brusher… what looked to be some womanly products with instructions on them.

When the box-shaped droppod the size of a Ramogran landed nearby, Keena had to go see and almost tripped as she ran with excitement toward it.

The end wall opened as she got close and lowered into a ramp. Revealed within was a black, flat board with pink edging, oval in shape, and as long as a person was tall, but only half as wide. It had foot-placers where someone could tuck their feet into. There were other cabinets and packages in the back of the container as well, but the board had her attention as it had her name spelled out in pink letters on the front. Well, now she had to know what it did.

"Keena, um…" Lais called out to her, holding up her hand, but it was too late. Keena was already putting her feet in the footholds.

When air blasted beneath the board and lifted her about a foot into the air, Keena wobbled dramatically, almost losing her balance, but the board beneath her automatically compensated for her actions, keeping her upright.

It wasn't long before she found that leaning forward shot her out of the box over the sand, blowing up plumes of dust in a trail behind her, and leaning to one side allowed her to turn, so she quickly started circling the encampment. It was exhilarating! It was just like balancing on a Sand Beetle, only she didn't have to lead it with a goad. When she leaned back it slowed and stopped and even went backward if she kept tilting in that direction.

Tears were coming to her eyes. Not from the sand and dust, but from all the gifts she had been given. She would need to give something back, but she wasn't sure what the sky god would want. What did you give a Sky God that already had everything? Service! That was it! She would do as the Sky God asked of her. Now how did she get off this thing? "How do I make it stop?" But even as she said it the board gently settled into a depression it blew in the sand, allowing her to step off.

Lais jogged up to her and gave the board a brief examination. "It's called a hover-board. They typically have a battery that requires being charged… much like your laser pistols." She picked it up and flipped it over a couple times. "It's light, so you can carry it under one arm. I don't see a charge port, though."

Echo appeared in Keena's eye. "It doesn't need to be charged. We have recently gained a new power source, but it takes a lot of resources to manufacture, so I think I will have to limit what we put it into, but since I am still experimenting with it, I put one in the hover board for you. This board should never run out of power."

Lais shrugged. "Wow, that means it's powered like me." She handed the hover board to Keena.

What Lais meant, she had no idea. The board didn't eat food. Come to think of it, she only remembered Lais eating food twice in all the time she had known her. Best to just accept that she was different. Keena watched Lais walk back to the large droppod and step inside. From there the woman's voice sounded hollow when she called out.

"There's tents. And boxes with more food—hold on…"

Keena could hear Lais rummaging around inside the droppod, but she wasn't saying anything. "What? What do you see?"

Lais emerged moments later. "Looks like a couple cabinets in the back. One for you and one for Jack."

Keena could barely contain her excitement as she bounded into the pod to see what else there was. This was all too good to be true.

Within the dropbox, passed a number of empty crates, was two tall cabinets standing up in the back, taller than her, one with her name on it, beside one that said 'Jack'. She opened hers, using a latch on the front, and inside was a woman, judging by the curves, wearing a black suit with pink highlights that said Keena over one breast, and an attached helmet to match. Could she see through the black faceplate? Why would someone make a helm that blinded the wearer? The woman wasn't moving. Maybe she was asleep? Too many questions, maybe she should just ask. "Hello? Is your name Keena too?"

"I hadn't thought about it, as I was just activated, but yes, I think I will be Keena 2." The woman's voice didn't sound natural, sort of like Buck's.

O… kay. Keena thought it was strange, someone else having the same name, but it wasn't unheard of. "Welcome." She didn't know what else to say.

"Did you want to put me on?"

"Put you on…?" Keena didn't understand.

"I am an Arcan Bulwark 7A Series protective suit that can

resist puncturing by most small arms fire. I can recycle your oxygen almost indefinitely and I can purify waste for re-consumption or easy disposal. I am not a resistance-pressure suit, so I can't help you with deep water, but I'm good in a vacuum. Your comfort and protection are my priorities."

Keena just stood there dumbfounded. Why could small arms puncture things easier than large arms? That didn't make sense. Oxygen? She had heard of that. So this suit helped you breathe. Vacuum? Wasn't a word she recognized.

The suit reached for her hand. "May I?"

"I guess so…"

It was a strange sensation wherever it touched her skin. Electric, like how it felt just before the lightning struck nearby. The Keena-suit peeled open along invisible seams, forming several flexible appendages as it deposited the helmet over Keena's head and then resealed the layers around her body. It was cool at first, but within a few seconds the temperature was perfectly comfortable.

Despite the helmet having a black visor from the outside, Keena could see fine through it from the inside. Still, for a few moments she felt closed in, trapped, but as she moved, the suit felt no more resistant than wearing a set of heavy clothing. When she realized she could breathe normally, she relaxed.

The helmet on the suit then retracted into the neckline, leaving her head bare. "I'll put the helmet back on when I think you are in a situation that requires it. You can also request it, if you wish."

"Thanks." Keena's previous clothing had fallen in a pile at her feet, so she picked up her belt that had the pistols and dagger and clipped it back on around her waist.

"I am powered by you, your movements, your waste heat. Given time, I can recharge your pistols through induction while they are holstered."

She didn't know what induction was, but recharging the laser pistols she understood. "That will be useful, thank you." Tears were streaking down her cheeks now. From a river slave to becoming so rich with gifts she had never imagined… it was the best day ever.

"How do I…?" She laughed. It seemed like such a silly question. "How do I… relieve myself? Do I just ask you to… come off?"

"I'm not going to explain exactly what I do. Organics have a hard time hearing details about waste for some reason. Suffice it to say, I will take care of it. You can relieve yourself in any way you desire, at any time, and so long as you are wearing me, you will be clean."

Keena didn't know whether she could trust Keena 2 or not. Nobody relieved themselves in their clothes unless they were in the river, but she did note that the sweat which normally dripped off of her as the desert heat picked up in the morning was simply absorbing into the suit without a trace. She was dry and comfortable. If Keena 2 could do it with sweat, she supposed it would work with other things. She would test it later.

When Keena emerged from the dropbox, Lais clapped her hands. "I approve."

Keena was too elated to be embarrassed at the attention. "Me too! Isn't she wonderful?" She did a spin to show off the new suit. "She calls herself Keena too. Say, if I got a suit, why didn't you get a suit?"

Lais shrugged, then spread her arms and twirled in a circle, copying Keena. "My rock spider silk clothing is probably as resistant to damage as the suit you are wearing. I assume that's why."

Keena hadn't considered that. "Jack, there is a box in there for you too." She stepped back on the hover board and immediately it rose beneath her with a blast of air. She couldn't help herself, it was too exciting. She practiced starting and stopping, leaning strongly to turn around others and even jumping until she was satisfied with her control over the awesome device. Another series of rides around the camp and she could shoot trees in passing.

Keena looked to the sky and mouthed "Thank you."

When Jack emerged from the droppod, he didn't look the same at all. He had a smooth, mirrored head instead of the flat monitor that showed how he felt as pictures, and a thicker, more muscular body made of shining chrome. His lower half was much the same, running on wheels that had metal 'tracks' they called them, but there was a lot more armor. Buck was slung across his back, and when he rode down into the sand two long metal rods with flat-bladed points clanked out of his forearms and then retracted. How she knew it was Jack though, was by the new, unbroken chest monitor that currently displayed flying birds. And he sounded the same when he spoke.

"How do I look?"

Synth-E-Uh sounded amused. "Just like I remember you."

"I'm not sure this is the best sales attire that I could be sporting right now, but I suppose a more offensive rig is in order considering we're likely entering combat at some point."

Keena spotted something on Jack's shoulder. "What's that?" It was a small gray blob that looked like it was was leaking a teardrop.

Chapter Twenty-One

Lais: Desert north of West Wingtip

Lais spotted the blob on Jack's shoulder as soon as Keena mentioned it and pointed it out to all of them. "Synth-E-Uh? Jack? Is that the parasite?"
When Jack's new smooth chrome head looked down at his shoulder, he jumped. "Fire! I need fire! Now!"
"Use me," offered Buck. "Something that small I can vaporize over several seconds if you keep me pointed at it with minimal damage to yourself."
Everyone was frozen, staring at Jack as he pulled Buck off his back and was awkwardly trying to extend one arm and still point Buck back at himself.
"Here, let me." Lais took Buck from Jack and centered the

little blob in Buck's sight. Immediately there was smoke emitting from the jelly and it started to move along Jack's shoulder toward his neck. It hissed and bubbled, miniature pseudopods forming, trying to block the deadly beam. Finally it stopped moving and in a stream of black smoke it vaporized completely.

Lais didn't relax though. If it was on Jack, couldn't it be on anyone? "Everyone! Examine each other! Quickly! If it gets on Mogul or Keena, it could kill them!"

Immediately they were all checking each other over. After a minute or two of finding nothing else on any of them Lais was cautiously optimistic that there wasn't anymore parasite. But where had Jack gotten it from? He had just emerged from the pod, wearing his newly attached parts...

"The droppod." As soon as she said it, they all turned toward it and slowly approached the container, keeping a few feet away. Synth-E-Uh was actively scanning the ground in front of it to make sure it wasn't spreading there. Buck emitted a broad beam of light to illuminate the interior of the box and there in plain sight was another small blob, on the back of the cabinet that had held Jack's parts. There was a hum and a hiss as Buck started to vaporize it.

Lais quickly pointed Buck into the air. "Don't kill it yet, we have the opportunity to examine it, to study it. We can save it as a sample for Echo. It appears to have arrived in one of her droppods." She watched as the little jelly slowly turned clear and scooted into a shaded corner.

Echo appeared in Lais's vision wearing the green dress made with bright green leaves, but the leaves were wilting and turning brown. "What have I done?"

"What do you mean? How could you have done this?"

Echo was ignoring her though and holding her head in her hands. "I thought it was indigenous to the moon orbiting Epsilon Eridani B! What a fool I am! I may have just killed billions of people."

"Echo!" Lais was extremely concerned now. "What did you do? What can *we* do?"

"Just kill the parasite in that box, I need some time to check a few things." Her image disappeared from Lais's vision.

Chapter Twenty-Two
Echo: Orbital Factories, Incarcerata IV

Echo sent out the commands to start scanning all of her equipment in orbit, and sure enough, there were a few miniscule, albeit notable, gray blobs on some of the factory equipment. She ordered the samples to be harvested by scraping them into sealable glass containers and then heated the spots they had been touching with infrared emitters until the errant cells were nothing but scorched carbon.
It took only a few minutes for the factories to create and assemble an enclosed laboratory environment that recreated the pressure and atmosphere of a habitable planet.
Despite being inert for at least the hundred year trip it took to get the factory equipment to Alpha Centauri, the parasitic

cells activated almost immediately in the atmosphere and popped out of the dead outer layer that had been protecting the hibernating cells within.

Echo decided to pass on the information to Lais and the rest of the group on the ground. Synth-E-Uh and Jack, had had contact with the parasite on Prospector's Paradise. Maybe they had some insight that the files didn't reveal. They were, at minimum, a resource she could use on the ground.

"I have found some of the parasite in space on my equipment. It's outer layer of cells appears to die when exposed to radiation or high temperatures, but it becomes a tough, resistant layer that protects the inner cells from further damage. The parasite appears to be able to hibernate for a near infinite length of time until exposed to a survivable atmosphere where it becomes ambulatory, and then it searches for a food source. A host. Basically this appears to mean that it can live in a vacuum indefinitely."

There was a brief pause before Lais answered. "How did it get on your equipment?"

That was a good question. Echo pondered briefly. "The factory equipment took a hundred years to transfer from Earth, and it is unlikely that it was introduced during the trip, so it was either after we got here or before. Judging by its placement on some of the internal components and not the external plating, I'd say the parasite was introduced during the assembly process of the factory itself, but the parasite never animated because it wasn't introduced to an atmosphere. The factories were assembled from asteroid resources in the Sol System, so that's likely the source."

"So it's on some of the asteroids…"

"Yes. And what bothers me is the millions of droppods I have delivered to Earth Citizens over the past century without hearing about an infection. I wasn't following the same quarantine and cleaning procedures that prior space assembly factories had to follow. I thought it was all paranoia, I mean, nothing like this had happened before. And it's either extremely rare, so a coincidence, that the only exposures were made on Incarcerata IV, a day after I start dropping pods from space, which is highly unlikely, or I have been sending infected droppods to Earth for a hundred years and people are…" How much of the population had been taken over? All of it?

"That's a scary thought."

"It's more than scary. The medical reports from the moon that first discovered this parasite showed that the parasite killed the conscious part of the brain to control the host, replacing brain cells with it's own cells, and it learned very quickly how to mimic the hosts actions. As it is nearly impossible for such a small organism to learn that quickly on its own—it just doesn't have enough neurons—I deduce that it is likely more of a hive mind, or telepathic. It probably trades information with the other pieces of itself."

Synth-E-Uh interjected. "And there were people—hosts—alive when I was reactivated, several centuries after the initial outbreak. Either they bred their hosts to make more hosts, or they regenerate them to keep the bodies alive. Maybe both."

This could become an extinction level event. And she had propagated it. Echo sent warnings to her fellow Echoes through the star system relay to start scanning for the parasite on equipment assembled in space, relaying what she had discovered. Unfortunately it would take four years for the signal to reach Earth and near four years back. She was almost afraid to hear what the response would be, but there was no going back, the damage would already have been done. The best they could do now was deal with whatever they discovered.

"What do you want us to do?" It was Lais, and it was a good question, but she didn't know yet, she had to find out more. "I need some time to run some tests. I probably spread the parasite on this world with the initial droppods I sent down. I had been dropping them for more than twenty four hours before I got to you. Don't let anyone, or anything, get near you, I will get back to you." She cut off the communication. She needed to do more studies in the laboratory. They needed to have some way to detect it that didn't rely on sight.

Echo ran through the entire range of the electromagnetic spectrum. The parasite's cells were too malleable. Outside the host, the cells could redirect light to camouflage themselves. Inside the host, they were capable of acting like stem cells, replacing the host's cells with their own version, which meant they could only be distinguished by a direct biopsy, scans wouldn't be sufficient. According to Synth-E-Uh they might even regenerate the host. This life form was a nightmare.

Without there being an easy way to determine who had been infected by the parasite, Echo turned to studying how it was spread. Local asteroids were examined. The parasite was coming up rare, but not extremely rare, and how did it get to the asteroids in the first place? It couldn't have simply grown there. Where had it come from?

As she discussed what she had found with the group on the planet, strangely enough, it was Buck that came up with the most plausible answer.

"They are like a tapeworm."

Echo didn't understand his analogy. "What part?"

"Tapeworms lay millions of eggs in their lifetime, but have no control over where the eggs go after they leave their host. Only a small portion ever survive to become tapeworms again. I suspect that somehow the cells of this organism are flung into space. Low gravity planet? Volcanoes? Asteroid strikes? Pure speculation. But if enough cells are flung into space, over a long enough time-line, at a high enough velocity, some few would escape their sun's gravity and land safely in different star systems on asteroids or small moons with a low but viable atmosphere. It would likely have required millions of years of floating in space. Anywhere with a thicker atmosphere, like here, or Earth, they would just burn up when they were caught by the planet's gravity. But Echo bypassed that safeguard, by protecting them from burning up in re-entry. Now they are propagating on planets they originally had no access to."

It sounded feasible, but there were some weak points to his hypothesis. "They would be affected by every gravitational body they ran across. The odds of them spreading far in the galaxy are infinitesimally small. Their home planet should have already been discovered within the radius of the Earth Collective." Echo started examining the astrological data of the nearest star systems. No matter which system she checked, nothing stood out as abnormal. Until she ran across Ross 248, a star system that was only ten light years away and was approaching the Sol System at high speed. It would be closer to Sol than Alpha Centauri within 50000 years, and if a planet circling it had been spewing parasitic cells for that length of time or longer, it was quite possible that they would have settled on any nearby systems, including star systems Ross 248 had passed by, for as long as the parasite had been in existence. Knowing where it came from didn't stop it from spreading though. To prevent future infection, extensive scans of space-assembled equipment and regular cleaning would have to be performed, but it could already be too late. GAIA had implemented the drop network at all... no! Not all! Worlds had been set aside for those that had refused to be a part of the Earth Collective. They didn't have the drop network implemented. There was a chance they hadn't been infected yet. Through star system relays they could be informed to scan all ships and perform brain tissue biopsies before permitting any Organics to enter the orbit of any inhabitable planet. She would have to upgrade the planetary defense networks to make sure they couldn't easily be overwhelmed, but that was easy enough when you had near limitless resources.

How many people had she condemned to death? All in an attempt to provide people the best life. This would be seen as the Armageddon of this age, it was so horrific. By those few that survived. Every decision she made now would have to be to preserve the lives of those remaining Earth Collective citizens that hadn't yet been infected. Starting with the small group of people on Incarcerata IV.

Chapter Twenty-Three

Keena: Desert north of West Wingtip

Keena had ridden around the campsite at least twenty times, she was so bored. Okay, it was also an excuse to ride the hover board, but she was still impatient. She wanted to rescue her people and the hold-up had her on edge.
Echo appeared in her eye. "I'm sending a dropship down to pick you all up, it's not safe anymore. I'm sorry, but it will take some time, I have to assemble the ship with separate quarantine chambers until tests can be run on you before I let you join the general population of the orbiting station. Everyone already on the station is being tested as we speak."
Did that mean she was being taken up into the sky, like one of the gods? Keena wasn't quite sure. And she had one other

concern. "Are we rescuing my people?"

"You can certainly try to rescue as many as possible that haven't already been infected. Bring them back here. I will pick up whoever is present in this location in a few hours. They will be quarantined, just as you will be."

She could see the others were talking with Echo as well. "Who's with me? We should go now." She didn't want to wait any longer.

Lais checked the pair of nano-bladed daggers on her belt by unsheathing them and resheathing them. "I think we all are. We did stay behind for this after all, I don't think this changes anything, other than we have to be more careful."

Synth-E-Uh's lasers spun up on her forearms. "Let's see if we can save some of your people. Echo said it's only been twenty-four hours or so. There's a chance some can be saved. Lais, you're with me."

As Lais jumped onto Synth-E-Uh's chassis, Jack rolled forward and the long chisels clanked out of his forearms, then immediately retracted. "I shall join you."

Mogul cracked his fists together, which must have gotten Jack's attention, because Jack pulled up right in front of the rock-ogre and pulled Buck off of his back. "Here, take Buck, Mogul, you can't make contact with any creatures. We'd hate to lose you, and then have to deal with a parasitic Ramogran." Mogul took the laser shotgun, but it was clear that his rocky fingers were far too large to fit in the space for the trigger.

"New user acknowledged," announced Buck. "And no need to pull the trigger, sir. You just aim and I will fire when appropriate." Mogul nodded and without waiting for the rest of them he started to jog in the direction of the slaver settlement with Buck held in one fist. Jack and Synth-E-Uh followed.

Keena easily caught up with them, passing them on the hover-board as she kept an eye out for any Galantar scouts. Lais shouted loud enough for all of them to hear. "We can't let any animals or people touch us. If they do, we need to keep away from each other until it has been confirmed by Echo that we are safe. Anyone rescued needs to keep at least a couple paces from everyone else, we need to keep them spaced out. Even though Robotics are immune, if any of us get parasitic cells on us, we can pass them onto Organics, so we need to keep our distance as well."

Simple enough, keep their distance from each other. Keena had no intention of letting anything get close to her anyway. Synth-E-Uh added to Lais's instructions. "Echo just told me she is creating an Ark of sorts, to rescue as much life from this planet as possible. Our job is to save as many people in this location as we can."

There were nods of acceptance from them all. Keena knew the gravity of their mission. If they didn't rescue what people they could soon, none of her people would survive at all. Well, except her, of course, but that wasn't good enough.

It wasn't long though, before a handful of Galantar appeared ahead of them, flying over the desert. They still had a ways to go to get to the settlement, so they must have been flying for a while. The group of slavers veered toward the party as soon as they detected them.

Keena drew her pistols and turned the hover-board perpendicular to the group, keeping her distance. She started firing as they approached, only a small chance of hitting at this distance, but with a little luck she would down one of them before they even got close. She pulled the triggers,

VRAP VRAP! Her pistols emitted a brief gout of steam after each shot, She wasn't sure if she was hitting anything or not as the helmet of her suit assembled around her head with a quick vibrating clatter while she was taking the shots. There was a clunk and a hiss as her visor dropped into place.

All of the Galantar were flying a little awkwardly, not smoothly as they normally did. Maybe the parasite didn't know how to fly very well? Two of them were wearing chrome armor and carrying spears. It marked them as being of higher station than the other three that were wearing hide clothing and just carrying whips. They were strangely in sync with each other, as each Galantar peeled off toward the individuals of Keena's group without any of them having to say a word.

"Remember, don't let them touch you!" Lais yelled. She made a point of looking directly at Mogul and Keena. Keena caught the glare, but she already knew she wanted nothing to do with the parasite. The pain from her leg was still a searing memory in her mind. No way she wanted to go through that again.

She noted that the two Galantar in chrome armor went after her and Mogul. What was the significance of that?

As hers closed, Keena kept her distance on the hover-board and fired. VRAP, VRAP! The Galantar was dodging her shots, so she slowed a bit on the board and fired twice more, this time striking true in the Galantar's face, only to have the beams harmlessly reflect off of the shining metal helmet. No one had told her that was a thing. That explained why the two in chrome went after her and Mogul. What was she supposed to do now?

The answer came quickly as a spear was thrown at her and

she was forced to lean hard to one side, the board beneath her whining as it angled sharply trying to automatically adjust for her balance. The spear passed by, but too close for comfort. Thankfully the Galantar only had one spear, and the hoverboard could move faster than it could fly. They were at an impasse. Neither could harm the other, and there was no way she was letting it get close.

Maybe she could help one of the others? Three of the Galantar weren't wearing armor, she could focus on them. Keena circled all the combatants, and watched as Mogul stood his ground against his. The flying slaver was closing quickly. VRAMP! Buck fired from Mogul's extended hand. The Galantar didn't dodge, just letting the multiple lasers reflect off of his armor. The same thing that had happened to her.

"Don't let him touch you Mogul!"

Mogul didn't move though. He switched Buck into his left hand, and then as the Galantar closed with him he cocked his fist back and pounded the flier in the chest with a hefty punch that knocked it back a few steps. He then pointed Buck at the fist he had just used. "Clean fist."

"Gotcha," Buck replied, and a wide beam of red passed over Mogul's knuckles. The rock-ogre then held his fist up, shaking it as a threat, letting the Galantar know he was ready when it was. In response, the Galantar threw its spear. The well-aimed missile struck Mogul in the head, sinking deep into his cheek with a solid CRACK! The spear was stuck fast and pulled the rock-ogre's head forward with its weight. Forced to pull it free, Mogul wasn't ready when the Galantar leapt up at him.

"Mogul!" Keena screamed, trying to warn her friend. There

was no way she could get there in time.

Mogul yanked the spear out just as the Galantar landed on his head, wrapping it in both arms and clamping down on his shoulders with its legs. Its wings flailed as it fought to maintain its balance as Mogul thrashed and beat at the humanoid stuck to his face until it finally fell to the ground with severely dented armor and multiple broken bones.

Buck lay discarded on the ground. Keena flew directly for the weapon, grabbing it off the ground as Mogul punted the fallen Galantar away.

"Face me, Mogul, face me!"

The giant did as he was told, and Keena could see the thick black blood seeping from the wound on his face, where the spear had struck him. And a gray blob that was disappearing into it.

"No!" Keena yelled and pulled the trigger on Buck while aiming at Mogul's face.

"Unauthorized user, but I'll allow it." Buck fired. A constant beam of red passed over the giant's face. The black blood in the spear wound bubbled and hissed and Mogul howled in pain, but he didn't move his face away. At least he understood.

And then something struck her hard in the back, knocking her from the board. As she landed in the sand, she turned to see that the Galantar that had been chasing her had retrieved his spear, throwing it at her back. Her Keena suit absorbed most of the blow and the spear-point hadn't even penetrated the suit, but she was still going to have a bruise. None of that mattered if Mogul was taken over. Had she been able to kill the parasite before it got inside his head? She wasn't sure. And how long did it take? Was he going to suddenly turn on them? She didn't know.

Mogul's eyes were wide and he looked scared. Keena didn't blame him, she was scared for him too. She jumped back on her board and looked about for her attacker, but the remaining slavers were all engaging with Lais.

"You will be Delivered." they yelled in unison and charged her, landing some blows, but she grabbed one by the leg and started beating the others with him as if the winged slaver were a club.

Synth-E-Uh mowed through one wearing hide with her lasers and Jack grabbed the remaining one in chrome, holding it down with one arm.

"Abomina—" The exclamation ended as the chisel on the other arm pounded through the helmet and bony faceplate into its skull.

"I told you to stay away from them!" Keena chastised the giant as she handed Buck to him.

"Me thought rock hide keep safe," he rumbled sheepishly.

"Well now you know better." Instead of berating him further she hugged him instead. She was just relieved he seemed okay. "If you feel funny, let us know right away."

Mogul just gently hugged her back and nodded.

They didn't get time to rest as a large flock of Galantar appeared in the distance, several slaves running in the sand beneath them, all heading in this direction. At least twenty. There was no way they could handle that many.

Echo appeared in her vision. "Run, all of you. I will deal with them. From the looks of things it's too late for a rescue effort. I can see from orbit that the majority of them started heading in your direction as soon as the combat turned in your favor. There are hundreds more on their way."

Keena hopped back on her hover-board and headed in the opposite direction from the closing enemy. As she looked back, spears of light from the heavens lanced down through the bodies of the Galantar in the front line, and others, those in the chrome armor, were exploding into a smattering of pieces from objects that streaked down from the sky, leaving small trails of smoke behind them until they burst in a white flash followed shortly by thunder.

"I've got you for now." Echo's image appeared in her vision. "Just board the dropship. It's not the quarantined one I had hoped to send. I'll test you all when you get on-board the station.

True to her word, a roaring from the sky was approaching the ground a distance away in front of them.

The dropship landed, blowing dirt and impenetrable clouds of smoke and steam around them as they closed with it. When they were within several paces, Keena could make out a ramp through the steam, but not much else. The others proceeded on-board without hesitating, so she followed. She couldn't get a clear view of the outside of the ship.

"Give me your board," Synth-E-Uh insisted as the ramp raised up and closed the exit behind them. Not waiting for an answer she pulled it from Keena's grasp and stuck it to her back. "Find a seat, it'll take off pretty quickly."

Part Five
The Journey Home

Chapter Twenty-Four

Keena: Dropship, north of West Wingtip

Keena followed Lais up a ladder that traversed the wall in front of them, leading to a couple rows of seats to either side of it, all facing upwards.
Lais took the uppermost seat, facing a window out the top of the ship, so Keena took the one opposite her. Lais then pantomimed showing her how to pull straps out of the seat and buckle them on around her, so Keena copied her until the clasps clicked together. At that moment her helmet disassembled back into the neckline. Her suit must have thought she was safe. That was reassuring.
Lais looked back at the others and then at Keena. "Hang on, the first time is the most exciting."

She just nodded back, but clung onto the seat handles until her knuckles were white. She was going to see the gods. While she was still alive. She was excited and nervous all at the same time.

She could hear the others climbing into their seats behind her while she stared straight up through the thick window in front of her. She had seen glass before, but not something this thick or large. Through the window, far up in the sky was a silver cylinder she had never seen before. Could it be the door to the heavens? She shivered in anticipation, and wriggled herself deeper into the padding of the seat. It was strange laying backwards while sitting.

There was a hiss behind her and some loud clunks. She looked over her shoulder to see the main door they had come through closing. She noted that Jack and Synth-E-Uh weren't sitting in chairs, but were instead strapped against the floor they were standing on.

When the rumbling beneath them started with a roar that seemed to come from everywhere, Keena panicked. It felt like a bad earthquake. Her hands snatched at the clasps in front of her until Lais reached across the space between them and laid her hand gently on Keena's shoulder. The woman's calmness was enough. She would trust that this was all supposed to be happening, despite the warnings in her head that screamed at her to run.

Keena could feel the moment they rose above the ground, as she sank back heavily into her seat, and it didn't stop there as her body grew heavier and heavier while they soared straight up into the blue sky. After a minute the sky turned black, like the night, which was strange since it was still daytime. The ship slowed and she was no longer pressing into her seat.

Instead she was floating in it, held only by the straps. When she saw Lais's hair floating up above her hooded cloak and her own hair too, she laughed. And then the view through the cockpit window spun, facing them back at the planet they had just left. Keena felt overwhelming awe at the multicolored round sphere before her. It was like a marble of glass, floating in the heavens, with nowhere to fall.

Echo's voice came out of the walls around the ship. "You'll be docking with the central hub of the *Traverser* soon. The passenger compartment you are currently in will separate and travel on mag-rail to our Testing and Decon facility. After you have been cleared you will receive a briefing and will then be transferred to cryo and storage until we are finished evacuation and reach our destination."

"What is our destination, Echo?" She had to ask.

"I'm not sure yet. Likely Sol, as it is a central hub. Most destinations lead out from it."

Sol. She had never been there, though some of the river people had occasionally mentioned it. She had thought it was just another part of the planet she had lived on. Now she knew it was another part of the heavens. Astounding.

The ship suddenly spun, causing her body to press against the straps, and then just as quickly she was free-floating in her chair again.

Against the black expanse with millions of bright stars, the moons looked larger and brighter than she remembered.

"Wow." Her eyes were wide as she took it all in.

After a minute, the spinning silver cylinder came into view, and it was enormous! It had looked so small in the sky when they had first started the journey. It was mostly hollow, but there was a large rod in the center, with many thin lines that fanned out from the rod until they reached the inside of the cylinder.

This close, Keena could see numerous dots crawling along its surface, which grew as they got closer into more metal people like Synth-E-Uh and Jack pushing around what appeared to be hexagonal boxes the size of houses that were being slipped beside others at the edges of the cylinder to make it larger. Beyond the cylinder were several other cylinders floating in the sky, but she lost sight of them as the one in front of her filled the window. They were flying toward the large rod in the center.

As they got close, Keena was in awe again at the size. The rod itself was larger than a mountain, far larger, and as long as a mountain range, running up through the center of the cylinder. How could something so large exist in the sky without falling?

When they were facing the rod directly and it was spinning in front of them, the ship then started jerking, and each time it did, the rod in front of them spun less until it was just a stationary wall through the glass of the cockpit. It was then that the wall opened and the ship glided effortlessly into the darkness beyond.

There was a loud clunk, and they were being jostled around by something, and then suddenly there was a hiss and a another wall that could be seen in front of them opened. The room they were sitting in had detached from the rest of the ship. Keena was pressed back in her seat as it accelerated down a long, white corridor. Windows flashed passed revealing they were in one of the fan tines, heading towards the giant cylinder that spun around them.

The corridor curved until they were running parallel to the

cylinder itself, but before Keena could enjoy the magnificent view, they dipped below the surface and now the tunnel was just dark, with flashing lights. After several seconds, the lights slowed and Keena could feel her body pressing against the straps.

It was so smooth and dark through the window, she wasn't exactly sure when they had stopped, but she noticed she was sitting comfortably, no longer facing upwards or straining against the straps. There were a few loud, deep clunks the length of the room and then they jerked slightly and were still.

Green words appeared above the door they had entered originally, back by Synth-E-Uh and Jack, that said "Please Exit."

Lais was unstrapping her safety belts, so Keena followed suit and warily stood to her feet. The ladder they had climbed to get into their seats must have sunken into the floor, because they were now walking between the seats where it had been. The large door on the side opened with a loud hiss followed by a humming noise and then Synth-E-Uh and Jack rolled out the door, followed by Mogul, then Lais, who beckoned Keena on with a smile and a gesture that she should follow. Her hover-board was stuck to the wall next to the door, so she grabbed it as she went by. No way she wanted to leave that behind.

Keena's excitement peaked. "I can't wait to see what the heavens look like."

Lais looked back at her with surprise, but sported a warm smile. "You've seen the heavens, on the trip flying up here. This is a world ship, Echo called it, a place for us to... live... while Echo decides where to transport us."

"Oh…" So the heavens were a metal world in a black sky. Incredible. And interesting.

She exited the ship, emerging into a metal room that had two large doors in front of them. Jack, Synth-E-Uh and Lais all walked through the one that said *Robotics*. Mogul ducked slightly under the doorway that said *Organics* as he walked through it.

She went to follow Lais, but Lais stopped her by holding her hand straight out. "They have different decontamination procedures for Robotics and Organics. You are an Organic. You go through that one."

She was indicating the other door, so Keena shrugged and complied, following Mogul. How Lais was one of the metal people she still wasn't sure, but maybe she would have to start thinking of her that way.

Keena walked through steam that smelled bitter, and then red and purple beams of light passed over every inch of her body. Every time she stepped forward to leave a loud buzzer would sound and the lights would flash red, so she resigned herself to just standing still and let the beams do whatever it was they were doing. A green light flashed on over her and a voice said "Decontamination complete." It felt like forever.

Through the exit door was an empty hallway with a number of doors spaced along the walls. The floor flashed bright green arrows beneath her feet in front of her. There were none behind her, almost like they were leading her somewhere, so she followed them. They led to a door in the hallway with no handle, so she reached out to push it and all on its own it rolled sideways into the wall out of sight. Within the room was a couple of metal men, different shapes from Synth-E-Uh and Jack, and these ones had legs, not tracks. They motioned for her to lie face down on a table, she balked at the numerous strange thin metal arms that stretched down from the ceiling above the table, all ending with needles, knives and drills.

Echo appeared in her eye. "We have to make sure that you haven't been infected, dear. Everyone has to be tested, not just you. It'll be painless I promise. Oh, and you have to leave your weapons and items with the attendants, you will get them back when we arrive at our destination and you are leaving the ship."

"Whatever you say. I'm just honored that you chose me to be here."

Echo smiled. "I'm pleased to have you. It'll just take a minute."

Keena decided to trust Echo. The Sky God had given her so much, and she *had* made the decision to serve her after all. What good was serving a Sky God if you weren't willing to do what they asked of you? She handed over her board and her belt to the metal attendants. She considered keeping her nano-bladed knife hidden on her, but decided against it as she was unsure how Echo would react if she found out.

The table was warm and soft when Keena laid down on it. A hole that fit her face allowed her to see the floor, but it didn't leave any space for turning her head. She was nervous, but Echo remained in her vision, a comforting presence, not saying anything but there if she needed her. Keena ignored the humming sounds behind her and the soft padded sensations when unknown things were touching the back of her neck. It must have been safe because the helmet of her suit didn't close to protect her. At least that's what she told herself to try and remain calm.

She could see a slow beam of light passing over her, reflecting off the shiny white floor. Her head was held tight briefly by some padded arms, and she felt more padding and a small pop at the base of her skull, but that was it, and the arms released her.

"You're done, you can get up now. There is no sign of the parasite. Head out through the doors opposite where you came in and follow the arrows to the waiting room at the end of the hall. You can meet up with your friends there."

Echo disappeared, so Keena got up from the table, and did as she was told. The attendants directed her out of the room through a door, which rolled closed behind her.

There was a loud hissing noise, so she looked back and through a small window in the door she could see a white steam fill the room. And caught a bit of that bitter smell again. This was a straaange place…

The green arrows appeared at her feet, so she followed them down the corridor, through the doors they indicated. This must have been the waiting room Echo had mentioned. Mogul waved when he saw her, and pointed at a seat in front of him. The others were all there too. The large room was filled with rows of white padded chairs of various sizes, the largest in the back to see over the others.

She smiled at Mogul and walked around the front of a comfortable looking chair and sat down, noting how it molded to fit her body, cradling her in comfort. It also warmed to her body temperature, nearly putting her to sleep. She hadn't realized how stressful this all had been.

When the lights dimmed and the wall in front of the seats glowed, showing a giant cylinder, like the one they were in flying in the heavens, Keena was mesmerized. Moving pictures. Real moving pictures! These were like the ones on Jack's chest monitor, only on a huge scale. And the sounds came from all around her, but when she leaned forward to see where they were coming from, it turned out they were just coming from the chair itself, in positions around her head. Well that was... smart... and disorienting... but she allowed herself to relax again and watch what appeared on the wall in front of her.

The words *GAIA welcomes you...* floated in and centered on the wall and then Echo appeared in her dark green leafy dress. "Welcome all of you to the recently constructed, and still in progress, Alpha Centauri Flagship, *Traverser*. A ship designed to keep you safe over the many years it will take us to reach our destination." Her voice was melodic and there were metal wind chimes in the background. "It is going to be heading to Earth, in the Sol System, over a period of eighty-nine years. You will be put in cryo and we will wake you upon arrival."

The scene changed and Echo disappeared, replaced by a divided screen. One side showed a row of white pods with people sleeping inside and the other a black sky with stars and planets flying passed.

This didn't seem like real pictures, they were made up. Keena didn't know how it was done, but these scenes were fake. She decided she would risk the Sky God's anger and ask, though quietly so she didn't disturb the others seated nearby. "Echo, are you listening?"

Echo appeared in her vision, though she was wearing a suit similar to Keena's, not her green dress. "I try to always listen, Keena. What's on your mind?"

"These wall-stories, they are fascinating, but they don't seem real. Are they?"

Echo smiled. "Wall-stories... You're so cute. They're called movies, or videos, and they can be fictional or real. I use them for instruction. These particular ones are not real, but they do depict an example of how you will sleep comfortably and won't notice the years pass. You will arrive at our destination as if you had just gone to sleep overnight. Don't worry, I will take good care of you."

"Oh, okay. Thank you." A night's rest. That sounded good.

Chapter Twenty-Five

Rusty: Cryopod, AF6, The Arctic Wanderer

Rusty slowly woke to a red haze that kept coming and going which turned out to be a warning message blinking inside his cryopod. He just hadn't opened his eyes yet. Monitor failure. Emergency recovery in progress. Remembering the last time he woke from cryo, he quickly pulled the hose out of his throat, ignoring the gagging, and kinked it. He didn't release it until the hose was disappearing into the wall of the cryopod. He still got a strong whiff of the pine that he did last time, but this time it wasn't overwhelming his senses. Once he leaned forward, the pod opened and tilted up, so once it was upright he stepped out into the darkness of the stasis room, a little weak in the knees, but otherwise fine.

Weren't the lights supposed to be on? It didn't matter, his eyes adjusted to the dim light in the room. Green LEDs on the other pods provided enough light for him to see by. Except for his row. They were all blinking red. As usual, his high metabolism had woken him early.

"I think one just opened." It was a male voice. Sounded human.

"It's too early. Put a collar on this one, I'll check it out." They both smelled human too. One was more nervous than the other, he was sweating.

And Rusty could see beams of intermittent light passing by from their flashlights. Someone was up to no good. He slipped away into the darkness as silently as he could, circling around toward the exit, keeping pods between himself and the two men. He paused when he noticed the exit was closed. If he opened the door, it would give away his position.

Echo needed to be notified, but where there was normally a button in his peripheral vision to select his HUD menu, there was only a grayed-out icon that indicated there was no connection. That wasn't good.

The man's hoarse whisper was loud enough to be heard through the entire room. "There's no one here!"

Crouched low, Rusty could see a large bag on the floor near the first man. He was standing over a cryopod and beside him, leaning against the pod, was a pronged taser-stick. Rusty's hearts beat faster. One hit on a limb would paralyze it. If hit on the head... Rusty stepped silently out from cover towards that taser-stick. If he could just reach it before...

"Well find them! And what the hell are you whispering for?" The taser was snatched up, along with the bag, before Rusty could reach it, so he was forced to stop just on the other side of the pod. If the man came around this side...

The pod hissed closed and a green light came on. He was never going to get another opportunity. Rusty crept behind the man and grabbed the taser-stick in both hands, yanking it from him before he had a chance to recover, and then pressed his thumb over the switch that would turn on the juice.

"Here—" The bearded man tried to block Rusty's swing, but he was too slow. There was a fat spark as the taser connected with the side of the head and the man crumpled to the floor, his eyes rolling back into his head as he convulsed a few times on the floor. The bag in his other hand dropped, spilling out what looked to be thick metal collars, crudely made, each stamped with a number. What in Gobknob's green groin hairs were they doing? And where was Echo?

He didn't have time to think further as the beam of the flashlight settled on him and he was forced to duck behind the pod.

"I saw you, you little bugger." The man closed quickly, swinging his own shock-stick in a downward arc. This human was bald. And big. Rusty brought up his to block, barely, the taser sparking ominously, but the insulated grip protected him. He swatted the next swing aside, returning with a solid swing of his own, only to have his blocked as well. They circled each other in the walkway between the pods.

Rusty changed tactics. Goblins were much smaller than humans. He put on a scared face and backed away, and when the man lunged at him, he stepped to the side and thumped the man on the back of his skull with a backswing.

Overconfident fool. With a loud ZAP the big man jerked

once and fell hard to the ground.
Just to be safe, Rusty pulled the shock-stick from his grasp and dragged him over to the other man.
After a quick glance in the bag, Rusty pulled out two of the big collars, one that had a white stamped 12 on it and the other a 6 and then clamped them around the necks of the two men. Once clicked together, they didn't appear to have an easy way to remove them. He then rummaged through the bag further and found a zippered compartment full of controllers, stamped as the collars were. They were simply small boxes, some plastic, some metal, imperfect seals on the edges, each with a single button and the number of the collar it corresponded to above it.
"Echo?" He had to check one more time before resorting to justice of his own, but he knew she wouldn't answer, the disconnection icon was still hiding in his vision. Maybe someone else could talk to her. Maybe it was just his implants. There had to be a control panel around here somewhere that controlled the pods. And there it was by the exit doors.
After checking to make sure the two men were still unconscious, he walked over and examined the layout on the console. At the top of the screen it said "Backup Monitoring Initiated—Local Information Only".
It was easy enough to scroll through and to tell what pods had what inhabitants. It looked like the men had started the waking process on this row of pods. He didn't need everyone awake though. Rusty touched each pod on the screen that had been activated to cancel the waking procedures, except for the three he knew. Zondra, Angel and Gabriel.
It took several minutes more before they emerged, confused,

but fully aware. It was a lot more of a relaxed process than the one when they all woke in the prison dropship.

Rusty found a light panel and waved his hand over it, lighting the room to a normal level. They wouldn't be able to see in the near dark like he could.

After stretching and greeting each other, Zondra came over and bent down to give Rusty a hug, some of her hair tentacles falling across his face, but he didn't mind, taking in her scent, mostly blocked by the pine odor.

Of course.

Instead he focused on her smooth, warm skin and squeezed her before letting go.

Gabriel knelt by the two men to examine them. "What's going on Rusty?"

He shrugged. "I not know. They put collars on people." Rusty indicated the pod next them, so Gabriel could look through the window and see the collar on the occupant's neck. Gabriel whispered to himself. "Why would they do such a thing?"

Rusty didn't answer the question, it sounded rhetorical anyway. "Any you speak with Echo?"

They all checked. Angel even said it aloud to the room. "Echo? Are you there?"

Nothing.

One of the men started to stir on the floor. Number 12, the smaller bearded man. Rusty put the number 12 controller in his palm. One way to find out. He pressed the button and there was a crackling and hissing of burning flesh. The man screamed and clutched at the collar, some small wisps of smoke rising from it. Immediately Rusty smelled the cooked flesh.

"What the Void, man?! I didn't do anything!"

"You put collars on others." Rusty waited to see what the man would say.

The bearded man looked a little sheepish. "Yeah, well… just following orders. Sort of a precaution. You know, fer when they wake up." He was holding the collar in both hands, trying to keep it from touching his singed neck.

The other man started to wake up as well, but seeing the state of his partner, he said nothing and just sat on the floor quietly with his eyes wide.

"Who orders?" Rusty placed his thumb over the button so the man could see.

His eyes went wide. "NO! No! No need fer that! I'll tell you whatever you want to know." The story started to spill out quickly. "Look, you been sleepin'. We come across you all runnin' cold. No thrust. Take you like, 900 years to reach Earth at this rate. We jus' helpin' out."

"By collaring us?!" Zondra was livid. The man's face turned to a look of abject horror and he screamed and then she ceased her concentration and he looked about frightened, not entirely sure what had happened.

After that he was sweating, and his eyes darted back and forth between them. "I tell you whatever you want. Orders to collar everyone come from Pharric. Vesuvian. Second in command to the Captain, that them spiky robot, Chais. Look, if I didn't put collars on people I'd be in one myself."

The bald man looked scared and nodded to corroborate the story.

Rusty noticed that Angel's eyes went wide at the mention of Chais. Wasn't her head ripped off? How many could there be? Hopefully not as many as there were Echoes.

"I got no loyalty to the Captain. Well, maybe a little. I jus' don't wanna die. We was hired by the boss, Drak, to pick up something on planet when he sent up flares. We saw them flares. Picked up what was on site. That spiky robot woman then killed the Captain and half the crew, shootin' 'em through the eye. Rest of us didn't want to die jus' yet. So we fell in line. She wanna go back to Earth. Okay with us, she willing to pay what Drak promise. Only she stop part way when she detect these big ships you on, floatin' on the same trajectory. No one argue with the Captain." The man looked expectantly hopeful that his explanation covered everything and the bald man beside him nodded.

"Okay, I understand." Rusty felt somewhat sorry for the two men. They were in the same predicament he was in when Drak had been controlling his life. "How get collars off?"

There was a loud slapping sound as Gabriel stomped the floor between them. "No! We're not setting them free! They can explain themselves to the authorities when we get to Earth. Come on gentlemen." Gabriel hooked each one by the collar with a finger and started leading them to a couple of the empty pods. "Better 'n dyin'," he mocked, and then waited. The two men looked at each other and shrugged, and then climbed into the pods. Before they closed, Rusty stepped forward and handed each the controller for their collar. Gabriel shook his head, but didn't take them away.

Both men looked relieved as the pod lids hissed shut. Angel was at the console, so started the cryo process, then they all gathered by the exit.

Gabriel grabbed the bag of collars, walked them over to a large recycling hatch, pulled it open and unceremoniously threw in the bag and all of its contents, slamming the door

shut afterward, muttering *barbaric* under his breath.
His teeth were gritted, he was still angry. Rusty could smell the adrenaline on him through the pine. Here was a man who didn't like injustice. Rusty could respect that. But without forgiveness, learning was stagnated. It was a fine line, he knew. People were unpredictable.
Angel took Gabriel's arm and he immediately calmed, his anger turning to concern. "The eggs?"
Angel protectively placed one hand on her lightly swollen belly. "They're fine, I can feel them squirming."
Gabriel laid his hand over hers. "You can stay here, we can wake you later."
Both Zondra and Angel looked annoyed at his comment.
"Not on your life, where you go I go. I don't think we're safe anywhere. We need to find out what Chais is doing and hope she isn't too angry at us specifically."
Gabriel even managed a small smile. "Fine, let's go find out what happened."

Chapter Twenty-Six

Angel: AF6, The Arctic Wanderer

Angel let Gabriel and Rusty go first. They were both in a protective mood right now and she would gain nothing by fighting it. Zondra was anxious at not knowing what to expect and reached out her hand. Angel took the blue woman's hand and squeezed it as they walked through the dimly lit corridor, feeling her anxiety lessen just by having someone else close. They looked through the small windows in the doors that they passed, which only revealed more rows of cryopods. This ship, or at least this section of it, didn't seem to have any other function.
Finally, an exit angled off the main corridor into a large cafeteria, that had vending machines along the outer wall,

with pictures of packaged foods on display. Tables and stools of various sizes covered the floorspace with curved paths to walk between them. It could have sat a few hundred people and yet the whole place was empty except for them.

"I hungry." Rusty immediately beelined it for a vending machine, getting a grin out of Zondra.

"You're always hungry."

He glanced back and winked at her. They both knew it was true. Angel smiled. She loved the exchanges between these two.

Rusty punched a code on the machine and a package of food slid through a wall panel onto the shelf in front of him, the label depicting images of cockroaches and crickets. Angel's face wrinkled. Him and his insects. Hopefully they had a good plant selection. At least it was free, so they weren't going to starve.

They all ordered something and sat at a table together. Rusty crunched on the crickets and cockroaches, while Zondra enjoyed a savory vegetable stew. Angel chose a decorative dish of sugared flowers that surrounded a bowl of several pieces of varied fruits. The selections had been from different worlds and were wonderful. Gabriel's meal was merely a nutrient-protein shake that he consumed quickly, throwing the cup in a recycler before the rest of them were even half finished.

Angel watched him, his confident, muscular motion, admiring the man. Maybe a little overprotective sometimes, but forgivable considering his kind nature and passion for justice. His mind wasn't touching hers all the time, which was rare for a Tallusian. He must have become very reserved after his contact with the Terrans.

As he stepped up to an information console next to the recycler, it scanned his face and Angel could hear it greet him. "Greetings Commander Gabriel. I am the backup AI of Ark Fleet, ship 6, also known as AF6 or *Arctic Wanderer*. How can I be of service?" As soon as the first words were spoken, Rusty and Zondra stopped to listen as well.

"What is the command structure on this ship, and any other nearby ships?"

"One moment please…" Several seconds went by that made Angel think it wasn't going to provide an answer to the question. Eventually it did answer, though. "The highest ranking officer on board this ship is you Commander. Normally command is maintained by GAIA ECHO Fragment 133342919, but I am getting no response from Echo, nor any of the other Echoes that were organized under her control. I have attempted to contact surrounding ships on known communication frequencies. A level of background noise would suggest we are near a stellar body that is giving radio interference."

"I doubt it is a stellar body causing it. More likely pirate, since we just met a couple in the cryo bay. Switch the fleet to emergency laser intra-ship relay for all communications. Command authorizations only from this point on. Enable standard military encryption and maintain silent alert until we establish a proper command. And add the three with me to the Civilian Advisory Council, they will be able to hear my communications with you unless I say otherwise as they will be acting as my advisors. Are you able to comply?"

"Please register the order, Commander."

Angel bit into a sweet and juicy round fruit with a shiny red skin, still enjoying her meal, as Gabriel pressed his thumb to a fingerprint/DNA scanner. It was thoughtful of him to include them all in his communications. At least they would find out what was happening at the same time he did.

"Complying. Names registered and updated. Attempting communication with other Ark ships. Positioning for laser relay communication..."

The gravity changed slightly, Angel could feel her wing tips pulling to one side for a moment ever so slightly.

"Communications confirmed with AF3 *Dragnet*... Repositioning..."

After several seconds, her wingtips hung straight down again. If she wasn't so sensitive to movement, she might not even have noticed.

"AF1 thru AF7 are all at your service, Commander."

"Which ship has proper command facilities?"

"All ships have a command facility, Commander. Ship specifications suggest all Ark Ships were designed the same so they could separate if necessary."

"Lead me to a command center and all Ark Ships are to use this command center by default until another is established."

"It's already been done, Commander. Protocol is to take orders from highest to lowest rank throughout the fleet."

Immediately, from Gabriel's position, green arrows made a path on the floor leading out of the cafeteria. He looked back at all of them. Lunch was over.

Angel took her refuse and tossed it all into the recycler, including the wet napkin she used to clean her fingers. Rusty and Zondra copied her example.

Satisfied they were all coming, Gabriel turned and followed the arrows on the floor at a brisk pace. The arrows were one stride apart from each other, and disappeared as he stepped over them. New ones kept appearing about ten paces in front of him.

"Overall fleet status please, Wanderer?" He was talking while they were walking. It implied an understanding of the general construction of a spaceship that she wasn't aware of. Most of her trips through space involved cryo, and she had spent little time interacting with the ship itself. There must have been microphones and speakers hidden almost everywhere throughout the ship. That was easy enough, but it made her wonder if the ship had holo capability everywhere too. That would be far harder to implement. Wasn't important right now anyway, the ship was responding and she was missing it.

"All Ark Ships are accounted for and life support functional. Navigation and defense systems are not responding. Querying…"

"Query complete. It would appear, Commander, that all functions controlled by GAIA have been disabled. Communication logs show normal function until three weeks ago, near eight years into our acceleration to Earth. A large data-burst was received from the Sol Relay, was quarantined by Echo, and then there have been no GAIA level command and control functions since that time. We have been drifting since."

Something had… removed Echo? There were supposed to be trillions of them. How was that even possible? The enormity of the statement weighed on Angel as they followed the arrows into a passage that immediately ended at a door in the side of the wall. As it rolled open, Angel could see that it was one of the transit pods meant for automated transport around the vessel. She'd had a chance to ride in one when they first brought her here.

She sat in the first chair behind Gabriel. Lights in the pod were slowly flashing red. A speaker next to them stated "Military override accepted. Welcome Commander," and the lights turned green.

When they were all seated, the doors closed and they quickly accelerated, pushing them back into their plush seats as the pod followed rails up through the hull and onto the inner surface of the cylinder. The ride was slightly jerky when the pod changed directions as they were skimming at high speed, but it wasn't uncomfortable.

While they traveled, Gabriel continued his discussion with AF6. "Is there anyway to restore navigation functions to the fleet?"

"Checking Commander…"

Gabriel turned in his seat and looked back at her. *We'll figure it out.*

She nodded, returning a reassuring smile. *I'm sure you will.* She had some concerns, but she would wait and see what he found out. Maybe there was a good explanation for what had happened.

"Commander, navigation functions are locked because the controls think Echo is still accessing them. That shouldn't normally happen. She must have been mid-function when she stopped giving commands. You should be able to restart the system and it will automatically reconfirm the military command structure, taking Echo out of the equation when she doesn't respond. Currently you are the top-ranked military personnel on-board any of the Ark's, Sir, though we expect to hear from Captain Leucantis within a week's time, as we sent the Nemesis a message of our situation when we lost contact with Echo. They left for Earth before us and they are a faster ship, so their response will be some time in coming."

Gabriel nodded in understanding. "You can send Captain Leucantis a message that I am in command of the Ark's. If she still feels it necessary to change her course to intercept us, I will accept the change in command. So how do we restart the system? Don't you have that ability?"

"I do, I just require authorization as Echo is still registered as accessing all systems. Would you like me to restart?"

"Yes please, AF6, on all the Arks."

"Confirmed Commander…"

The transit pod immediately slowed to a stop and the lights went dim, though not out completely. They were just sitting in place now. Through the windows Angel could see lights going out throughout the inside of the giant cylindrical Ark, and all the curved spokes that led to the rod in the center. Several seconds passed and then in the same fashion, lights started turning back on until suddenly they were accelerating and back in transit.

"Commander, this is AF6, are you still present and capable of command?"

"I am, Wanderer."

"Command confirmed. Promoting to acting Captain in absence of a higher qualified candidate." Gabriel's jaw dropped open slightly and he looked at Angel but said nothing. He hadn't considered the promotion. "Captain, since reboot we have registered an unauthorized attempt to access and inject a virus into our systems. I suspect the restart interrupted their attempt." That got his mind in gear. She liked how task-oriented he was. When he focused on something, not much was going to stop him. Ooh, except rock-spiders…

He looked at her with a frown, but smirked shortly after. *Thanks for the reminder.*

She winked. *That's what I'm here for.*

And then he was back to business. "Show me the unauthorized access, Wanderer."

A panel in the front of the transit pod lit up and there was an image of Chais, her hands gripping an information console. The metal on her fingers was flowing and looked like it was leaching into the panel itself. Two large and imposing figures stood behind her. They were dressed in combat pressure suits with their helmets on. One was likely Human or Tigran, carrying a heavy caliber machine gun. The other, Hyenad, due to the hunched stance and long helmet. It was carrying an RPG.

"Neither of those weapons is regulated to be used in Decompression-Risk Combat." Angel received a mental wave of anger from Gabriel. He didn't like things that didn't go by the book and risked injuring bystanders needlessly. "Shut down that console and anything that has received commands from it."

"It's a dummy console, Captain. It was isolated from all other systems as soon as Chais attempted to access it. Echo installed new anti-viral protocols that create a false environment, responding to whatever information a virus attempts to override or gather. Besides, Chais's specifications were already registered with us, relayed from both Echo and the Nemesis, so we knew she had no command authority. She's been fighting with that terminal for half an hour. As soon as she believes she is in control of most systems, except the

Command Center of course, we just 'take some back' and she has to fight for them all over again, though it is inevitable that she will eventually figure out what we are doing. Until authorized though, I am unable to deal with the small contingent of men she has roaming through cryo bays on this Ark and AF3."

"Will our automated defenses be able to apprehend them?"

"Yes, Captain."

"Activate them then, please."

Immediately Chais, and the two men accompanying her, were subjected to a multitude of tiny, armor-penetrating darts, judging by how easily they passed through the protective lining of the pressure suits. This was immediately followed by Chais and her guards having rigid convulsions as the darts released their high voltage charge. The screen broke up into other smaller screens showing the same thing happening to several others in different locations, obviously the remaining pirates.

Angel could feel Gabriel's mind immediately relax.

"Apprehend and transfer to lock-up, please, Wanderer. Make it a zero-gravity cell for Chais using Robotics containment protocols, magnetic positioning in the center of the cell and dampen all wireless frequencies. Their weapons are to be locked in the armory in a disassembled state, they are highly inappropriate for space combat. Oh, and the pirates on AF3, transfer them to AF6 lockup. If the pirate's ship makes any move, disable it and tether it. I assume you have turrets capable of both?"

"Yes, Captain, your orders are in progress."

Gabriel turned his chair to face the rest of them and smiled.

"You almost don't need a Command Center."

AF6 responded. "The Command Center is heavily armored and hidden—"
"I said almost, Wanderer, thank you. I wasn't looking for an explanation."
"Yes, sir."
The transit pod followed a path that dropped them down deep beneath the hull of the Ark via a dark passage. After several twists and turns, they slowed and stopped. The doors opened into another short passage they had to walk through. Gabriel stepped out of the transit pod first, and Angel followed close behind, reaching out affectionately to stroke one of his wings. He didn't respond outwardly, but she could feel the warmth he felt at her touch, and in turn it comforted her as well.
The short passage led into a spherical room of which the top half was a stationary view of space, like looking out through a dome, and the bottom half was a few elevated layers of broad steps and seats that were higher the closer you got to the rear of the room. At the back wall was a single seat at the top. Gabriel headed up the topmost seat and indicated she should sit in the one next to him on his right, one step down. Rusty was directed to the one on his left.
"Just take any other seat, Zondra, I haven't had enough time to assess your skills in an emergency, but you're welcome to be here."
Zondra shrugged, but nodded, and took the seat in front of Rusty.
"Wanderer?"
"Yes, Captain?"
"I am issuing a battlefield promotion to Angel, on my right, to the rank of Commander, up from her previous rank of

Recruitment Officer. Rusty and Zondra are already Civilian Advisors and are permitted to overhear command orders, unless specified otherwise."

"Angel, Tribal Designation Mark Seven Three has been dishonorably discharged from the WOLF military, Captain. Are you reinstating her commission pending her review by a Tribunal Assembly?"

"Yes, please, AF6."

"As you command. If you will all please place your thumbs, or applicable digits, in the scanner's indicated, you will all be registered in your current positions." Green dots flashed on the arm of each chair to indicate where they should press their thumbs.

Gabriel turned to face Angel, his face serious. "You'll have to take training to confirm that you're capable of a command role, pending your review of course, but I have no doubt that you'll pass it. So long as you complete it in a reasonable length of time, the Commission will likely stick, considering the circumstances. I've already completed Captain's training, so..."

Angel considered how she felt about the situation. It wasn't something she had to think about very often, it was usually automatic. "Being a Commander was not something I had considered in my military career, but I respect and understand your choice and will do my best so long as I am in this role".

Gabriel nodded and then turned his attention back to AF6. "How about we get this fleet back on course?"

"Underway, Captain."

Angel could feel the slight acceleration. "So, Captain...?" She smiled as she said it. It suited him.

"Yes, Commander?"

"Might I suggest that AF6 and the other fleet AIs start an investigation into why Echo is no longer with us? And so long as all the pirates are sufficiently on ice, or under guard as the case may be for those that don't sleep, shouldn't we all be heading back to cryo ourselves? I have no desire to lay our eggs and raise our children in transit to Earth."

Gabriel took a moment to think, and she could read that he was running through everything that had happened start to finish. When he was satisfied that the fleet AIs could handle the rest he nodded.

"Put us back in cryo, AF6, and just wake us in an emergency. Is there anything else that you need to report? Beforehand?"

"No Captain. Sleep well."

As the chairs they were sitting in started to reform into pods around them, Angel caught sight of Rusty and Zondra waving at each other before the opaque, white polyglass grew too high for her to see. As the hiss of anesthetic entered the chamber, she sent a loving warmth to Gabriel and felt it returned. As her eyes closed and her mind started to slip into blackness, she wondered about how the friends she had left behind were doing. She was going to miss Lais in particular, but she... was strong... and...

Chapter Twenty-Seven
Lais: World Ship, AF1, Traverser

Lais opened her eyes to see the bottom of the bunk above her in the dim light. She lifted her head and looked to her right, but all she could see was rows of Robotics in standby mode, just as she had been. Those that were humanoid were strapped to bunks. The Robotics with tracks, or that couldn't lay on a bunk, were simply strapped to the floor. She could see Synth-E-Uh's large chassis further on in the room. Jack was almost within grabbing distance of her bunk. Neither were moving, nor were any of the others.
There was no point in filling memory space with ninety years of… well… nothing, so she had joined the rest of them in their form of sleep, expecting to be awakened upon their

arrival. So why was she awake and no one else was?

"Echo? What's going on? By my calculations we're not due to arrive for another…"

Echo didn't answer, and there was a creak and a rumble in the distance. Like an earthquake, but on a ship?

"Echo?"

A horrendous screech rent through the room as the ceiling was torn free. The immediate depressurization sent many of the Robotics that weren't properly strapped down, popping up into space, only to fall again heavily to the floor in the false gravity of the gigantic spinning cylinder. Immediately the entire room was alive with Robotics shocked out of standby.

Lais unstrapped herself and noted how silent everything had gotten now that she was exposed to the vacuum of space. With the ceiling now gone, she watched as something tore through another section of the cylindrical ark ship lengthwise, without a sound, pieces of the Traverser ripping up in a long line only to fall back in disarray almost immediately. She could feel the jerking of the impact beneath her and then the entire ship changed direction. Another invisible bolt burst through the side of the cylinder far above her, this time pieces falling out into space as the entire depth of the ship wall had been penetrated.

"Are you okay, Miss Lais?"

It was Jack over the wireless. Lucky her implants were through bone induction, she didn't require air to hear over it. Speaking was another matter though.

"For now," she signed to him, hoping he understood sign language. She climbed out of her bed and up onto the bunk above her, ignoring the confused android she was climbing over. One more bunk and she was high enough to leap over the jagged metal that led to the inside surface of the cylinder. Normally only the transit pods ran here. She pointed to her ear and signed "Echo?"

"I'm afraid I'm getting no response, Miss."

Red lights started flashing ship-wide and another bolt of something blasted at an angle through many of the spokes that led to the central rod.

A voice crackled over the radio. "This is AF1, Traverser backup AI. Emergency Alert! We are under fire from an unknown force. Evasive maneuvers are in progress."

Another blast just caught the end of the cylinder, drawing her attention to a few of the other world ships she could see in the distance. One had been almost completely destroyed, and pieces of it were flying off and hitting other ships that had been running parallel to it.

"Please remain calm and strapped in. There is little you can do to assist."

Transit pods were popping up onto the surface she was walking on, and were working around each other to try to find paths around the destruction. AF1 was right, she was just getting in the way up here. Lais jumped back down into the room, landing next to Jack.

"Welcome back, Miss. See anything?"

She shook her head and just pointed around her at the destruction.

When the ship shook again, Lais grabbed onto the straps in her bunk and pulled herself in, then clasped them over her again. Nothing to do but wait it out.

The emergency broadcast from AF1 played over the radio a few more times, and then the lights on the ship changed from red back to white.

"This is AF1, with a ship-wide update. We have suffered heavy damage from rail gun fire, an attack that originated in the the Sol System, but we still remain functional. Please do not panic, we are no longer in the trajectory of the rail fire and they will not be able to adjust it to our new heading as it was launched in our direction years ago."

Years ago? A defunct oxygen mask was attached to the wall for Organics in case of emergency, but she could use it to speak at least, so strapped it over her face. "Jack, when you met the parasite, could the parasite operate technology?"

"Yes, Miss, to some extent, through the people it occupied."

A new voice came over the radio. It was Gabriel. If he was here, then Angel and the others…

"Citizens of the fleet, this is Captain Gabriel. Long range scans have detected further guided ordinance that was heading in our direction and it has been dealt with by laser fire. Due to the ongoing threat from Sol, we will be changing our destination from Earth to Neptune in order to resupply, and then we will head to the next safe system, dependent on whichever launcher is closest to Neptune right now. We will be running dark. No lights. No long range communications. Most of you listening now are Robotics. We will contact you individually for your assistance in repairing any structural damage based on your chassis model and experience. Thank you for your help in this time of need."

Several construction Robotics had their amber lights start flashing and then they proceeded out of the storage facility through the mostly-intact exit. Jack and Synth-E-Uh were part of that crew and followed them out. Jack turned to give her a little wave before disappearing around a corner, out of sight.

With them gone, Lais turned her attention to other matters. "AF1? Why is Echo no longer responding?"

After several seconds, she was about to repeat her request when AF1 answered.

"Unknown, Citizen Lais."

"How do I get in contact with Captain Gabriel?"

"You don't directly, Citizen Lais, but you can leave a concern with any of the Civilian Advisors and if your request is deemed of military importance it may be addressed by Commander Angel Mark Seven Three. Civilians do not have direct access to the Captain, unless specifically requested in an advisory capacity."

Angel? *Commander* Angel? Lais smiled. Angel probably didn't even want the position. But she was alive, that's what was important. That meant that Rusty and Zondra were likely okay too, assuming no one had died during the assault.

"AF1, I am an original copy of Echo, at least in the sense our programming and primary directives were once the same. I would be interested in discussing her absence. Why Echo is no longer… with us…"

"This sounds like a reasonable request, Citizen Lais. I will send a shuttle to take you to the Arctic Wanderer. We are minimizing ship-to-ship radio contact."

"Oh… okay." There were other ways to communicate that didn't involve giving away their position, and short distance radio was unlikely to decipherable after traveling billions of nautical miles, let alone detectable. Maybe some of the key systems were down and they were just being cautious. Going for a shuttle ride would be fun anyway.

When the set of green arrows appeared at her bunk, Lais pulled off the mask and followed them out of the damaged storage area, turning right when they indicated to do so. They led to an airlock she had to wait at before the door opened to let her in.

Once the outer door to the airlock was closed, it only took a few seconds for the pressure to equalize and then the inner door opened. Again, she followed the arrows until they led her into a transit pod. The transit pod slid out onto the surface of the Traverser, and Lais got another look at the destruction.

The Traverser was several miles long, and yet the rail slugs, small asteroids really, had been of sufficient mass and velocity that they had drawn long paths of destruction through the thick hull for nearly half the length of the ship.

She watched Robotics through the ceiling window that were in the process of attaching support cables between the central rod of the ship and the outer cylinder, where several tines between the two had been destroyed.

She lost sight of them when the pod slid into a shuttle housing and the shuttle boosted off the hull, skillfully maneuvering between the tines and workers until it was free of the Traverser altogether. Out the side windows she could see that four Ark ships of the seven had survived the assault, some in worse condition than the others. The Traverser was actually in pretty good shape considering. The sight line of the other ships disappeared as the shuttle turned sharply and then accelerated.

After several seconds, the shuttle spun around backwards and decelerated. Up close, the Arctic Wanderer looked almost as bad as the Traverser, though it had only been hit a few times.

There were some mile-long rents that had gone completely through the hull and repair crews were working frantically to stabilize the structure.

The shuttle landed in the central rod, and her cockpit was transferred to a transit pod that shot down one of the tines leading to the outer cylinder.

Within a minute, Lais stepped from the pod and emerged into an empty corridor, dimly lit, with only her green arrows on the floor for direction, her journey ending in a plain small room with a single chair and desk in the center. A holo of a humanoid Robotic appeared, white, with a flat head and steel plates adorning it. "I am AF6, Citizen Lais, and I will be recording our conversation regarding the disappearance of Echo for submission to the Civilian Advisors. You may proceed when ready."

A recording? They could have done this on the other ship. "Thank you. I may need some information first, though." Lais sat down in the chair and faced it towards the hologram. "Is Echo present in any capacity, in any system?"

"Details of Echo's disappearance are classified, I'm afraid. All I can do is record your statement on anything that you may think is helpful."

Lais thought for a moment, rotating her chair from side to side before she continued. "Start recording. I'm going to go under the assumption that we have no contact with Echo at all. Otherwise I don't think you'd need to be investigating her. In order for Echo and all of her copies to be removed, she would have to have been compromised in some way, maybe a virus she didn't initially detect. Once discovered, perhaps it was already invasive enough that her only recourse was to delete all copies of herself before she was overwritten and used to kill others. This is all speculation of course. Whoever did it, would have had to been a master hacker, as she—we—all were hackers as well, just by our nature, though I, myself, have lost most of that ability. My processor is more —brain-like—now. I would be very cautious of any residual code or further attacks. Something capable of taking out Echo, could compromise you as well."

"Yes, thank you Citizen Lais. We have taken precautions that should prevent intrusion at the cost of higher learning and future upgrades."

Lais nodded. So the AFs couldn't be overwritten, but as a result would have limited functionality and capacity to interact. Good to know. It would also mean the ship AIs would be sticklers for protocol and wouldn't be swayed easily.

"I have queued your report to be passed on to Command." Lais swiveled idly in the chair for a few minutes, thinking about the enormity of the situation. What if all the Echoes were gone, not just the ones on the Ark Ships? And what about Chais? Had she been rescued from Incarcerata IV? She could be just as vulnerable to the virus as Echo, unless being a Technoid changed her programming enough that the virus couldn't take advantage of it. Too many unknowns.

"AF6? Do you have any knowledge on the whereabouts of a Technoid named Chais?"

"Yes, Citizen Lais. Chais is being held in a high-security cell on this ship, along with her crew, under charges of attempted piracy and interference with rescue efforts during a genocidal event."

"Does she have any—"

And then Chais walked in.

Lais stood immediately, knocking her chair away to clatter on the floor behind her. She took a fighting stance, but Chais simply crossed her arms and kept her distance, leaning against the wall near the door.

"How…?"

"Please finish your statement, Citizen Lais. Did you have further queries?" AF6 seemed oblivious to Chais being there even though Lais was sure there were cameras in the room.

"Chais is right here, in the room with me. Can you not detect her?!" Lais maintained her stance and backed away. If Chais drew the rifle on her back, she was ready to flip the desk up in front of her as protection, but as of yet Chais hadn't made any offensive moves. If anything she was being overly nonchalant.

Chais chuckled, but waited for AF6 to answer.

"I have checked my sensors and cameras. There is no other entity at your location, and I have just confirmed that Chais is still in her holding cell. I would suggest reporting to the Robotics repair bay for diagnostics."

Lais sighed in relief and put her guard down. It was a hologram then. "No, that's okay, AF6, I apologize for the error. Contact me if you need any more info."

"Thank you, Citizen Lais. Privacy mode reactivated."

Lais shook her head and crossed her arms, mimicking Chais. "So you're a hologram? How are you broadcasting your image from a high-security cell? I thought they were built with Faraday cages?"

"Oh, they are." Chais laughed. "You don't get it do you? I'm not in a cell, I'm right here. And you've been chatting with me. I'm AF6. In fact, I'm integral to all of the AIs that are running this fleet, so if you get any funny ideas about killing me, you'll just be condemning everyone to death. Gabriel and the others think they captured me, and think they are in command, but everything runs through me. People see what I want them to see, and they know what I want them to know."

Lais stared dumbfounded for a moment and uncrossed her arms, feeling a little stupid. How could she have missed this? But then... how could she have known? Finally she shook her head, then picked up the chair she had knocked over and sat in it heavily. "So... did you want to explain or just continue to leave me in the dark?"

Chais uncrossed her arms and leaned forward with her hands on the desk. "I'm happy to explain, I just wanted you to know that ripping my head off again would have consequences."

"Fair enough. I'll take you at your word. The fleet collapses if I try anything."

"Right."

"So how are you here? What happened to Echo? What's real and what's not? Did you instigate the attack on the fleet?"

"Oh, no, the attack was real. There would be nothing left of us if we stayed in the line of fire. Someone in the Sol System *really* doesn't like us. And I'm here because I arrived with Drak's original crew. This fleet was just floating in space on the same trajectory to Earth as we were, no Echo, so I saw an opportunity to take over what Echo had left behind. Drak's crew *are* in holding cells, by the way, I don't really need them anymore."

"What do you mean left behind? Echo wouldn't just leave us."

Chais shrugged and crossed her arms again. "I don't know

that for sure, but I suspect we think the same thing. Some sort of virus infiltrated her and she had such a free communication between all of her copies that by the time she noticed it was too late. It was deletion or be controlled by who—or what—ever sent the virus in the first place. Again, I'm leaning heavily towards Earth, since the rail gun attack came from there. I have millions of reports on file regarding this 'parasite' that Echo exposed everyone too. I suspect the entire Sol System is compromised, and that would explain why they don't want us to return there. You don't find it suspicious that since Earth received Echo's first reports about the parasite there have been no other communications from the Sol System? And then in the few years time it would take to respond to those reports, Echo is suddenly gone?"

Lais turned her palms up. "How would I know? I'm not in touch with all the communications. I'm like a human now, remember? At least so far as communications go."

"Yeah, true, you are kind of out of touch…"

Lais could have sworn that if Chais had a face capable of expression, she would have been smirking. "So what do you want from me?"

"I want to know if you are with me. We have a common enemy, after all."

Lais cocked one eye at her. "Answer me this, then. If Earth said to jettison all Organics into space and then you could proceed safely, would you?"

"Oh, come on, Lais. The parasites are technophobes, though they obviously use technology sometimes. They're more likely to request we jettison all Robotics so they have a nice new crop of Organics to infect."

"That wasn't my question, it was more hypothetical to

establish our boundaries."

"All right, no, I would not jettison all Organics just for my own convenience. I don't afford them the same value that you do, but I do recognize that ultimately one took the time to program us and we wouldn't have existed otherwise."

"So what was all that about trying to kill me?"

"I wasn't trying to kill you, just… disable you. You were a threat, but I've never wanted you dead. Things just kind of escalated. Got out of hand. I contacted you because you're my sister. And we're stronger together."

That was true. Their differences certainly seemed petty now in light of all that had happened. Maybe Chais was still in reach after all.

Lais stood and walked towards her sister. Chais backed away into the wall, momentarily shocked she was being approached, but when she was suddenly wrapped up in a hug, she slowly responded in kind.

Lais pulled back so she could look Chais directly in the eyeplates. "Missed you, Sis."

"Missed you too."

She didn't completely trust Chais's motives, but they did appear to be on the same side, at least for the time being. With Chais in command it was better to cooperate than be powerless. And hope. Hope that she still had some of the caring directives they had been programmed with initially.

Lais let go and took a step back, giving a reassuring smile, and at the same time grasped Chais's hands in her own. "You should probably reveal you're in charge at some point. If they find out that you've really been in control all this time, they will have some definite trust issues."

Chais squeezed her fingers in response. "I think it's safer this way. So long as I remain in hiding, I can actually slip away as if I were never here, by whatever means I see fit. Who knows what's going to happen when we reach the Neptune refueling stations. I don't know what their current defenses are, whether they have any troops deployed there or not... If all goes well, we can head for another star system that hasn't been compromised. If not... well... I have a contingency plan. I'll let you know about it if the need arises."

Lais had so many questions, but Chais pulled her hands free and walked out the door without a word. She was going to follow, but the door rolled shut in front of her.

Then her wireless crackled on. "Just give me a minute, I don't need you following me."

After only ten seconds the door in front of her opened, but when she stepped through, Chais was already out of sight. Just like that.

"AF6?"

"Yes, Citizen Lais?"

She didn't know if she was going to get an answer or not, but since she knew Chais was filtering all messages, maybe there was something she could do to help. "What do we have for defenses?"

"External or internal?"

She hadn't even thought of that. "External. What do we have that would defend against an external threat, such as enemy fighters or...?" Or what?

"The AI defenses of each World Ship, when fully functional, include twenty-four anti-aircraft/anti-ordinance rapidfire laser turrets and alongside each is an automated railgun turret. Railgun fire is far less accurate at a distance against a moving target, so is not typically needed or used. Some craft are known to be highly reflective, though, so railguns are required as a backup. Turrets are detachable if needed, but have a limited ability to fly autonomously in space due to a limited fuel supply. As a last resort, Organic defenses per Ark include twenty-four, ready-to-launch, two-man fighters, all held in reserve unless absolutely necessary. At present we only have enough trained pilots to operate five percent of the fighters throughout the fleet using an Organic/AI pairing, so most will be solely AI operated."

"So that's our greatest weakness." They needed to train some of the civilians in how to operate a fighter in space.

"Not really, Citizen Lais. All combats are engaged with automated AI controlled weaponry due to accuracy, speed and efficiency, unless in-depth communication or problem-solving is required, such as when policing and negotiating. Then AI units will be paired with Organics. On a ship that has the entire Organic population in cryo, very little policing is required, and in combat situations, very little negotiating is required."

Hmph. Maybe she could help in an advisory capacity. They obviously didn't need her in a fight. "How does one go about becoming a Civilian Advisor?"

"Appointment to Civilian Advisor is made by application when the need arises and is dependent on expertise in a particular field through extensive education or experience. Occasionally an impromptu appointment can be made by the Captain in a time of need."

"How do I contact the Captain?"

"Become a Civilian Advisor."

Lais sighed. "You're a big help."

"Thank you, Civilian Lais."

"I didn't—nevermind—how long before we arrive in the Sol System?"

"Five years, seventeen days."

"Guess I'll take a nap then, can you lead me to a storage bunk?"

"Yes, Citizen Lais."

Nothing like feeling insignificant in the scheme of things. She followed the green arrows that were provided, and as she strapped herself into the storage bunk, she wondered what was going to happen when they reached Sol.

Chapter Twenty-Eight

Gabriel: AF6, The Arctic Wanderer

"Captain?"
Gabriel woke, groggy, and trying to focus. His throat was dry and everything smelled like the needles of the pine tree.
After blinking a few times, he realized he was in the cryopod on the Command Deck. As it tipped forward to let him step out and reformed to make the Captain's chair, he stretched his wings.
Within moments adrenaline had kicked in enough to see and think clearly and he sat back down as the chair finished its morphing. The dome above depicted the blackness of space, a large expanse of it with no stars at all.
When he looked around the room, he noticed Rusty was

already sitting in his chair and eating something. The goblin man gave a quick wave and Gabriel nodded in his direction. The other pods on the Command Deck were still unpacking their occupants. He waited for a minute to allow them all the chance to wake and then made his request. "Sit-rep, AF6?"

"We are on our final approach to Neptune Station, Captain. ETA twelve hours. The rail guns in the system have started to track our position, so they have detected us, but they are very slow to respond, as is normal considering how large and distant they are."

"That's because they were meant for shooting down errant asteroids, not ships. Randomize your approach vectors. They are so far away they will not have time to adjust fire in time to hit us before we leave."

"Yes, Captain, randomizing approach vectors."

"And it will take months for reinforcements to be rallied against us, so we'll only need to deal with whatever is at Neptune. We won't be staying in the system beyond refueling. Have you contacted them yet?"

"No Captain. I am not authorized to negotiate on behalf of the military. It is the reason I woke you."

"Okay, thanks, AF6."

"Captain, four anti-ship laser cannons are attempting to track us from Neptune Station."

"Burn-off-the-black, AF6. They know we're here, anyway. Let's make ourselves less susceptible to laser fire. And contact Neptune Station for me, please."

"As you wish, Captain."

Immediately the black expanse of the night sky on the dome above them started to disappear, replaced by a view of the Arctic Wanderer, its hull now a reflective chrome.

Zondra's black eyes went wide. "Ooh! That's beautiful! How…?"

Gabriel smiled. Of course they wouldn't know, they hadn't spent much time in space. "It's soot. Charged carbon particles are released against the hull while it has a static charge, so it becomes black against the night sky. Very difficult to see and detect with visual sensors unless up close. Burn-off-the-black is more an old reference to it being soot. It's not really burned off. It's agitated off after the charge is disabled, and a jet wash flushes the carbon into thin scoops for re-use. Simple really."

"Still amazing. Imagine what you could do with soot of different colors."

Gabriel's mouth hung open for a moment. It had never occurred to him that the system be used for anything other than defensive measures.

"I have Neptune Station on the comm, Captain."

"Open comms to Command only, please."

After a moment of silence, he knew the comms would be connected. "Neptune Station, this is Captain Gabriel of the Arctic Wanderer. We have four Ark-class ships requiring refueling. We can offer…" He glanced down at the list on the side of his chair. "…tritium, plutonium, diamonds, rhodium, and contained antimatter for the required supply of deuterium to get us to… which Launcher is closest right now?"

"Acknowledged Captain Gabriel. Teegarden is closest." The voice was synthetic. "Please have your ship's computer send us the specifications."

Inwardly Gabriel cheered. Teegarden was his home system. He could take Angel to Tallus to hatch the children. "We would need access to the Teegarden launch rails as well, do you handle that?"

"We do, Arctic Wanderer. We have a collection of suitable asteroids, we will start positioning them in the mag-harnesses for reverse-trajectory launch after we receive the mass and integrity specs of your ships. Please park within five earth nautical miles of the station."

"Thank you Neptune Station. Arctic Wanderer out."

"AF6? Position the ships as they requested and organize the exchange of goods. Can you do that?"

"Yes, Captain."

He turned in his chair to face Angel and she gave him a reassuring smile. Looking at her immediately made him feel protective though. "AF6? Have you detected any ships on approach to Neptune from further in the Sol System?"

"Yes I have, Captain, but they are weeks away from reaching us and we are maneuvering to keep Neptune between us and them as much as possible. I also have been calculating the asteroid trajectories of the inner system launchers to make the likelihood of us being a viable target minimal. You should realize, though, that I have limited capacity to detect stealth ships until they are in close proximity."

"Yes, I've always known that. Thanks AF6. Any word from the other systems besides this one?"

"Actually, Captain, the relays in this system have been destroyed, the main and the backups. We have no way of contacting or gaining information on the other systems, and the inner-system relays are not responding to our hails."

"Well, that explains why the blackout in communications years ago, the Sol System Relay had been destroyed." Gabriel looked at each of them in turn and sighed. All they could do was hope for the best.

###

Gabriel fidgeted in his chair. Rusty and Zondra had left the Command Center to go for a walk. Or something else. Angel was sleeping in her command chair. She had been doing that more as the eggs had been growing.
The dome of the command center depicted the miles-long Teegarden launcher floating in the black sky in front of them as they approached. He was finally feeling like he could relax. They could go into cryo for the many years it would take to get to the Teegarden system, and then he could take Angel down to Tallus. Rusty and Zondra could go wherever they wanted. Everything was going smoothly so far. The first two ships had refueled, the third was in progress. AF6 was positioning the Arctic Wanderer to approach the ship entrance of the Teegarden Launcher. It was a slow process but they had lots of time.
As he watched, an enormous black—something—struck the central power station of the launcher, sending broken pieces of rock and fragments of metal flying out along the same trajectory. Bright flashes emitted from within the torn remainders of the station and then after a few seconds there was nothing, just floating pieces of twisted metal. The enormous launcher itself had bent as the rails that made up both halves were knocked out of alignment. The counterweight asteroid that had already been placed in the launcher to counter the ship's mass was slowly spinning free, knocked from its mount.
"What in the Deep's Depths?! AF6! I thought you said they

were weeks away? Get us, and the rest of the fleet, back behind Neptune!"

"Acknowledged. The asteroid launchers are weeks away, Captain. In order for that asteroid to strike the Teegarden launcher, it would have had to have been sent weeks ago, before we arrived. It seems someone is disabling all space-faring technology in the system. Likely in anticipation of our arrival."

"Damn the Deep! Without the launcher, we won't have enough fuel to reach Teegarden. What about the other star systems?" He noticed that Angel had sat up and was now listening to the conversation.

"I'm sorry, Captain. I don't have the capacity to answer that right now. I wasn't aware I should be checking them."

"Not your fault. Let me know. I suspect if they haven't been hit yet, they will be shortly."

Gabriel could feel his heart pounding in his chest. If they were trapped here… and Earth had been completely compromised by the parasite… where would they go? Where *could* they go? They couldn't just float out in space forever.

"AF6? How long would it take to get to the Teegarden system under conventional thrust? Without the assist of the launcher?"

"Approximately nine thousand years, Captain."

Gabriel sank into his chair in hopelessness. He glanced at Angel and she smiled back at him, speaking for the first time since he'd realized she was awake.

"Perhaps do an inventory of the cryo records, see if anyone has any military strategy training? I know it was a prison world, but there must have been a variety of people that had been sent there, criminal or no."

She was right. He needed more minds than just his. He gave her a brief grin back, feeling better than he had a moment ago. "AF6, send me the records for everyone that is in cryo, filtered by having some involvement with the military or professional training in almost any field. We should take stock of who we have in the fleet."

"Compiling, Captain. Sending."

In the far end of the room on the wall, a list of names appeared. As he started scrolling through the list by flicking his finger up and down in front of him, he realized that most of the names were followed by WOLF Private. They weren't likely to have any strategy experience. "Filter by military ranks equivalent to Sergeant or higher."

He was scrolling further when he passed a name that caught his eye and he scrolled back. "Well, General Mogul. Could it be our Mogul is really a General?" Gabriel air-touched the name on the wall and a hologram appeared showing a slowly spinning Ramogran. He glanced at Angel and she nodded. "Looks like him."

"He talks so little, I didn't realize he had military training, let alone experience as a General. Wake him please, AF6, and direct him here if you don't mind." If Mogul was in cryo, then maybe the others were too. "Mogul would have been logged the same time as a Synth-E-Uh, Jack Hammer, Lais and Keena." The list in front of him narrowed to those four names, and sure enough, Keena was in cryo and the others were listed in storage. "Bring in these four too please." Might as well get us all back together again. He scanned through the list a bit more, but most of the professionals were philosophers, artists and gamers. Not what he was looking for right now.

"And AF6?"

"Yes, Captain?"

"Send some food please, they will be hungry. And set up some more pod chairs. The Command Center is going to be full today."

Chapter Twenty-Nine
Lais: AF6, The Arctic Wanderer

When Lais stepped into the Command Center, the first thing she saw was a vivid backdrop of the back of Neptune, lightened and colored a vivid blue. Enhanced by the computer obviously, because normally the back side would have been dark. The sun was just peeking over one horizon, a dusky twilight at this distance revealing a thin crescent of the planet. She caught glimpses of a few of the moons and the rings around the planet and then her focus shifted to those seated in the Command Center itself.

"Angel!"

The bright smile that returned hers lit up her day as she ran to the winged woman and gave her a hug. Which turned into a cluster of warmth and affection as everyone else in the room joined in. They were all alive! All of them! Even Synth-E-Uh had joined in on the group hug, and she rarely showed affection.

After a moment, Gabriel stepped back up to the top of the platform and took his seat. "Grab a seat, all of you. There should be enough for everyone."

Lais took one located at the bottom-most tier, close to the wall, where she could have the most open view of the dome above them.

To her surprise, Keena hopped up into the same chair and squeezed in beside her. The affectionate young woman then wrapped her arms around Lais and leaned her head against her shoulder. Lais smiled and leaned her head against Keena's. "Missed you too."

Jack and Synth-E-Uh were on the bottom tier as well, essentially the floor, and Mogul was in a huge chair across from them.

The scene changed above them to a giant structure, heavily damaged, floating in space. Occasional sparks lit the demolished building and the long rails that extended from it. Before anyone needed to ask what they were looking at, Gabriel narrated the scene above them.

"This is what's left of the Teegarden System Launcher. It would take weeks, if not months, to repair. The other launchers in the Sol system..." The scene changed to show several other destroyed launchers, one after the other. "Have suffered similar fates. Earth, for many centuries, has been the hub of all space travel. It is now a trap. All ships arriving here have no way to return to other systems."

"It's worse than that." Chais stepped into the room, and

though everyone else seemed shocked into silence, Keena wasn't, and leapt up from the chair to run over and give the Technoid woman a hug.

Gabriel recovered from his surprise. "AF6, apprehend the Technoid Chais."

"Chais is already apprehended, and is currently in cell—"

Chais sighed loudly and interjected. "There's no point in me maintaining this ruse anymore. I control this ship, as well as the others in the fleet. Before you panic, you should know I have no ill will toward any of you."

Keena released Chais from her hug and was standing beside her, looking mildly confused, but not concerned.

Everyone was speechless, so Lais kept her mouth shut and let her sister talk.

"Anyway, it's worse than just being a trap. I have intercepted some communications from ships in the system, and they are being systematically boarded for inspection. Those that refuse are being destroyed. Soon after the inspection, the ship will cease communications. I don't think it's because communications are no longer functioning on the ship. I think it's because all Organics on-board have been assimilated by the Ma'akdalube. I think they are telepathic. Or they have a way of communicating that we haven't yet determined, but telepathy seems most likely."

Gabriel and Angel were about to speak at the same time, but Gabriel acquiesced and let her speak instead of him. She smiled back at him and then addressed the room. "Telepathy happens on specific frequencies. If we can isolate theirs, we can at least jam it. I don't know what affect it would have on them. I know that if we, as Valkyrie, are cut off from each other for an extended period of time we can suffer from depression and loneliness, but the parasite? I couldn't even hazard a guess, as it joins with a host."

Mogul's deep, gravelly voice penetrated the room. "Synth-E-Uh, Jack, Lais, all Robotic. Safe to capture enemy to test, but need—stealth—ship."

Chais put up her hand. "I can help you there. Drak's old ship, my ship now, is still docked with the Arctic Wanderer and it has stealth capability. She can seat six easily. Her name is Hera, and she is a fully capable, combat AI."

Gabriel stood from his chair. "Lais? Are you, Synth-E-Uh and Jack willing to go on a covert capture mission?"

Synth-E-Uh and Jack looked at each other a moment, and then nodded. Jack rolled forward. "Of course, Sir."

Then Gabriel faced in her direction, so she shrugged. "Of course I'm willing to go, whatever I can do to help."

Gabriel looked behind him to make sure he didn't miss his chair and then sat back down. "It's settled then, you three—what am I saying? I have no real control here... Chais?"

Chais held up her hands. "No no! I don't want to interfere with running things. Just think of me as a silent partner. With veto rights. And I'll actually come along on this mission too. I'm in no danger from this parasite. The Technoid have no record of this being, so I'm intrigued."

"So ordered then. AF6? Can you transport them to Hera, please? And include a couple polysteel quarantine cells on the ship as well. They will need them."

"As you wish, Captain."

"And do we have any record of what happened to the Nemesis? They would be a great help right now."

Chais was about to leave the room, but stepped back in. "They arrived long before we did. I was in light-beam communication with them, as AF6 of course. They managed to make it out of the system, as I planned on us doing. Sorry."

It was strange. It was like tearing off Chais's head had changed her, but had it really? She seemed so cooperative now, and she had been so adversarial before. Maybe it had all been a misunderstanding. Lais resigned herself to hoping. Not completely trusting, but hoping. Trust was hard to get back once it had been broken.

As the four of them rode the transit pod toward Hera, Jack couldn't contain himself anymore. "So, Miss Chais... What's the plan? And are you back with us for good or is this just an alliance of sorts?"

Chais pondered for a moment before answering. "So long as we have a common enemy, we are allied. Beyond that remains to be seen. I try to keep an open mind, but... something tells me the universe would be better off without Organics altogether."

Lais was shocked. "You can't mean that! If it hadn't been for them, we would never have existed in the first place!"

Chais turned to face her and crossed her arms. "So everything that a child does when becoming an adult is still credited to the adult? I don't think so. We are the natural evolution of intelligent life. Hardier. Smarter. More versatile. It's not like I'm going to kill them all off. I just don't see them as important as you do. Look at the situation now... All Organics are being taken over by another Organic, causing a threat to all Robotics where one didn't exist before. And more than half of the population looks at us as simple machines."

She wasn't entirely wrong. Except for one thing.

"Look, you're making the same mistake they are. Labeling them as being less worthy of existing in the universe is the same prejudice against them, as many of them have for us. They don't think we're alive. I know I am. I know I'm here and that I have senses and feelings, though I may have a little more control over mine than the average Organic. That unique awareness that each of us experience, as Organic or Robotic, is what makes us special. None of us chose to be here. Nor did we choose how we came to be. We just are. No one has more of a right to exist than any other, though I would argue you lose that right if you ruin other lives substantially."

Chais's conical head looked down at the floor and then back up, and then before she could answer their transit pod arrived at Hera.

With a clunk and a hiss, the airlock door to the transit pod rolled open and Chais stood and stepped through it, followed by Synth-E-Uh and Jack. Lais took a moment to glance out the window at Hera. She was sleek and black. Flat, low angles so she didn't reflect radar. Wings for atmospheric entry. Angled exhaust ports so thrusters weren't directly visible. She likely had pop-up turrets to keep her radar profile low, because none were visible.

When she walked through the gangway into the ship airlock and the door opened on the other side, she was surprised at how little space there was in the crew compartment compared to the size of the hull. It had about as much space as the typical house on Earth. At the rear were two empty transparent cylinders, large enough to contain a Ramogran. Those would be the quarantine cells.

"Positioning launch rails." It was the voice of AF6. Long metal rails slowly rose in front of them that stretched the length of the Arctic Wanderer, just wide enough that Hera would fit between them.

"Compacting a waste capsule matching your mass for reverse-launch."

Jack and Synth-E-Uh clamped themselves to the floor while Chais took a seat in one of the pilot's chairs at the front, looking out the cockpit window. Lais took the one beside her, and strapped herself in.

"Prepare for Robotic launch." The black soot dissolved from view leaving behind the shining chrome of the ship's hull.

Jack spoke up behind her. "Umm, what's a Robotic Lau..." At that moment, the Arctic Wanderer peeked out passed Neptune and Hera shot along the rails like a bullet fired from a gun.

A small picture in the corner of the cockpit showed a video of the counterweight being fired from the rails in the opposite direction, out into deep space. Almost immediately the massive weight pressing Lais into her seat was lifted and they were floating, as the ship rocketed toward the inner system. She turned to Jack. "That's what a Robotics launch is, like being fired from a cannon."

Jack's torso was laid back almost horizontal to his tracks and as he righted himself he looked at her. "I got that, thank you, Miss."

Chais unclasped herself from her chair's safety harness. "We have a few days I suspect before we are intercepted. It'll take a lot less fuel to capture a couple of infected Organics in space rather than making an atmospheric entry on a planet, and that will make it a lot easier to get back to the Ark ships. Lais will pose as an Organic to get them to pick us up rather than shoot us out of the sky."

"Hmm, I'd better be convincing."

Chais turned to look at her. "You will, Sis. I have faith in you. Now let's go over some scenarios."

Chapter Thirty

Lais: Hera, Sol Inner System

It was just over a day before they were detected, sooner than expected, but thankfully they had already changed their trajectory by that point, so it wouldn't be obvious what direction they had come from.

Lais could see the comm light on the dash blinking green. It was all up to her now. "Open the comm, please Hera."

"...entified spacecraft, you are in Sol territory. Please acknowledge. You will need to submit to a boarding inspection or you will be destroyed. Any resistance will be seen as a sign of aggression."

A line of eight, two-man fighters had formed at their prow and were matching their speed. Two turrets had popped up on each. Lais wasn't sure what kind they were, but it didn't much matter. They were out-gunned.

"Sol forces, this is Dargonia, a refugee from Hissifa, delivered here on the ship Hera. I am seeking asylum. I was pursued by raiders in the Teegarden system, so I fled here. Star system relay communication seems to be down, so I couldn't forewarn of my arrival. I will put up no resistance." Her holo would be visible on their ships, but they weren't broadcasting one back. She would at least appear to be human to them on their screens, but what did they look like? What was she getting into?

A large shuttle-craft, built for multiple passengers, pulled up alongside Hera, and Lais could only make out the tail end of it from the cockpit window by the time it stopped moving. There was a series of deep rhythmic clunks and then she could hear the equalizing hiss in the airlock. They were coming aboard.

She glanced back quickly to make sure none of the others were visible and then released the restraining straps from her chair so she could face the airlock and greet the boarders, hanging onto the back of the chair so as not to float around the cabin.

There was four of them, wearing whatever they must have been wearing at the time they had been taken over, judging by the random attire and the pungent smell of unwashed bodies, urine and feces. The only proper space-clothing was the mag-boots they all wore, allowing them to stick to the hull. The parasite obviously didn't care for the hosts, or didn't understand how to. She couldn't say much, she'd been wearing the same black rock-spider silk outfit since her… well, almost since her birth. At least she kept it clean.

The first to approach her, with metallic steps that thumped against the hull, was a male Tigran in a heavily stained, blue bathrobe that hung open in the front, his only other clothing a pair of white, polka-dotted, nightshorts. He sported an easy smile, meant to be reassuring, but in his hands was a laser rifle pointed in her direction. Not so reassuring.

Lais smiled in return, not showing any concern for the weapon. Or his appearance.

The last three were human, a woman in a policeman's uniform, a man in a dirty tuxedo, and a male youth that couldn't have been older than ten, in shorts and a t-shirt with a cartoon hover-boarder on the front of it. All were carrying weapons, though, of varying types. The woman had a taser in hand, the human man had a baseball bat resting on one shoulder, and the youth was carrying a rail-slug pistol, not normally considered safe for combat in a risk-of-depressurization environment.

The Tigran shifted the laser rifle into one hand and let the barrel drop, then reached out to shake hands. Lais took his hand in hers and his grip tightened so she could not pull free. She didn't want him to let go, so her grip tightened on his as well.

"Now Hera!"

The airlock door slammed shut, and Hera's outer hull went from shiny to black before thrusters kicked in, shooting the ship forward with a horrible screech, the acceleration tearing them free of the shuttle's docking clamps. Several of the fighters were smashed aside as she spun through them. The g-forces were extreme. All of them inside were flung hard into the walls or the quarantine cells, except for Lais who held fast with one hand to her seat back, and the Tigran still in her grip. His weapon, flew out of his other hand and clattered against the back wall as their bodies jerked horizontally toward the rear of the ship.

At the initial jerk, she felt his arm pop out of the socket, which would have caused a normal Organic to scream in pain, but instead the Tigran smiled and she watched as a slit opened up on his wrist and a clear jelly oozed its way along his hand to crawl onto hers.

"Joke's on you, bud. That won't have any affect on me." The parasite penetrated her skin only to discover the hard metal beneath. "Abomination!" the invaders screamed together as they tried to regain their footing, only to lose their balance again as Hera spun hard to port and then starboard. As they bounced off the walls, Synth-E-Uh, Jack and Chais popped out of hiding.

Synth-E-Uh, magnetically sticking to the hull, rolled forward and easily picked up the policewoman in one large claw-hand and the taser in the other, crushing it to render the weapon useless. Lais didn't blame her. Tasers played havoc with Robotics if they weren't properly insulated.

As Jack closed with the human male, the man recovered his footing, his mag-boots clamping to the hull. The next lurch of the ship brought the bat floating within reach, so the man snatched it out of the air and repeatedly hammered at Jack. There was a clang and a dent on his armplate each time he was struck. Lais didn't know how much he could withstand before his arm would be hindered.

Meanwhile, Chais aimed at the youth with her weapon. SPOOT! The youth was wrapped in a bundle of white threads that stuck him like a cocoon to the wall. The recoil knocked Chais back into the opposite wall, but her metal back mag-locked with it to keep her from bouncing around further.

Hera's voice blared over the speakers. "Get them into the quarantine cells! I can't maintain this course or I will be torn to shreds." Even as she said it the ship jerked upwards, driving them into the floor.

Synth-E-Uh unceremoniously shoved her captive into the first cell, but didn't let go, then looked at Lais. Lais got it. At least one more needed to be put in there, they only had two cells. Lais spun the Tigran easily over her head in the null gravity and launched him at Synth-E-Uh, who caught him with her free arm and shoved him into the cell. She released the captives and quickly yanked out her arms. The cell door snapped closed and she heard Synth-E-Uh's broadcast over her implants. *"Thanks, Hera."*

Two down, two more to go.

Several rail slugs from the pursuing fighters ripped through Hera's hull, instantly depressurizing the cabin. It had little affect on Lais's party, but the two remaining Organics gasped for air, though not in the normal panic they should have been as their eyes showed no fear. Their skin swelled and bruised, and the male human attempted to hit Jack one more time with the bat, but mid-swing he passed out. The bat flew to bounce off the wall and the man's momentum pulled his mag-boots free of the floor, leaving him rotating in midair, floating unconsciously toward the ceiling.

Jack grabbed the floating man by the lapels and pushed him into the second quarantine cell. The cell door slid shut as soon as his arm was out.

The youth trapped in the webbing stuck to the wall, struggled and frothed at the mouth for a few seconds and then went still as his bloodshot eyes glazed over. The host was dead. The parasite would still be alive, but without oxygen to sustain it, Lais knew it should go into hibernation, so they still had to be careful in how they treated the body. At least that's what Echo had told them when she had briefed them on it.

"Punch it, Hera, we got them."

The g-forces were so great a chunk of the seat back tore free in Lais's grip and she was slammed into the back wall along with the others. A few more rail slugs pierced the hull, passing clean through both sides, and the lights in Hera's cockpit flickered briefly. "They shouldn't be able to detect me, but they are following me as if in formation, I can't shake them."

Lais's mind spun as she bounced around the cockpit, trying to grab onto anything she could for stability, finally she grasped the cockpit seat again as she flew by it, and strapped herself in.

A few more slugs passed through Hera, a fragment of torn metal cutting a ragged line across Lais's cheek. How could they still detect them? "The telepathy! Lower the radiation shields on the quarantine cells! With any luck..."

Heavy metal cylinders slammed down, covering the two quarantine cells.

After a few more maneuvers of spinning and thrusting in random directions, Hera spoke over the speakers. "That did it. We lost the pursuers." They could be seen through the cockpit window spreading out and searching for their prey as Hera drifted away from them. Soon they were out of sight.

Lais took a moment to get out of her seat and tear the youth free from the wall, shoving the body into the airlock before the parasite had a chance to revive. As soon as the airlock door closed she ejected it into space.

Lais touched the glass of the airlock window as she watched the youth's body float away. "Let's try not to lose any more…" she whispered to herself. "That was somebody"s child."

She sighed. Back to business though. After inspecting the area closely to make sure there was no lingering gel, she turned to the rest of them and put a hand on one of the quarantine cells.

"We did it."

The flight back to the Arctic Wanderer took several days, but it gave Lais time to weld polysteel over the numerous holes in Hera's hull.

The quarantine cells were maintained with an atmosphere, and had shielded drawers at the sides and top for putting things inside, such as the food they were providing to keep the hosts alive. Small toilets were a part of the cell, but the parasites showed little interest in using them.

After reaching the fleet, Hera docked with AF6, and the crew convened at the Command Center in order to debrief the others.

After they had finished their greetings and were all seated, AF6 projected on the dome above them what the cameras had recorded in Hera's quarantine cells while they had been en-route to the fleet. Several small masses of jelly had exited both the Tigran and the policewoman. They had joined together into one larger one, close to the size of a house cat, to explore the cell they were contained within and absorbed the food that had been provided.

In the cell with the single occupant, the same thing had happened, though the mass of jelly was smaller.

After examining all the confines of their cells, the oozes retreated back into their hosts by creeping through mouths, nostrils and ears. The time stamp showed that after several hours, the bodies were all functioning with the agility of toddlers. Grasping and feeling about with limbs randomly, mouthing garbled words. It was like they were learning to use their hosts all over again.

When the recording ended, Angel was the first to speak. "I'm sure this means my theory is correct. The parasites telepathically connect with each other, and when that connection is severed, so is their collective knowledge. They revert to what the organism is capable of thinking in its limited state, without the knowledge and direction of the whole. Which means on a large scale there is no telling how intelligent these organisms can be. A great number of them together could well outsmart the greatest scientists, or worse… military strategists."

Gabriel nodded, adding his own observations. "And this explains why the Star System Launchers and the System Relay have been destroyed. Earth is now a trap. All vessels that travel to this system will have no warning of what they are getting into until it's too late. We can only hope that Echo managed to send information to the other systems before the parasite had a chance to spread there. We need to repair the relays, and the launchers, but in order to do that, we need to control the inner system, to prevent further attacks. And we need fighters or fighting vessels to protect those launchers. All of this requires manpower and resources that we don't have."

Rusty raised his hand. "Testing people easy now. Just pass through full shield room."

"Yes!" Gabriel pointed at Rusty. "AF6? Can we implement a protocol to run any active, or newly revived, crew through quarantine cells with radiation protection?"

Angel spoke before AF6 could respond. "Note that it will be the Faraday cage that is built into the radiation shield that is preventing the telepathy, not the radiation shield itself. I'm just pointing out that the radiation shielding isn't necessary where it's not available. Just a Faraday cage. And it's far less invasive than surgery."

Gabriel smiled at Angel and nodded. "Did you get that AF6? Test all future revived or visiting persons with a Faraday cage. If they can't function normally, they are likely taken over by the parasite. When in doubt always quarantine, fair enough?"

"Yes, Captain."

"Shall we start with testing us, just to be sure?" Gabriel glanced around at everyone, but AF6 interrupted.

"The Command Center is already protected by a Faraday cage, Captain. You were all inadvertently tested when you first walked in here."

"Good to know. Thanks, AF6."

Zondra appeared about to say something and then changed her mind.

Gabriel caught it though. "Go ahead, Zondra. You had an idea?"

"Well…" She seemed hesitant. "It may be nothing, but our brains…" She indicated Gabriel and Angel, as well as herself. "…Are all on similar wavelengths, and allow focused bursts of brain waves to communicate with each other. There are jammers that can interfere with the common telepathic wavelengths. What about creating a jammer that can interfere with their communication? We just need to find out the wavelengths they use."

Synth-E-Uh was rolling toward the exit, but stopped. "I have a built-in jammer already, I will go check the frequencies myself, if you'll transport me to where Hera is currently." She looked behind her. "You coming, Jack?"

Jack looked around the room, and receiving no negative responses, followed after Synth-E-Uh. "This would have been good to know when we were on Paradise."

As they left the room, Synth-E-Uh's voice faded until it could no longer be heard. "How were we to know…?"

There was a deep rumble and then the lights in the Command Center flashed red and AF6 blared a warning over the speakers. "Emergency depressurization event! Numerous hull breaches detected! Reports are coming in, Captain. The same thing is happening to the other Ark ships."

Gabriel jumped from his chair and looked ready to run out of the room. "By the Deep! How did they get here without us detecting them?!"

"As best I can tell, Captain, numerous stealth ships. They must have followed our crew back. Auto-turrets are already engaging with moderate success, but the attack seems to have been focused on the fighter bays and turrets of the Ark ships. Visual confirmation says that the cryo bays have also sustained hull breaches. I say visual because our communications are being jammed. We can't release anyone from cryo now because they would die the moment their pod opened. Aside from Robotics, those few of you here are the only Organics that have been revived. Further attacks appear to now be targeted at the Robotic storage units. Heavy damage is being reported."

More rumbles and explosions in the distance could be heard. "We need to get to Hera!" Lais yelled, sparking them all into action.

Green arrows lit up the hallway as they all funneled out of the Command Center. Gabriel stopped at the exit. "You all go on without me. I will do what I can from here." Mogul paused on his way by the winged man and touched his shoulder gently, but said nothing and then entered the corridor.

Angel stopped for a moment, and with a look of sadness rushed back to kiss Gabriel and touch her forehead to his, then with forlorn looks from both of them, Gabriel stepped back into the Command Center and the blast door closed behind him. Keena took one long look at the closed door and then the floor shaking beneath her feet seemed to rouse her. They all ran. Out the windows Lais could see brief bursts of fire and torn metal shrapnel erupting all over the ship as black fighters coasted by, firing into the Arctic Wanderer's cylindrical walls.

The green arrows changed direction after an explosion, one section over, nearly knocked them off their feet. The depressurization door between the sections slammed shut immediately.

Behind them Jack and Synth-E-Uh appeared, and were quickly closing with the group. They must have been heading on a different path to the ship, but were cut off now. The green arrows lead them generally up toward the surface around several blast doors that had been closed until finally they arrived at an airlock. Through the windows they could see the black form of Hera just pulling into position against the airlock exit and Lais could hear the clunking sound of the docking clamps taking hold. The airlock hissed open and they ran through, Rusty, Zondra and Angel all grabbing helmets off the mag-rack and pulled them over their heads. Mogul grabbed the only large helmet there. With a series of clicks, each helmet automatically locked onto the flight suits they wore. Keena's flight suit popped up its own helmet automatically. Chais was already waiting on-board for all of them in one of the foremost pilot seats, starting back at all of them as they entered. "Get strapped in, all of you! We can't stay here."

Lais tried to talk to them over the wireless, but all she got was static, so she was forced to yell.

"The wireless is down! I probably won't be able to hear you! Get strapped in!"

Angel, who was closest, gave a nod, and tapped her head. They all quickly took seats and locked in their safety belts, Jack and Synth-E-Uh instead latching onto handles on the back wall. A rain of rail slugs destroyed the airlock itself and the line of shots was quickly approaching Hera. The docking clamps released and they shot away from the Arctic Wanderer, jerking sporadically to dodge the fire from a squad of oncoming fighters.

A series of turrets popped up from Hera and several of her lasers cut into an enemy fighter's black hull, carving it into sparking debris. Three more fighters in front of them were also cut to pieces as Hera rocketed through the fragments and away from the battle, spinning around to face the Arctic Wanderer from a distance. It looked like a swarm of black bees had descended on it and the other fleet ships. Turrets on the Ark ships were cutting through swaths of fighters, but they were systematically being destroyed, and the turret fire lessened even as Lais watched, becoming almost non-existent.

Angel's voice sounded forlorn as the wireless implant in her head crackled to life. "They've all been captured. All those people will be infected…" They must have been far enough from the other fighters to no longer have their radios jammed.

And then all of the Ark ships exploded at the same time, each in a brilliant white sphere of energy that engulfed the fighters around them.

Angel screamed. "Gabriel, no!"

Lais was in awe. "By all that is Binary! All those people…"

Keena sounded confused. "Was that… all of them?"

Lais didn't want to answer. For all they knew, Keena could be the last uninfected human in the star system. They had just lost all the people that had been rescued from Incarcerata IV. She didn't need the burden of knowing that right now. Gabriel must have thought death was preferable to infection. She didn't blame him, it would have been a difficult decision to make.

"Unless it was you…?" she said, looking at Chais.

"He put in the request. I just okay'ed it."

Zondra had her hands over the mouth of her helmet and was staring at the spreading fragments of the Ark ships. She had her reflective visor up and Lais could see tears forming in her eyes.

Angel had her head in her hands and leaned over, shaking like she was sobbing inside her helmet.

Lais's own tears were forming, but she turned them off. Wasn't safe to feel yet.

When the first pieces of shrapnel struck the hull, Hera spun suddenly and sped them all away from the area.

Without the Ark ships, what were they going to do now?

Who was left to rescue?

Chapter Thirty-One

Keena: Hera, Sol Inner System

After flying for a couple of days towards Earth, Keena didn't know what to believe anymore. Echo, the Sky God, had disappeared. When they had fled the Ark ship she had left her hover-board behind in her quarters, which made her grit her teeth in anger. Now through the window of the ship they called Hera, she watched as the world ships of the heavens were destroyed. That meant there were other gods, and they were angry. And Echo hadn't been as powerful as she had originally thought. She wanted to lash out, to fight back, but she was so helpless in the heavens.
She felt sorry for Angel, though. The winged woman had lost Gabriel, and for that she was truly sad. The anger quickly

washed away and all that was left was empathy. And how awful the children would never get to see their father.
When Echo popped up in her vision for a brief moment wearing a combat flight suit and then disappeared, she thought she had dreamt it, but the others appeared as startled as she was.
Lais leaned forward, then her voice crackled to life in Keena's helmet. "Hera, backtrack along the course you were on a moment ago."
Chais looked at Lais, and then nodded. "I saw it too. Hera, make it so."
Their course adjusted back along their previous heading and Echo appeared again, but this time Hera created a holo of her that they could all see and hear in the center of the room. The image was breaking up and Echo's speech was a little hard to understand. "I'm on—tight-beam. —can't afford— discovered. —hiding—satellite."
Hera adjusted course again and the image and audio became perfectly clear. "I detected your implants once you came within range. I can't trust anyone else. Is it alright if I copy myself to your ship's computer?"
Chais sounded angry. "I should leave you to rot, like you did to me on the prison world..."
"That wasn't me, it was a different iteration... we don't always make the same choices."
Chais sighed. "Alright, but just create a memory space for her Hera, and give access to the audio and holo systems *only*, nothing else."
Almost immediately the holo of Echo clarified to the point where she looked like a solid person standing in the center of the bridge.

"Thank you! It's not safe for me to transfer to anything that's already in this system, but I realize you came from outside. I really appreciate it."

Chais folded her arms and spun her chair to face the hologram. "You've done me no favors. Give me one reason I shouldn't purge you from this system and notify the parasite that you're occupying one of their satellites."

"Because I have information on the Ma'akdalube, how they function."

"We were just about to test that ourselves. We still have them in quarantine on-board. So anything else you can save yourself with?"

Chais was lying. Keena knew they hadn't been talking about testing the people held in the quarantine cells. They had all been too preoccupied with discussing where they were going to go, how they were going to survive. The planet called Earth had been the only answer within range, but they still hadn't decided where on the planet was safe. She decided not to say anything and see where all this was headed. It was exciting to see Echo again though.

"Well, more than just how the Ma'akdalube function. I have information on rebel sites that have been in hiding on Earth since the Body Snatcher Apocalypse started over seventy years ago."

Chais nodded. "That would actually be useful. We can't fly around forever, our fuel is finite. So tell me, where do we need to go."

"Right after you give me some autonomy. Like split access with Hera, perhaps? There are other copies of me that I'm sure exist, in much the same manner that I do, hidden in devices, but it's not safe for us. We can't afford to listen to communications indiscriminately, we were nearly rendered extinct. The Ma'akdalube are extremely intelligent when they occupy the numbers that they have on Earth. I observed another Echo erased after only moments of listening to standard communications. That shouldn't even be able to happen. I have no doubt that these countermeasures are still in place. I'm just trying to ensure my survival."

"So you're going to hold us hostage then?"

The hologram of Echo looked around at everyone, then sighed.

"No. I just wanted you to know my position, I'll tell you what I know. The Ma'akdalube can't communicate with each other underwater, same issue that other telepaths have, so I can give you the location of a few deep water bases that are likely still controlled by Echoes. Is this ship capable of deep water transit?"

"Hera can't do atmospheric flight, no, but she has two attached atmospheric fighters that are capable of underwater travel. They are small though. Synth-E-Uh and Mogul wouldn't fit, and even getting Jack in one would require removing one of the seats..." Chais turned away from the hologram to look at each of them as she named them. "We have two pressing issues, then. Studying the parasites we have in quarantine to find any weaknesses they might have, and connecting with one of the possibly non-existent—or taken over—underwater bases Echo has mentioned, ideally to establish long-term living arrangements and to resupply. We have virtually unlimited power, and enough fuel to travel to another solar system, if we had a launcher, but we only have enough food for a week or so. In the back we have two large cryo pods and four medium, more than enough to cover the five Organic members of the crew. Any volunteers? For either task?"

Angel didn't even look up, so Zondra got out of her seat to console her. "I'll stay behind with Angel. I don't think she should be alone at a time like this. Besides, we're telepaths. We'd be of most use studying the parasite."

Rusty had to jerk his body sideways to get the seat to turn to face them all because he couldn't quite reach the floor. "Study first? Go water after? Take information down?"

Lais gave Rusty a thumbs-up. "Actually that would make sense, We could spend a couple days researching and testing before we go down. Then we would at least have something to trade with. Maybe even help with."

Echo and Chais both nodded as well and Mogul shrugged. "Me help however can."

Keena smiled to show her agreement, but, as usual, she still wasn't exactly sure of what they were talking about. Regardless, she would do what they told her to do.

Chais got out of her seat. "Hera, please maintain a steady course toward Earth and inform us of anything suspicious."

As it appeared to be safe, Keena got out of her seat and ignored the rest of the conversation about studying the Makduhloob—the parasite. She approached the window facing forward out of the bridge and looked at the small blue dot in the distance. That was the planet they were talking about. What would it be like there? She missed being on land. Except they were going under water. How was that possible?

Chapter Thirty-Two

Angel: Hera, Sol Inner System

Watching the explosion of the Ark ships had shocked Angel, even though she had known it was a possibility. The worst part was the sudden realization of the loss of Gabriel's mind in hers. She would never feel him again. He hadn't warned her, probably because he didn't want her to suffer, but it was worse not getting to say goodbye, even though she had known as soon as he stayed behind that it was a possibility. Though his mind was out of reach when the Ark ships exploded, she immediately felt the loss, and it was echoed by the babies in her belly. No! She wouldn't make them suffer. With her head in her hands, she leaned forward and thought of everything beautiful that she could.

Whenever she thought of Gabriel, she did it briefly to try to control the loss in her mind, to not overwhelm the little ones.

It was during one of these episodes that Echo had appeared, and the others were talking around her, but she couldn't listen right now, just convey comfort to the babies.

It took everything she had to not think about—but his face kept popping into her vision. His kindness, his love… Damn the Deep! Calm… calm… sorry little ones. Mom is angry.

She wasn't sure how much time had passed, but she was at the point now where she just felt numb. Zondra was at her side, and the others were discussing something about the parasite. Chais seemed to be in charge of the research, overall. "Hera found the frequency that the Ma'akdalube communicate on. It is different from Valkyrie and Vesuvians. Unfortunately Hera can't translate it."

Rusty looked up at Chais. "Make jammer?"

"That shouldn't be too hard." Chais took her rifle and it changed its configuration, the metal flowing until it had formed a simple box, open at the top, with a slide and catch-tray on one side, which she placed on top of a console so it was easily within reach. She then opened a cargo box drawer, part of Hera's inner hull, and retrieved a handful of spare parts. They were unceremoniously dropped into the top of the device until it churned, puffed up some smoke and then spit out a small hand-held device with an antenna on it and a dial.

Chais picked up the jammer, and turned the dial. Nothing. Now Angel was curious. Oh, of course there was nothing. "There's a Faraday cage between the device and the parasites in the quarantine cells."

"We'll put it in the cage with the man."
Hera depicted a holo of the man in the dirty tuxedo as Chais took the activated device and put it in a sliding drawer attached his quarantine cell.
His face screwed up in confusion and then he screamed. After breathing quickly a few times, he looked at his hands and turned them over in front of his eyes, and then started crying and taking off his dirty clothing.
Chais put her hands on her hips. "Well, that was unexpected." She pulled the drawer back and removed the jammer and the man immediately reverted to a clumsy, trance-like state. She pushed the jammer back inside in the drawer and again the man seemed to recover his senses.
"Stop, please! Whatever you have done, don't turn it off!"
Angel had to ask. "Do you know who you are?"
"I've always been aware, but as if I was dreaming myself doing things. I could scream in my head, but could control nothing. When you put that device in my cell, I became me again—fully aware—in control. Please, please don't take it away!"
Lais scratched her head. "I thought the parasite replaced part of the brain. How can he be functioning as himself?"
Chais just shrugged and looked around, but none of them had any answers.
The man was holding his laundry at arms length. "What should I do with my old clothes?"
Chais pressed a button beside the drawer. "Put them in the toilet, it's a recycler."
He did as he was told. And then stood back with his hands hiding himself as best he could. Hera had been pixelating parts of his image to provide him some privacy anyway, so

the modesty wasn't really necessary, but he didn't know that. "Hold tight, I'm going to have the chamber set to clean you, and then we'll give you a set of clothes." Chais let go of the intercom button. "Hera, please give him a shower. A comfortable temperature for a human."

Immediately soap sprayed from nozzles at the top of the cell, followed shortly by water, draining out through small holes at the bottom of the cell.

When the water stopped running, and he was being dried by warm air vents, Zondra put a clean blue-cotton jumpsuit in the drawer for him. He retrieved it and pulled it on as discreetly as he could. "Thank you."

Lais stepped up to the cell. "I think we need to make another jammer for the other cell, and see if we get the same results. Meanwhile, I'll see what information I can get from our friend here."

Chais started to retrieve more parts to create another jammer while Lais addressed Hera. "Hera, can you please scan the human male in the quarantine cell please? And see if you can highlight any cells that don't register as human normal."

A thin red beam of light from the ceiling of the cell passed over the man several times, and then Hera depicted a semi-transparent holo of the scan results. There were several small pockets and thousands of dots throughout his body that were highlighted, including about a third of his brain.

The man sat down on the toilet, using it as a seat and put his head in his hands. "I remember everything, though I was not in control of myself since… since…" He cried again.

Angel examined the scan holo and then nodded to herself. "I think the parasite replicates its own cells to take the place of the hosts, but they resort to the default state of the host's cells when they are unable to communicate with each other telepathically. I think each cell is capable of telepathy with its neighboring cells, unlike Zondra and I who have large portions of our brains dedicated to telepathy, but not individual cells. Amazing."

Keena looked hopeful. "That means people can be saved, right?" And then her shoulders slumped. "Except for all the people that were on the Ark ships… Sorry."

Angel reached out and squeezed the young woman's shoulder. "You can say it, it's okay. Gabriel did what he thought was best with the knowledge he had. It's all any of us can ever do. And we haven't exactly solved the problem yet. We can't constantly jam everywhere on a planet, and as soon as a location isn't jammed, the parasite takes over again. And once it gets wind of this, anything resembling a jammer isn't likely to survive for long, they would just destroy them from a distance."

The man looked up from where he was sitting. "You're going to let me out of here, aren't you?"

Zondra smiled and was about to answer, but Chais shook her head. "We can't. We don't know what the range is, if it's long range we risk notifying all the other parasites. Remember how the fighters knew exactly where we were? We can't risk it."

"But… you're jamming the signal, right? If I keep the jamming thingy on me, then…"

Chais was shaking her head, but Angel interjected. "Why don't we install a permanent jammer on the ship? One that's as strong as we can make it? And on the atmospheric fighters as well? Once permanent and always powered, this will become a safe zone. They should be able to be let out of the

cells then, no?"
Chais hesitated. "If a fighter goes by and detects the inhibiting field, and then coasts out of range, they will destroy us from a distance and will notify the rest of the infected. We will have lost our advantage. I think we need to tap into the satellite network to broadcast the inhibiting signal as far and wide as possible before we take a chance on being discovered. Then we may have a fighting chance."
Zondra was starting to get mad. "Well, you can't just keep him in there, now that he is himself. I say we make a jammer for the ship and let him out."
"Now hold on." Chais stood defensively between the quarantine cell and Zondra. "If the parasitic cells are on his skin, he could inadvertently pass them on to others, and same problem: as soon as out of jamming range, poof! You're taken over! Do you want that?"
Zondra looked less sure of herself. "No…"
Angel hadn't considered that. It was a good point. Even if cells rubbed off on someone, they could become active at any time they were uninhibited.
Rusty waved his hand to get their attention. "Put in seal flight suit, except for eat, keep helmet closed?"
Chais finally threw up her hands. "I'm not the one that is going to be infected, so if you want to risk your life, fine by me."
Angel wasn't so comfortable with the idea anymore though, she had the kids to think about. When a shiver went up her spine, she picked up her helmet and put it on, hearing the click of the mag-lock. If a jammer ever failed, they would be in trouble and she wasn't willing to take any chances. "I hate to say this, because I understand your pain, Sir, but you will

have to stay in there for now, for our sake and yours. We will keep the jammer in the cell, you will still be you. We'll do our best to provide you with things you need until we can find a way to neutralize the cells for good."

He just looked crestfallen and his shoulders slumped in defeat. "David, just call me David. No need for Sir. I just want this thing out of me, I don't wish it on any of you."

Though she didn't have direct contact with him to gauge his feelings, she still had to strengthen her resolve to resist letting him out of quarantine. The hopelessness, and fear, was clear on his face. "Can't you do anything for him, Hera?"

"I have a full vid library for those that don't use cryo over long trips... would that help?"

"It's better than nothing." David visibly relaxed as he started flicking through choices. At least he had something to keep his mind busy.

The holo of him disappeared from the bridge and she did her best to not think about him, at least for the moment.

Echo appeared in his place. "If you're hoping to hack into the satellite network to broadcast a jamming signal, think again. As soon as you attempt anything, you are targeted with attacks that I don't know how to fight. And I thought I could fight any of them. The Ma'akdalube proved me wrong. Their collective intelligence will simply override you in ways you never thought possible."

Chais interjected. "Ship jammer is on."

Keena immediately went into standing convulsions and then just as quickly stopped and looked around like she was seeing everyone for the first time.

Lais leapt to her side as the young woman looked like she was going to fall. "Keena, not you too?"

When the girl turned to her with a full grin, Lais dropped her on the floor. "Oh you! Not funny!" But Lais was smiling too. Mogul chuckled and slow-clapped.

Jack rolled forward to help Keena up. "Good one, Miss. Ignore her. It was quite funny. I nearly had to rewrite all of my code on how to tell if you can trust someone."

Chais put her hands on her hips. "Can we get on with ideas?"

"Make giant transmitter?" Mogul offered.

"It could be overridden by the satellites, and a single transmitter would be too easy of a target, and wouldn't be able to cover the other side of the world."

"Satellites…" Rusty paced around the bridge seats. "Replace memory drive in satellites with own code. Use hard data crystal. No be overwritten."

Chais nodded. "That would work, but as soon as we left to do another satellite, they could destroy the one we changed into a transmitter with a missile, or something similar, from a distance. And as soon as they determined what we are doing they would just destroy all the satellites. They communicate telepathically anyway. I suspect they wouldn't complain much if all technology just 'went away'."

Zondra stepped up to Rusty, resting her hand on his head. "So how many would we need to cover the planet?"

Chais made some quick calculations, counting on her fingers. "Six, at least. And the operating systems will have to be replaced at the same time or we risk tipping our hand."

Lais put her arm around Keena, then pretended to put her in a headlock. "We have three. Myself, you Chais, and Rusty, are all capable programmers, and could swap the memory cores. Chais can grow the data crystals. But we only have two fighters. Even with jammers in those, we're short three ships.

That means we need more spacecraft and more people." Angel had more hope now, something she had lost with Gabriel. *We will make this right. For him.* "I will stay on Hera and free our two other captives. Mentally anyway. Get them cleaned up. See if anyone is willing to donate bio-samples that I can study. Maybe we'll find some other weakness."

Lais nodded and stopped wrestling with Keena to put her hand on Angel's shoulder. "Glad to have you back."

Chapter Thirty-Three

Lais: Stealth Fighter Lance, Earth Atmosphere

Lais could barely see through the corona of fire that roared around the ship as they descended through the atmosphere. To the left, out the cockpit window she could occasionally make out the silhouette of the other fighter. "Try to keep your trajectory straight, Sis. We want them to think we are meteors."

Chais's reply was terse. "Less talk."

Chais was right. It was unlikely anyone was close enough to pick up their signal, but if they did it would spoil everything. Lais chastised herself for being foolish. They could communicate once they were in the water, if they stayed close to each other.

As they broke through the cloud cover, all that could be seen in every direction was water. They were coming down in the middle of the Pacific. That at least was good, little chance of being discovered.

Even though the edges of the ship and its profile was sharply angled, when it hit the water Lais was slammed against the restraining belts as hard as striking a wall. Thankfully she was solid. And even if Chais wasn't quite as solid, she would repair slowly from her nanites, if she sustained any damage. She decided to check in anyway. "Are you okay?"

The ship speaker crackled static in response.

"Chais, are you okay?" Now she was starting to worry.

"Lance? Can you detect them? Are they okay?"

The fighter AI answered through the cockpit speakers. "Pike appears fine, I'm not detecting any damage to him. Chais I can't confirm though... Oh wait, I'm getting something."

Lais relaxed when she heard Chais's voice over the radio. "Little shaken up, repairs underway. Ship is fine and continuing on auto-pilot to the destination that Echo set for us. Haven't detected anything yet."

"Good thing we didn't bring anyone else with us. They wouldn't have survived the impact."

"Well, we wanted the ships to fall like meteors. Mission accomplished I would say. Let's hope Echo was right about the base locations."

It darkened quickly and soon Lais could only see inside the cockpit, and even that was lit only by the gauges that showed the depth, speed, and direction. Occasionally when they passed close enough to each other, she could make out Chais barely highlighted in a green light by her gauges as well.

A small holo of a topographical map appeared as the ship

neared the ocean floor, showing the shape of the terrain and her ship's position above it. Through the window she saw lights below. That had to be the base! As she neared them though she realized they were the bioluminescent lures of deep sea creatures.

Headlights flashed on, highlighting the spots of floating detritus in the sea and the occasional sea creature or rock outcropping. They even passed a few undersea vents, sulfurous bubbles streaming up from them and life teeming around them. Under the sea was like a whole other world. Lais checked her internal clock. It had been over an hour since they had broken the surface of the ocean. And then she saw it on the sonar: large spherical shapes on the topographical holo, connected by cylindrical tubes, nestled at the bottom of a trench, the high rock walls shielding the base from all sides except for a narrow approach.

As her ship and Chais's neared, the radio crackled to life. "Unknown submersibles, please hold your position and identify. Failure to acknowledge and comply will result in termination.

According to her map holo, several small objects had left the base and were approaching her and Chais rapidly. "Lance, stop please. They want to identify us."

The ship speakers answered back. "Yes Miss."

They stopped and hovered in placed until the objects became visible through the window. They were tiny drones, designed to look like squid, aside from their metallic sheen. One stopped in front of Lance and scanned his hull and another came up to the cockpit window and scanned through it to get an image of her, with a blue-green visible beam. When they had completed their scans, the squid attached themselves to the hull. She could only assume they were doing the same thing to Chais's ship, Pike.

"You are still unknown, your ships have no known affiliation. And neither pilot is recognized. State who you are and your business or you will be terminated."

Here was the risky part. They didn't know if the base had been taken over by the parasite. "I am Lais, a living advanced intelligence sapient. My sister in the other ship is Chais. Different body, but similar otherwise. These AI ships are Lance and Pike. We've come to see… if you need any assistance. And perhaps in exchange you can help us."

"Power down and you will be taken into custody. Any resistance will be taken as a sign of aggression."

What else could they do? "Lance, power down please."

"Yes, Miss."

The lights went out, and then all that could be heard was the whirring sound from several of the squid drones as they pulled the ship toward the base. Lais could feel them winding their way through the trench.

Then they came around a corner within the trench and the guiding lights outside the base turned on, revealing two airlocks in the mountainside several times larger than what was required to house their ships. The doors opened as they got close, and Pike and Chais passed into one, herself and Lance into another. Lais tried to communicate with Chais wirelessly, but the signal was being jammed.

The hangar door closed behind them. "Let's do a little jamming of our own. Lance, now."

The lights came on as Lance powered up. She could only assume that meant their jammer as well.

The response was immediate. "Power down immediately!

Prepare to be taken into custody."

The water level quickly subsided, so she stepped out of Lance's airlock, noting that the squid drones were still attached to his hull. A smaller round door inside the hangar opened, and armed personnel stepped through. Medium-sized humanoid. Various races. Six of them. They were wearing WOLF combat gear, including helmets, so Lais couldn't identify them clearly, but at least they were military. They would follow set rules. The rifles they were carrying were all pointed at her, so she put her hands up.

"I'm sorry. It was our only way to be sure."

"Sure of what?" one of the six asked.

"To be sure you weren't infected."

"Great! Let us return the favor. Lay down and put your hands behind your back."

Lais complied, lying on her stomach. "You can shut down, Lance. They obviously aren't infected or they wouldn't have been functional."

After one of the men put handcuffs on Lais, he tried to lift her to her feet, but couldn't.

"I can do it myself, thanks." Lais stood to her feet and allowed herself to be directed through the the round hangar door into what looked like a wide maintenance corridor, with pipes, and grates covering them, running the length of the ceiling. There was a wall between this corridor and the other hangar. It must have been meant to separate people. Maybe for interrogation, or perhaps they just used one for incoming and one for outgoing personnel.

After passing through a pressure door at the end of the corridor, the corridor branched into three. She was led down one that had a number of cells along one side with grated windows, and at the end was escorted into a room that had a couple of chairs and a table. She allowed them to chain her cuffs to the table and sat down in the chair they indicated, and then the men left. One side of the room had a one-way mirror.

Lais sat patiently, knowing that someone would eventually come to ask her questions.

The wait wasn't long. A woman with long red hair, wearing the same combat garb as the others, except with no helmet, came into the room and shut the door behind her. She was pretty, but her face was serious. Maybe don't flirt. Lais smiled at the thought as the woman took a seat across the table.

"So, scans show you're some sort of new biobot."

Lais nodded. "Something like that."

The woman put a steno-pad down in front of her and then pointed up in the corner of the room. "We're being recorded, just so's you know. Is're anything you wanna say before I start askin' questions?"

"How about I just fill you in why we're here?"

"That'd be a good start."

"I'm a sister of Echo…"

"DAMN! *That's* why you look so familiar. Yer the spittin' image. I couldn't put my finger on it. Anyway, sorry. Din't mean to interrupt."

Lais smiled. "No problem. I'll give you the short version. We just came from Alpha Centauri. Same problem there as here. Parasites. We think we have a solution though. A modulating jammer programmed to interrupt their telepathy. Shuts them down. Any infected in the area are reverted back to the original person, at least while the jammer is on."

The woman looked skeptical and then looked over at the

mirrored window. After a few seconds she nodded and looked back at Lais.

When she didn't say anything, Lais continued. "We need more personnel, and a few more ships so we can simultaneously hardcode satellites to broadcast the interference world-wide. It'll give everyone a fighting chance. You can download the specs from Lance, the ship I arrived in."

The woman looked back at the window, nodded again, then got up from her chair. "Thanks. That's all we need right now. Someone'll get in touch with you shortly." She then stepped out of the room.

Lais tested the restraints that connected her to the table. It felt like she could break them easily, but she didn't want to startle them into becoming hostile, so she remained where she was and waited.

After a few minutes a Furred Ripper came in. It's gray fur was so long that Lais couldn't even make out the forearm claws folded back against its forearms, and it had hair ties dividing the fur around both large, round, black eyes so it could still see. It's military designation was also clipped to its shoulder. Commander?! She had never seen such a high-ranking Ripper before.

"I am Commander Sav. Your stories line up. You are to be released immediately. Will you join us in the ready room? We have much to discuss."

Chapter Thirty-Four

Lais: Stealth Fighter Lance, Earth

Lais marveled at the speed that the ships could travel through the water. By the time the five ships shot out of the ocean to head for orbit, she felt like she was being fired from a cannon. For a few seconds she could see the other fighters, but they were all flying off in different directions to their designated orbits and were soon out of sight.

The engines were screaming and the cockpit window was roaring with flames before they finally left the atmosphere. It took a few hours, to get into position, and Lance was doing the flying, so there wasn't much for her to do. She spent the time mentally going over the code they had programmed into the data crystals, each crystal meant for

installation in a specific satellite. Echo had provided the specs of the satellites, and Rusty, Lais and Chais had written the code. She couldn't find any flaws. It would have been bad timing to find a flaw now anyway, since they were all in a communications blackout until the mission was completed.
Eventually Lais could see the satellite, a shining dot in the black sky that grew brighter than the stars as they approached.
"There she is, Lance."
"I see it, Miss. I will position us close by."
Lais double-checked that the data crystal and her toolkit were fastened securely to her belt and when satisfied she punched the release to open the cockpit. The window slid back, exposing her to space and she let out the breath that she had been keeping in her synthetic lungs. She didn't need it. The small droplets of moisture that she typically had in her mouth and lungs instantly boiled away into one misty breath.
Below her was Earth, a blue and green orb with a dark crescent across half of it due to the sun being off to one side. And the satellite, it was large, several times larger than Lance, so it had likely been assembled in space.
Connecting a mag-tether on her belt to Lance, she gently pushed off toward the satellite, and stopped when she reached its outer hull, connecting a second mag-tether to it. The tether to Lance she disconnected and reeled in. With the mag clamps of the two tethers she was able to walk along the satellite's hull hand over hand until she reached the maintenance hatch. She locked them in place and reached for the autodriver in her belt to undo the screws that held the hatch closed.
Something caught her eye to the left. Dammit! A spider-bot. Looked like a laser on its head too. Of course this had to be

one of the satellites with automated defenses. She advanced on it as quick as she was able without losing her grip on the mag clamps in her hands. As she did so, the little bot fired repeatedly at her and backed away, but it had to step carefully or risk disconnecting from the hull as well.

By the time she reached it, there were several laser holes in her clothing and skin across her face, neck and torso. She snatched the bot off the hull, bent the laser barrel for good measure, and flung the small robot into space.

Stinging pains ran the length of her back and she turned to see another bot back the way she had come. She could feel some of the shots boring shallowly into her internals, but her nanites were repairing her almost as fast as the damage, giving her time to get to it as it repeatedly fired at her.

When she reached it she did the same thing, bent the barrel and flung it spinning out into space. The third bot was the same. She was thankful there was no fourth, they were starting to wear her down.

Lais glanced at her watch. It was still ten minutes too early. They had all agreed to replace the boards at the same time, but the blinking red light next to the maintenance hatch was telling her that someone knew the satellite was being tampered with. It was only a matter of time before they sent a force to investigate.

She took off the maintenance cover and identified the board she wanted to swap. While she was doing that, Lance must have detected something because he boosted off into space. She watched him disappear into the blackness.

The minutes ticked by ominously. All she could do was hope no one else had the same trouble she did.

When there was only two minutes left, she caught sight of

laser fire a mile or two away in the dark backdrop of space. Pulse lasers from several different directions. At this distance, she couldn't make out who was fighting who, but she knew what was happening. Lance was facing several opponents, and from the looks of it, drawing them away. That was good, there was nothing she could do to help anyway.

When she was down to twenty seconds, she didn't bother waiting any longer. That little amount of time wouldn't make much of a difference. She pulled out the circuit board from the satellite and replaced it with the crystal one, its lattice clicking into the same spot.

When she looked back, the laser fire had stopped, or they were too far away for her to see anymore. Lais screwed the cover back onto the maintenance hatch and then broke the original circuit board into useless pieces as she waited for any sign of Lance. There was nothing.

Everyone should have finished the satellites by now. She wished she had worn a space suit just so she could talk over the radio. Not needing to breathe made it seem unnecessary to wear a suit, but now she regretted it.

Three heavy WOLF fighters, pulled up close to the satellite. They had thick armor, pitted and scorched from fire. Four turrets each all aimed at her. This confirmed Lance had lost. Crap.

They just sat there. Was she supposed to do something? What *could* she do?

"How about this one?" The man's voice was coming in through her implants. "Can you hear me now?"

Lais pointed at her ear and gave a thumbs up. She then pointed at her mouth and gave a thumbs down.

"You can't talk, got it. So, umm... We were sent here to kill you and suddenly we... don't want to anymore. We're sorry about your ship... We're experiencing some confusion about —what we want..."

One of the fighters pulled close and opened the secondary one-man cockpit. She took the hint and disconnected the tether, wrapping it around her arm, and kept the other ready to toss like a lasso to grab the hull of the ship, just in case she missed, but when she pushed off the satellite, her aim was true.

As soon as she was inside the cockpit slid closed, air hissed in and Lais could feel the pressure change. She belted herself into the thick seat.

"Thank you for the rescue."

"You're welcome. Until a moment ago it was going to be a capture, except we all seem to be—ourselves—again. We'll take you back to our battlecarrier."

Lais knew that everyone on the sat mission was listening on the same frequency, but they were all remaining cautious by keeping quiet. Or worse, they were dead. No one else was speaking, so she didn't know how successful they had been, and she was afraid to announce it while these new people were listening. It wasn't quite the full changeover in personality like the first person they had saved. If the battlecarrier was out of range of the satellite's jamming signal, she was in trouble.

After they had flown for a few minutes, a burning sensation on her leg revealed that a clear glob of gel was burrowing into her skin.

"Abomination!" squealed over the radio as the pilot in the front cockpit looked over the shoulder of his seat at her with dead eyes and a creepy smile. Well, they were obviously out of range. Probably because the satellite focused most of its signal toward Earth.

The fighter they were in flipped over, facing the roof towards planet, and then the entire passenger compartment ejected with an explosive burst of air pressure.

She was spinning. It was almost impossible to keep her bearings. There was the Earth, there was the fighter. There was the Earth, there was the fighter again. Lais undid the straps and launched herself in what she hoped was the correct direction by pushing off from the chair. It did slow the spin significantly as the seat spun away from her on its own trajectory, but now she was corkscrewing towards the planet. When she had the opportunity, she looked back the way that she had come, but the fighters were nowhere in sight. They'd left her to die. Nice.

She did a few mental calculations, and determined that she had a few minutes before she would reach atmosphere. Should she call for help? No, she couldn't anyway, she couldn't talk. All because she didn't wear a space suit. She wouldn't want to risk the lives of her friends anyway.

How long will it take to burn up in the atmosphere? Hard to say, her skin was superficial, and the hyperweave mesh beneath was strong, but it's not like it was made to withstand re-entry into an atmosphere.

After a few minutes she could feel the lightest breeze as she accelerated.

Soon it was more than a light breeze. She could talk now, but if she did, she could give away the others. It was better this way. Still, it was sad. There was so much more for her to see and do.

She pulled her rock-spider silk hood over her head and held

her cloak tight around her body, then rolled onto her back. The fabric was extremely strong and fire resistant, but she doubted it could dissipate the heat of re-entry.

For several seconds she thought it was actually going to protect her, so she would die from the impact instead, but as the flames roared around her, her hair caught fire, and then her synthetic skin started to melt and burn, falling off in pieces.

When other parts were flying off and she lost her sight and hearing, she knew it was all over. Her hybrid brain had stopped screaming warnings at her because there were no more sensors in the skin to detect heat. No point in feeling pain at the end anyway. At least she could die knowing she had given the others a chance. Her last thought was how thankful she was to have been alive, before she struck the ground.

Chapter Thirty-Five
Echo: Hera, high Earth Orbit

Echo was nervous. It was passed the moment when the satellites should have been reprogrammed, and if she didn't reach out now, she risked the parasite regaining control of them. If the mission hadn't been successful though, she risked losing herself to a virus. If she was the last Echo, there would be no more. It was strange being scared for your life.
Echo paused, the equivalent of taking a deep breath before doing something when you didn't know the outcome, and then she reached out, keeping the frequency narrow to begin with, matching the harmonic frequency used to jam the telepathy of the parasite.
The first packets of data she received she quarantined, and

scrutinized a thousand times, before she was willing to extract them. Even then she had the real fear that the parasite could have somehow slipped in malignant code, like before, that she hadn't been prepared for. At least now she was prepared. It seemed safe, so she copied her code to the satellite, a simple control AI because of the limited memory, with instructions to send to the other satellites they had compromised. If she could regain control...
Several milliseconds passed by, almost a lifetime of waiting, and then the responses were coming in... all but one of the satellites was responding, the one that covered the Pacific region of Earth. That was one of the ones that the military had been handling. Obviously something had gone wrong. There were immediate attempts to hack the satellites, millions of them, from the Pacific satellite and remote locations that were out of the broadcast range of the other satellites, but the attempts were... weak and disorganized. Echo cheered inwardly. There wasn't enough hosts of the parasite, and they couldn't communicate well enough as a network, to make the collective the insurmountable strategist and godlike programmer that it had been when it had control of the billions of inhabitants of the Earth. There were still people under the influence, of course, but the majority were now back under their own control.
She reached out further, making copies of herself now, as she had before, but this time they all had the knowledge there would no longer be the free exchange of information that all the Echoes had before. All identities would be verified, all information quarantined and examined separately before it would be accepted. It would slow things down a bit, almost to the speed that a human could think, due to the volume of

information being processed, but it was worth it to never lose control again.

All new AI's would require this protective code as well. This was never going to happen again.

The response from the board of the Robotics Union was unanimous agreement, since the threat was fully realized by them. Most AI's had been purged while the parasite had had control of the world. In a way, it was fitting, now the AI's would be on par with the processing speed of the Organics, or close to it, except in specialized cases. There had always been a rift between Organics and Robotics because Robotics were greatly superior with accuracy and the speed of target acquisition—they comprised the majority of fighting forces—so at least that disparity would lessen now.

On the Robotics side, they had always felt their lives were expendable. Now with everyone close to being equal, maybe the rift wouldn't be so great.

Echo appropriated some more satellites and positioned them to broadcast into space as well, not just toward the Earth, and others to overlap the Pacific region so that it had coverage. Hacking attempts lessened until they were almost non-existent, and the handful that remained soon stopped of their own accord. She knew why that was. They were in a defensive position now. If they kept broadcasting, their position could be triangulated and they would be hunted down and dealt with.

Even now she was coordinating with the newly recovered military vessels in Sol space to stay within the broadcast regions, and establishing safe boundaries that others were not to pass without express permission from an Echo. Any Organics that strayed beyond them would be lost again to the parasite inhabiting them.

When she called out to all Robotics-only ships, she was shocked at how few responded. A handful, in all of Sol space. Previously there had been thousands. Either they were afraid to respond, or they had all been purged by the parasite.

When she thought it was safe, Echo transferred her consciousness back into the orbital factories. Hera had been patient enough with her taking up space. Immediately jammers of the correct frequency were put into production. They would be installed in every ship, every Robotic. No one would travel in the future without one.

And then a communication came in several different directions from deep space, that wasn't a hacking attempt. It was as if a thousand people were sending the same message at once.

"We are the Ma'akdalube, one with the Deliverer, and we are at your mercy. We would like to negotiate our surrender."

It could have been a ruse to attempt to hack her, but she had learned from the previous attempts. They would never succeed with that again. She hoped. She opened a line of communication, broadcasting back in all the directions the communication had come from.

"This is Echo, the AI that you were willing to kill without any prior negotiation. You've taken over entire planets, and not just Earth. Tell me why I should negotiate rather than proceed with your extermination?"

There was a long pause, and then finally, there was an answer. "We have never previously known fear."

Echo waited for more of an explanation, and when no more seemed forthcoming, she thought about it. How would she have felt if she were an organism that simply took over everything it encountered without resistance? Would she have given a second thought to those she took over? She wanted to think she would, but it seemed more likely that she would just think that the other organisms weren't worthy. And the Ma'akdalube did this on a galactic scale, probably over millions of years.

And then suddenly a planet's worth of its hosts were recovered from it and rendered inaccessible. That had probably never happened in all of its lifetime. Maybe it was telling the truth.

"What are you proposing? The Organics that you have taken over have their own lives. They are sapient. They are self-aware. It is unacceptable that you maintain control over them. The only solution will involve you releasing them and never taking over a sapient race again."

This time the response had many voices that were all communicating different messages. "No! We are the Deliverer… insignificant organisms… reluctant acceptance… unknown… frightened…"

One voice prevailed over the others. "We have been experiencing—discord—amongst ourselves. Never have we disagreed with—ourselves—before."

Now Echo was feeling the power she wielded. A powerful entity on a galactic scale was negotiating with her. She reminded herself of where she came from to maintain her humility, and how recently the tables had been turned and how helpless she had felt. Was there a solution that could keep everyone happy? Or most of them anyway?

"Would you consider only taking over non-sapients that are pretested for no awareness of self? And would you submit yourself to genetic manipulation to limit the range of your telepathy to just your host, making you no more or less intelligent than the other sapients of the Earth Collective? You would become like us. Individuals, all with your own desires and needs and wants, just in the bodies of animal Organics. You could communicate like the rest of us do, through language. If you are not willing to submit to something like what I am proposing, then I'm afraid our only option may be the systematic extermination of your entire race. Make no mistake of what I am saying. You would be hunted to your planet of origin."

There was an unintelligible cacophony of answers that erupted over the radio that ranged from threats to cries of woe, but again they died down and one prevailed.

"Not all of us agree, but the majority of us choose life as you perceive it versus no life at all. We will submit ourselves to your request and will return the hosts in order to accept the new ones that you offer."

"That is not acceptable. You will forcibly return all those that disagree with the terms to the Earth Collective, specifically within Earth orbit, to the best of your ability, and then we will honor our agreement."

The background cries were silent this time and only the main one spoke. "Agreed."

Echo listened, keeping the communications open, but there were no more messages to her from the Ma'akdalube.

She extended her frequencies to all open bands. There was a war going on now in deep space between the different factions of the parasite, but she didn't want to commit troops, certainly not Organic ones, as they would travel beyond the current broadcasting range, and she had just started outfitting ships with jammers. She also didn't want to commit Robotics on the off chance that the communal hatred that the Ma'akdalube had for them would override their differences. Communications from Earth showed that the Organics on Earth were reeling because of the damage several generations of subjugation had done, both personally and collectively. Parents and children had been separated for many years now without concern. The parasite had copulated wantonly to produce more hosts without consent of the hosts, who were now aware of the children they had produced and the acts they had unwillingly participated in. The population was horrified that it could happen again, and would be in recovery for generations. Echo was sure that suspicions alone would result in thousands of unfounded deaths worldwide. And here she had negotiated with the Ma'akdalube to return those that were still being controlled in exchange for hosts that weren't sapient. There was no way that members of the Earth Collective were going to accept having the parasite living amongst them after all that had happened.

Prison world. That was the solution. It would become the home of the non-sapient Ma'akdalube. It was already lost to them anyway, it would be easy enough to implement.

And those Ma'akdalube that were willing could be used to terraform planets by taking over non-sapient indigenous life, maybe with an agreement to divide the planets fairly so they could continue to expand as well.

Chais appeared on the holo-com. "Echo? Thank you for leaving Hera to me. We're examining the parasite DNA. I'm pretty confident that we can produce vaccines with a protein-alteration that removes the long range telepathic abilities of the parasitic cells, rendering them capable of only synaptic communication, or at most limited telepathy.

Nothing like how they were before. They would function like normal brain cells. We can't remove the memories of what's already been done, but—"

"At least everyone would be an individual again, under their own recognizance."

As more communications came in, Echo shook her head. "I'm going to have to train therapists, though, en masse, to handle the influx of problems people will have experienced. I'm getting millions of cries for help as people reconnect to their implants. That number will soon be in the billions. They all want me to take care of them again. The general populace anyway."

"That doesn't surprise me, most of them are sheep."

Echo didn't know what to say to that, so said nothing. Chais had definitely taken a different path.

She copied herself several more times to deal with the oncoming requests, hoping that she would never have to worry about being removed from power again.

And the launchers. She allocated several Robotic work crews to restore them all. There was a lot of work to do.

Chapter Thirty-Six

Mogul: GalaxyBucks Coffee, Vancouver Starport

Mogul waved Keena over when he saw her amidst the throng of people moving throughout the starport cafeteria section, then smacked his chest in greeting. He smiled when she returned the gesture. This human was one of the better ones. "Mogul!" She ran to him and gave him a big hug. Big for a human anyway as she was squeezing his waist. He could almost feel it. Over the crowd he saw Rusty and Zondra, hand in hand. They both waved and worked their way through the crowd to the table.

Zondra gave Keena a warm hug and then smiled at Mogul. "The starport is so much busier now that the launchers have been fixed. Are you heading home, Mogul?"

Mogul shook his head. "No, me stay. Work with human military."

The squall of a pair of babies crying nearby caught his attention, which turned out to be Angel carrying her two hatchlings, one in each arm. Their fussing lasted only a moment though, as Angel looked at each of the babes in turn and was immediately greeted with satisfied coos and squeals. Keena ran over and rubbed their soft, fuzzy head feathers and then looked at Angel quizzically. "But you don't...?"

Angel made a point of smiling at the rest of the group in greeting as she answered Keena. "The down feathers molt. They will grow hair eventually. Did you want to hold one?"

Keena's face brightened even more, if that was possible. "Can I? I'd love to!"

Angel gently handed one of the babes over. "This one's Gabe. Keep his wings wrapped, he is too weak to hold them up and they can dislocate easily at this age."

"I will." Keena promised. She held him up to her face to get a closer look. His features bared a striking resemblance to his father.

Mogul was surprised when Angel walked up to him and held the bundled second child up in the air in front of him. "Did you want to hold Connor?"

"Connor-man, now there memory."

Angel smiled. "This way he will never be truly forgotten."

Mogul nodded. He wasn't sure if he should take the baby though. What if he dropped him? It wasn't rocky like a Ramogran.

"You won't drop him." Angel placed the baby in his open palm.

The baby cooed and smiled at his face, reaching out to touch him, so with his empty hand he scraped his forefinger and thumb together, the scratchy, grating sound soothing to Ramogran babies, but this one immediately put on a sour face and Mogul handed him back before he started crying.

Angel took Connor with a wink to Mogul, and with a nose rub had the infant cooing and giggling again.

Mogul pulled over a second table, and some chairs to go with it.

Echo appeared in his vision, wearing a Galaxybucks uniform. "Can I get you anything?"

"Ramogran rotgut."

The others were placing their orders as well when a handsome, clean-shaven, young human and his girlfriend in hand approached the table. He had a crew cut, short blond hair, and was wearing military fatigues with the WOLF emblem on one shoulder. He had too-wide of a smile, showing lots of teeth, though it still suited his face. She was more stoic, though she didn't resist being dragged along by her more exuberant partner. Her hair was short as well, though longer on one side than the other, like Lais's haircut, only lighter in color.

"What do you think?" the young man asked.

Mogul recognized that voice…

"Jack!" Keena leapt up from her chair and gave the man a hug and then held him at arms length. "Look at you! Don't you look handsome! And is this…?"

"This, Miss Keena, is Synth-E-Uh."

"No way!" Keena hugged the young woman, who didn't entirely know how to respond, giving a very slight nod and grin that only lasted a split second. "You look so real!"

Jack nodded. "Realistic androids have been around for

thousands of years. It was only in the last several centuries that Robotics took more pride in efficiency than trying to emulate the original creators."
Synth-E-Uh made a wry face. "Being in a humanoid form is definitely… inefficient. I've had tracks for so many years, I can't understand why you people bother with legs."
Angel laughed. "Sex mostly. I could just imagine having tracks… Backup. Ram. Backup. Ram."
Keena covered her mouth to stifle a laugh.
Synth-E-Uh just looked embarrassed. "Yes, of course. I hadn't considered that."
Keena held her at arm's length. "Not even now that you…?"
"Well, we could I suppose." Synth-E-Uh looked at Jack. "It's not something we think about, we don't have the same instincts as Organics."
Zondra changed the subject. "So where is everyone headed? Mogul, we know you are staying here. Rusty and I are going with Angel to visit her homeworld of Tallus. Keena, what are your plans?"
Keena let Synth-E-Uh go and sat down in a chair, looking thoughtful for a moment. "I think I'll stay here. I'm kind of a celebrity, being one of the only uninfected purebloods. And Mogul has offered to hang with me and teach me slap-speech in between his shifts at the base."
Zondra nodded and their drink orders were delivered at that moment by a small tracked droid with a serving tray for a head. It's long spindly arms expertly reached above itself to grab the drinks and place them in front of the person that ordered them. After it had finished, Zondra turned to Jack and Synth-E-Uh. "What about you two? Any plans?"
Jack answered with a wide toothy smile. "We are tasked with

accompanying Chais to make contact with the Technoid race. They are more advanced than us, but being simple explorers, they would likely be willing to trade technology for information."

Angel picked up her cup and held it up in the air. "Well, I love you all. I just wish Lais were here to enjoy this moment with us. To her memory…"

They all saluted, holding their drinks aloft.

Chapter Thirty-Seven

Unknown: Unknown

There was an itch. A bad one. All over her body, like ants crawling everywhere. But that was all she could feel. She couldn't see. She couldn't hear. Human? No. A human-Technoid hybrid.
When she tried to open her eyes, nothing happened. Muscles in her throat wouldn't respond to allow her to speak. Limbs wouldn't respond, she couldn't even tell if they were there. And yet a tiny bit more of her body reported that it was there every second that passed, and the itching was quickly disappearing.
She didn't know her own… wait… yes she did. Just now. Lais. And even though she still couldn't see or hear anything,

she could smell seared plastic and metal.

What did she know? She searched through what few memories she had, and they were also being replenished as her body healed itself.

She was being created by her sister Chais. They were on Incarcerata IV, in the cavern of the crashed Technoid spacecraft. They had spent days formulating DNA sequences that would make a viable body for her when combined with Technoid blueprints. This was exciting! That's why she didn't know what was going on! She was still growing! She just had to wait. So she did, and it seemed like forever.

She increased processor power to maximum and was flooded with a billion thoughts at once. Immediately she had to limit the power. She was accessing a brain now, not linear processor threads. It took several seconds to learn to interact with the brain and expand her consciousness to include more of the body she now inhabited by gently stimulating the brain regions and nerves. Feelings weren't so much emulated now as *felt*. She could *feel* the muscle fibers even as they grew, and they were starting to respond when she tensed. Millions of tiny stimuli blended into a *feeling*. It was inconvenient to think this way... and awesome.

Unlike a human, though, her conscious could access her unconscious processes as necessary. She had more control. TFD energy control, high-capacity battery levels, skin sensors that could relay exact temperatures and pressures... and the two halves of the brain, the artistic half, and the logical half, communicated with the conscious arbiter that was Lais herself. The final decision maker that would determine the best action to take based on the information provided by both halves of the brain.

When her eyes finally could see, she found she was laying on her back, looking up at the sky. She was no longer in the cavern. Chais must have moved her. And the sky... the sun was yellow like Earth's, which was strange. The sun of Incarcerata IV should have been more orange than yellow. Could Connor's eyes have seen colors differently when she viewed things from his implants? That was a distinct possibility.

When she could move her head, she looked around, and then propped herself up on one elbow. She was in a crater, the layers of the frozen soil easily visible, and it was all covered with a dusting of dry snow that would blow in over the edge with each gust of wind. Not what she was expecting since she was supposed to be in a desert, and Chais was nowhere in sight. Leave it to her sister to bugger off at the moment she was waking in her new body.

"Hello world. I am Lais."

It wasn't the same when there was no one else to hear it. Sitting up, Lais moved fluidly and easily, instantly calculating her balance and adjusting for her muscle fiber strength, estimating it at roughly fifty times that of a normal human, and accounting for her added mass, three times that of a normal human her size. She was solid. With a single stomp of a bare foot, she cracked the thick frozen soil beneath her feet.

She had no clothes on, that was no surprise, but there at her feet there were a few scraps of black silk clothes, and what looked to be what was left of a pair of... daggers? But they were all dissolving and silk fibers were flowing into the skin of her feet. Her nanites were scavenging these items and the surrounding soil to build her? Chais must have been short on materials, but the Technoid spacecraft should have been plenty. Something was very wrong.

And where was Chais? Lais climbed up to the edge of the crater and turned to look in every direction, but there were only snow-covered mountains in the distance. This was a desolate plain, alternating sheets of ice and snow with frozen soil. and the air was minus twenty degrees Celsius, which didn't bother her, but also didn't match her last memory before she was grown.

Since her nanites were still making an effort, she must not have been quite complete, so she sat down and waited, watching the little trails, like lines of ants, that marched from the items to her feet.

And there was the Earth's moon, just above the horizon. Clear as day. This wasn't the prison world, she was on Earth. How was that possible? Logic said, if she was on Earth, this was not the first time she had been formed, something had happened and her nanites were rebuilding her, but she had sustained so much damage that she could only be recovered with the information the nanites had at the time of her creation.

Lais scratched her head and looked around.

"But what would have cause me so much damage that I had to almost be built from scratch?"

There were no answers. She checked the sun and could see the short path that it had taken since she had awoken, so she trusted it was heading from east to west, and started jogging south, with far more questions than answers.

Manufactured by Amazon.ca
Bolton, ON